PRAISE FOR THE AUTHORS

JENNIFER BLAKE

"Treachery, blackmail, and greed lace a plot that is made all the more intriguing by Blake's trademark overlay of sultry, deep-South charm."
—*Library Journal* on *Kane*

"The lush setting of the Louisiana marshlands and Blake's vivid prose will send newcomers back to the shelves to pick up the first three books of the series."
—*Publishers Weekly* on *Clay*

HEATHER GRAHAM

"This gripping tale strikes a perfect balance between romance and intrigue."
—*Publishers Weekly* on *Night of the Blackbird*

"Ghostly visitors and an English history book provide clues in this compelling, darkly magical tale of enduring love and reincarnation, which will please fans who want a holiday romance with a paranormal twist and a bit of a mystery besides."
—*Library Journal* on *A Season of Miracles*

DIANA PALMER

"The dialogue is charming, the characters likable and the sex sizzling…"
—*Publishers Weekly* on *Once in Paris*

"A love story that is pure and enjoyable."
—*Romantic Times* on *Lord of the Desert*

JENNIFER BLAKE

HEATHER GRAHAM

DIANA PALMER

With a Southern Touch

MIRA

ISBN 1-55166-876-9

WITH A SOUTHERN TOUCH
Copyright © 2002 by MIRA Books.

ADAM
Copyright © 2002 by Patricia Maxwell.

A NIGHT IN PARADISE
Copyright © 2002 by Heather Graham Pozzessere.

GARDEN COP
Copyright © 2002 by Diana Palmer.

Visit us at www.mirabooks.com

Printed in U.S.A.

CONTENTS

ADAM

One

The woman appeared from out of nowhere.

One moment Adam Benedict saw only the rutted, curving driveway of the address he was seeking, the next his headlights picked up the form of a goddess. She stood proud and fearless on the center strip of gravel, with her long hair drifting around her shoulders in the night breeze and the space-age silk of her silvery cloak lifting to reveal the alabaster paleness of her gloriously naked body.

Adam slammed on his brakes. The wheels of his SUV locked in a skid. Dust boiled up to obscure his vision, and he wrestled the steering wheel by instinct, swearing as he tried to avoid the woman. The right rear tire dropped off the graveled edge into soft sand. The vehicle spun, hit the ditch with a wrench that threw him forward against his seat belt, then jolted to a halt.

He sat for a long moment with his hands clenched on the wheel and his heart pounding. Then he released himself, swung open the door of the SUV and got out. A quick glance showed him that he'd missed the encroaching tree line by inches so no damage had been done. The ditch wasn't that deep; the four-wheel drive should get him out of it easily enough. He closed the door and took the long step up to the driveway's surface in a single quick jump.

The wide curve of wash gravel lay empty in the moonlight. The woman was gone.

The night was pleasantly warm, bringing out the rich, green scents of early summer. The dust he'd raised had almost dissipated, settling like dingy gray down on the bitterweeds and black-eyed Susan that edged the ditch. He walked forward, scowling as he set his hands on his hipbones and stared around him. Nothing moved among the dark trees. Though he listened hard, he heard no footsteps, no sound of rustling leaves, breaking twigs or startled night birds. He was absolutely alone.

Adam did not see visions. He was a logical man, an electrical and computer engineer who believed primarily in what he could see and touch. His thought processes marched in linear progression with few detours for imagination. He was as positive as anyone could be that there had been a living, breathing woman on the driveway. She had stepped out, stark naked, in front of his moving vehicle. So where the hell had she gone?

Yes, and what had she been trying to do? Stop him by running him off the road?

He shook his head at that idea. The risk of being killed was too great. Anyway, no one knew he was coming. It was a fluke that he was making the trip instead of Roan. Detective Jack Whitaker had expected Adam to ask his cousin, the sheriff of Tunica Parish, to pay this semi-official visit to the woman living at the end of the drive. Adam had decided to take care of it himself. For one thing, the annual Benedict family reunion was being held in nearby Turn-

Coupe in a couple of days. He'd also felt restless lately with a definite need to get out of New Orleans, spend a little time in the part of the state where he grew up. Mainly, though, he didn't like being manipulated. Jack was a good old boy and decent friend, but could also be a royal pain, always looking for ways to go around NOPD official channels or get other people to do his job. Adam made a practice of doing the opposite of what Jack expected once in a great while just to discourage him.

He liked taking part in a physical search now and then, too, instead of concentrating on the virtual methods of his high-tech database. What he didn't like was playing hide-and-seek on dark country lanes with crazy females.

She had been magnificent. Mystery and magic had shone in her eyes. The body he had glimpsed had been sweetly proportioned, with curves and hollows that made his fingertips tingle and the back of his neck feel hot. It would be a pleasure to meet her again, with or without her silver cloak.

For an instant, it crossed his mind to wonder if she'd been real, after all. Then he dismissed that doubt. He didn't imagine things. He'd seen her with his own eyes. She'd been there. The only question was where she was now.

Adam swung back to his SUV and climbed inside. It took a little doing to get back on the rough driveway, but he made it. A few minutes later, he pulled up before a rambling Victorian house with gables and a turret that was set back under giant oaks. A light glowed faintly behind the drapes that hung at an upstairs window, indicating that someone was still up.

He hesitated, mindful of childhood strictures

against bothering people at home after nine o'clock. New Orleans was a city of night people where such rules seldom applied, but Turn-Coupe ran on a more old-fashioned timetable. However, his mission was urgent. He opened the vehicle door and got out.

It took so long for his knock to be answered that he began to think it would be ignored. Then he heard approaching footsteps. Seconds later, the door was snatched open.

It was the goddess.

The knowledge was visceral, like a blow to the stomach. It was visual as well; he'd have known the hair, the even features and challenging stance anywhere. And yet, she was different. Gone was the silver cloak, replaced by faded blue jeans and a white T-shirt. Her hair was confined in a single thick braid that swung between her shoulder blades. The incandescent shimmer and glow of her had dimmed to something near normal and she looked tired. Still there was not a doubt in his mind.

"So this is where you went," he said with satisfaction.

Lara Kincaid surveyed the man in front of her with misgivings. His tall form and broad shoulders blocked the doorway, while the strength of his personality bordered on intimidating. The light from the foyer behind her caught golden gleams in the sun-streaked waves of his hair and revealed the rich sea blue of his level gaze. A haunting familiarity marked the set of his chiseled features, as if some distant ancestor might have served as the model for ancient Roman coins. Surrounding him was a mixed aura of red for courage and blue for fidelity, something she'd never seen before. Every instinct said he was a benign influence at the moment, yet she knew beyond a doubt that he had brought danger with him.

"I beg your pardon?" she said with noticeable coolness.

"When you vanished just now," he amplified with a crooked smile. "Though I'd love to know how you managed to get away so fast."

"There must be some mistake."

"Right," he drawled. "So what was the game? I could have killed you. Or put a dent in my own head when I hit the ditch."

"I haven't the faintest idea what you're talking about. Is there something I can do for you, or do you just show up at the doors of strange women and hold weird conversations?"

Irritation tightened his face, perhaps for her superior tone and lack of response to his conversational lures, but he became all business. "I'm Adam Benedict, and I'm looking for Lara Kincaid. Would that be you?"

"What if it would?"

"I'm looking for information about a relative of yours that I'm trying to locate, a woman named Kim Belzoni."

Of course he was. It was possible that she had made a mistake in antagonizing this man, Lara thought. Such errors in judgment were rare for her, but his presence was more disturbing than was comfortable. She controlled a strong impulse to slam the door in his face before she asked, "Why?"

"She's wanted for questioning in the death of her husband. Anything you could do to give me a line on her whereabouts would be greatly appreciated."

"I'm sure it would, if I had any idea where she might be. Also if I really wanted to see her go to jail."

"You've heard from her," he said with satisfaction.

"I never said that."

"It follows, since you know she's in trouble. Is she here?"

He stepped forward in a smooth movement that carried him over the threshold and into the small foyer with its mirrored Victorian console table set with an antique lamp topped by a fringed pink shade. Lara retreated instinctively, then stopped in annoyance as she realized what she was doing. Voice sharp, she said, "Don't be ridiculous. Really, I can't help you."

A whimsical smile, more charming than it should have been, curved one corner of his mobile mouth. "Maybe, maybe not. But I might be able to help you."

"I doubt that. It's late. I'll have to ask you to leave."

"Not yet," he replied, unperturbed. "We need to have a talk about what you're going to do when the others show up, the men sent by the Belzoni family. You going to let them walk into your house, too?"

"I didn't let—"

"You did nothing to prevent it."

"Because I know you're harmless."

That stopped him.

"Do you now?" he asked, the words carrying an edge under their softness. "What makes you so sure?"

"Maybe I'm psychic." She lifted her chin, her

gaze clear. She'd discovered long ago that it was possible to tell many truths under the guise of sarcasm.

"Then why am I here?"

Was it a test? Did she dare answer, or would that only bring more trouble than she had already? It made little difference either way; the challenge in his dark blue gaze was irresistible. "You're here on police business, though you aren't police. You're one of the so-called Bad Benedicts of Turn-Coupe, a family so used to doing whatever they please in this part of the country that you consider it a right. One of three brothers—there were four but one died—you were brought up some ten miles from here at the family place known as Grand Point. You consider the old house the next thing to a mausoleum, however, and much prefer your thoroughly modern condo in New Orleans."

"How did you—" he began.

She cut across his words without compunction as she closed her eyes to block out extraneous sounds and sights that might interfere with her inner vision. "You aren't married, have no particular relationship of the moment, mainly because the kind of women you choose aren't happy with being ignored while you concentrate on digital logic. On the other hand, you enjoy the company of women, particularly when you need distraction or feel in a protective mood. You would consider marriage if the right woman came along, but you've never been sure the woman of the moment was the right one."

"Now wait a minute." His clothing made a rasping sound as he shifted, possibly in mental discomfort.

"You have some consideration for my aunt, though you believe she will be safer in police custody. Your concern is real enough that you took a step you seldom bother with before coming here. You are…'' She paused, uneasy with the image before her.

''Don't stop now,'' he said in tight irritation. ''I'm dying to hear all the little details you've found out about me.''

''Armed,'' she finished as she opened her eyes. ''You're armed, at least in a manner of speaking. You have a .357 Magnum pistol in the glove compartment of your SUV, along with a license to use it.''

He met her gaze, his own grim. ''How do you know this stuff? Who told you?''

''No one told me,'' she said with the lift of a shoulder. ''Oh, it's easy enough to hear about the Benedicts and to place you among them by family resemblance. The rest of it I just know.''

''I don't buy it.''

''Suit yourself.'' His reaction was no surprise. Few people, especially men, wanted to think that their lives were open to someone of her ability.

''You know one of my brothers, Clay maybe, or his wife Janna. You have a contact of some kind at the New Orleans Police Department.''

''Wrong.'' Her smile was thin. ''I was born in Santa Fe, but moved back here after my grandmother died and left this old place to me a few months ago. Or left it to my mother, if you want to be precise. Since Mom swears she'll never set foot in Louisiana again, and I was interested in my roots, here I am.''

''I remember now,'' he said slowly. ''Your grandmother was old Granny Newton that everybody said was…''

''Was a witch. Exactly.''

''I was going to say everybody thought she was

crazy, because she called herself a white witch and practiced weird spells.''

"Wicca. She practiced wicca or white witchcraft, though she never called it that, not even when my mom got into it. She just chanted her spells and made her potions to attract good rather than evil. She also kept chickens and sold eggs and herbs from her garden, and started the little quilt shop that I still run in the front parlor.'' She tipped her head toward the room on the right where an array of colorful project books could be seen laid out on tables, with upright bolts of quilt fabric in rainbow colors lining the floor-to-ceiling shelves.

"She once gave Esther Goodman a spell to make me fall in love with her.''

Lara tipped her head in swift interest. "Did it work?''

"For maybe ten seconds,'' he said on a snort. "Until Esther made the mistake of crowing about what she'd done and how I couldn't get away from her.''

"You had nothing to fear,'' Lara said, unable to prevent a smile for his look of disgust.

"We were fifteen at the time. Esther is married to a plumber now. So much for potions.''

"They have advantages and disadvantages.''

"Which you know all about, since you've inherited Granny Newton's powers, or whatever you call it, as well as her clientele and her house?''

"You've got it.''

"In that case, tell me what I'm thinking right now, this second.''

It was the kind of dare that Lara hated, mainly because her ability to tap into her odd gift was unreliable under stress. The images, sometimes vague, sometimes strong, came easiest when she needed them least, or so it seemed. Still, she'd ventured this far in her candor, and continuing seemed as good a distraction from his questions about her aunt as any.

Lara closed her eyes again, opening her mind to direct impressions from the man beside her. At first there was nothing more than drifting patterns of his red-and-blue aura. Then she caught a flash of silver. Immediately following it was the full-blown image of herself in a fantastic cloak that lifted around her, swirling with the wind that tossed her hair while a full moon gleamed around her. Beneath the cloak, she was naked.

She reveled in her lack of confinement under the warm kiss of the Midsummer's Eve moonlight. Then Adam Benedict stepped close and circled her waist with a strong arm to draw her against him. His body was warm and electric with the passion that flowed inside him. She tilted her head back to meet his gaze, and was snared in the communion of perfect mates. Countless ages passed, measured only by the synchronized beating of their hearts, until slowly, carefully, he lowered his head and touched his mouth to hers. His lips were smooth, firm and incredibly sweet to the taste. They molded to hers with tingling fidelity. Lost in their sensual magic, she barely felt it as he brushed his hand from her waistline upward to the gentle curve of her breast. His warm fingers cupped her cool, bare flesh, capturing...

Lara drew a sharp breath and stepped back until her spine was against the parlor door facing. Her eyes snapped open and she glared at Adam Benedict in shock and accusation.

His eyes were closed as hers had been, so his lashes

rested in a dark fringe against his skin. At her movement, they snapped open. A startled look came into his face as he met and held her gaze. "What?"

"You kissed me. You touched me. At least you did in your mind."

"I…" he began, then stopped, pressing his lips together as his face darkened a fraction.

"Don't bother denying it."

He shook his head as a slow grin tilted his mouth. "So sue me. Just remember that you started it."

"I did nothing of the kind!" she declared firmly.

"You weren't flitting around in a state of nature tonight, driving us poor dumb mortals insane?"

"Never! At least, not like that. I saw you all right. I was caught for a second in your headlights, but not…not like that."

"The word you want is naked. And I know you were, because I saw you."

"You didn't. You couldn't have."

"I did," he insisted. "Fantasy may be your thing, but I'm not that good at it, believe me. I don't see phantom naked women while I'm wide-awake."

Lara stared at him for long seconds while he met her gaze with the same angry incredulity that was reflected in her own. She hadn't been naked out there on the drive. Still she'd sensed the approach of trouble and had been watching for it. She hadn't known the man in front of her, specifically, was coming. Then she had glimpsed him through the moon-bright windshield of his SUV. The strength of his presence and the aura of danger that surrounded him had held her mesmerized where she stood in his path. And there had been a brief moment when she'd imagined what it might be like to appear unclothed before him.

It was Midsummer's Eve, after all, the night when witches prowl and anything might happen. She didn't practice the wicca of her mother and grandmother, had never celebrated Midsummer's Night by dancing naked under a full moon, though the ancient witch's tradition, allied to her disturbing premonition, had driven her outside on this special night. That this man had somehow tapped into her momentary inclination, seeing her as she'd seen herself in her mind's eye, was near unthinkable. It had to be, because otherwise she had no defense. If Adam Benedict had the power to invade her thoughts, then he could do anything he wanted, take anything he wished from her, and there was little she could do about it.

The good thing was that he didn't seem to realize the potential of his mental processes as a weapon, didn't recognize that he had a telepathic element in his makeup, at least for her more audacious impulses.

Heaven forbid that he should ever find out.

Two

Lara's first thought was to get rid of Adam Benedict, to see him off her property and out of her life before it was too late. "It's the middle of the night," she said abruptly. "You'd better come back another time, maybe tomorrow or the next day."

"I'll be glad to go when you tell me what I need to know."

"I can't help you."

He watched her without moving, his blue gaze steady. "I think you can. If your aunt isn't here, maybe you could tell me where else she may have gone or who she might turn to for help?"

It was unlikely that she'd be able to eject him physically, Lara thought, and trying might make it appear that she had something to hide. What was she going to do? Even as she considered it, she said, "I told you, I've been living in New Mexico. Aunt Kim used to visit us out there now and then, and I've seen her once or twice here, but I've never even been in her house in New Orleans. I know next to nothing about her life there or the people she may call her friends."

"That may be true, but if you've talked to her recently, you're ahead of me. Besides, you may know more than you realize, things that could come out if you'd answer a few questions.''

"I doubt it. Really, I'd like you to leave."

"There's always a subpoena," he said, a harder note in his voice. "It would probably lead to a full-scale search of the premises, a messy operation you really want to avoid. Especially if you have nothing to hide."

It was a warning, probably the only one she was likely to get. Which would be better, to try to convince Adam Benedict that she had no useful information, or to risk him discovering that she knew everything? And did she really have an option when he stood as immovable as an oak tree there in the middle of her foyer? Added to that was the growing feeling she must know more about this man, get closer to him. She had no idea whether it was personal or connected to her aunt, but she had learned that ignoring such instincts led to trouble.

"I'm sorry," she said, forcing a smile as she came to a decision. "If I've seemed uncooperative, it's just that...that I'm concerned about Aunt Kim."

"Understandable. She's in a lot of trouble."

"You seem to know more about it than I do. Maybe you'd like to tell me exactly what's going on over a cup of coffee or a drink?" She waited with a tight feeling in her chest for his answer.

"Coffee is fine," he said, though something like wariness lay in the blue depths of his eyes.

"Good. That's good then." She gestured toward the sitting room on the opposite side of the foyer from her small quilt shop. "If you'd like to be seated, I'll make it."

"We aren't that formal around here, you know," he answered, his voice dry. "We can talk in the kitchen."

What he meant, she thought, was that he preferred not to let her out of his sight. That was fine, since she felt the same way about him. Flipping off the foyer light then turning to lead the way, she spoke over her shoulder. "Whatever. I'm not very good at this Southern hospitality stuff, as you've noticed."

"You'll get used to it. So you moved back alone?"

He was closer than she expected as they moved through the dim sitting room, near enough that the deep timbre of his words seemed to vibrate along her spine. Self-consciousness gripped her, so she became much too aware of the sway of her hips and the swing of her heavy braid down her back. She was also reminded of how isolated they were, and how little she knew of Adam Benedict. "If you're asking whether I have a significant other around somewhere," she said, "the answer is, not at the moment. So tell me again just how it is that you're interested in Aunt Kim? Are you some kind of private detective?"

"Not exactly. I run a high-tech information retrieval operation."

"Some job."

"More a hobby. I'm retired, work out of the condo."

She gave him a quick glance over her shoulder as she pushed through the swinging door into the big back kitchen with its tall windows draped with vigorous ivy, granite countertops, and vintage woodstove in one corner. "You can't be more than thirty-two or three, thirty-five at the most. Isn't that a little early for retirement?"

"Not if you hold the patent on an innovation in fiber optics."

"I see. High-tech, indeed. So information retrieval means computer snooping, I suppose?"

"You could put it that way," he agreed.

"Strictly legitimate? Or are you one of those hackers who slip in and out of secure databases?"

He didn't answer. When she glanced in his direction, he only lifted a brow as if daring her to comment.

"You must be good," she said with irony.

"I also create methods to keep others from doing it."

"*Very* good," she amplified. "Even so, I'm not sure how you found me."

"You showed up as Kim Belzoni's next of kin on her medical records. After that, it was easy."

She gave him a narrow glance as she took down the white ceramic coffee jar, then turned to measure grounds into the filter. "How convenient for you."

"Wasn't it though?"

"Especially since I never knew I was listed."

"She needed a name to put on the form. Maybe she chose you because you were closer than your mother."

Closer in affection as well as in distance, Lara thought. For all the infrequency with which she saw Aunt Kim, she was one of her favorite people. As the much younger sister of Lara's mother, Kim was only twelve years or so older than Lara, and had lived with the two of them for a time as a teenager. Lara's mother, divorced and bitter about it, had been a bit too domineering and openly critical for there to be much affection between the sisters, but Kim and Lara had been co-conspirators against the adult head of the household.

"If you checked Aunt Kim's medical records, then you probably saw that she was hospitalized recently," Lara said.

He nodded. "I'm aware that the husband put her there if that's what you're getting at. But if you know it, the two of you must have had a long conversation."

"You could say that." Lara paused a second before she went on. "She was terrified of him, you know."

"I don't doubt it, but that doesn't give her the right to whack him preemptively." His gaze was level, and exacting in its certainty.

"What about in self-defense?"

"Is that what she's claiming?"

He was still hoping she'd slip up and reveal when and where they had spoken, Lara thought, even as she answered, "I can't imagine Aunt Kim pulling a trigger for any other reason."

"Why would you say that?"

She gave the coffeemaker a thoughtful frown as she added water, then started it. "You have to know Aunt Kim. She isn't what you might call a forceful personality. Avoiding trouble is a lot more her style."

"Running away from it, you mean?"

"Don't put words in my mouth," she snapped, even as she realized that part of her instant irritation was because he was right. Her aunt was a past mistress of the art of leaving unhappy situations, especially unhappy marriages, behind her. The wonder was that she'd stayed so long this time.

"So where does she usually run to?"

"The question isn't where, but how. Aunt Kim is an extremely attractive woman." It was better to throw him that bone than to admit that she often turned up on the doorsteps of her sister or her niece.

"Meaning she usually finds a man to take her away?"

"If she wants one."

"And does she, as a rule?"

"I believe so." In fact, her aunt turned up with the men in tow, older men with flashy habits, younger guys with attitudes, and now and then a cowboy with more in his jeans than under his hat. Lara suspected that their admiration and the security they represented were more important than the sex angle.

"This lover may have decided to make her a widow. Is that it?"

Adam's gaze was narrow as he waited for her answer. She turned away from it to pick up a cake plate set with small rolled pastries. "It seems possible."

"Convenient, you mean. Unless, of course, he was persuaded to have that notion?"

"Oh, please."

He watched as she set the cake plate in front of him. "This wasn't her first marriage, was it?"

Lara shook her head. "Her fifth or sixth, something

like that. Didn't your database give you an exact count?"

Ignoring the last, he commented, "A hard woman to satisfy."

Lara glanced at him, but saw no sign that he was hinting at anything salacious. "Maybe," she agreed. "Or maybe she just dreams too big, expects too much."

"Could be she just likes variety."

"Or keeps hoping that someone, someday, will match her high standards." Lara stepped back to lean against the cabinet and cross her arms over her chest.

Adam Benedict watched her with sardonic consideration in his eyes. "You think she found somebody this time to make her dreams come true?"

"Nothing she said to me suggested it. The situation could be totally different."

"True," he agreed with a twist to one corner of his smooth lips. "But if Belzoni was bad enough that she had to kill him, what took her so long to decide she wanted out?"

"Wanting out is one thing, actually leaving is another. She was afraid he'd come after her, I think. He'd threatened to kill her and she believed him."

"She said that?"

"Not in so many words. But isn't it the usual scenario with an abusive husband?" Lara hoped the question would avoid further speculation about her aunt's motives.

"Or desperate ones who want to hold on to the women they love at any cost."

"That's all very fine from the male point of view,

but what sane man would want a woman to stay with him out of fear?''

Adam's gaze was straight. ''Maybe one who can't stand the thought of living without her.''

''You mean one who would rather see her dead than let her slip out of his control. Yes, and one who cares a lot more about his precious pride than he does her. If he really loved her, he'd want her to be happy. But then, if he cared about her happiness, she probably wouldn't want to leave.''

''People aren't that rational—or that altruistic.''

''If they aren't, they should be,'' she said defensively.

He watched her with unnerving appraisal. ''Idealistic, but true. Is that why you aren't married, you dream too big and are afraid of being disappointed?''

''Who says I've never married.''

''My database. Is it wrong?''

She'd known his mental ability and insight could be a problem. Not that she intended to admit that he was right, but it had in fact been her aunt's aimless bouncing from one man to another that had made her determined to wait until she found the right one. If real and lasting love was supposed to be a big dream, then she was guilty and unrepentant about it.

''What about you?'' she asked with a direct look. ''Don't tell me no woman is willing to settle for your narrow version of reality?''

His gaze widened a fraction as if in surprise or, just possibly, the unwelcome knowledge that he had his own expectations. Silence stretched between them. Finally, he shrugged. ''All right, the personal question was out of line and I withdraw it. But I'll tell you what I'm looking for in a woman anyway. I want someone who will laugh with me and let me hold her when she cries, someone who values love and desire, tolerance and compassion, who doesn't mind work and can take pleasure in its rewards. I want a woman who can look at life, and at our lives together, as the greatest adventure in the world.''

She gave a short laugh as she gripped her arms tighter around her to ease the odd pain around her heart. "And you call me an idealist!''

''Oh, she's out there and I'll find her,'' he said, the blue-and-red aura around him almost glowing with the intensity of his conviction. ''The only question is whether such a paragon will have anything to do with me.''

He'd said nothing about the appearance or background of this perfect mate. No doubt he'd expect a patrician beauty of good family, with conservative beliefs, commitment to church and civic service responsibility and a history of discriminating, even virginal, sexual conduct. He would have no use for the daughter of a New Age mystic with a distaff family record of weird habits and odd practices. Not that Lara had any particular interest, of course. It was just that a man's choice of friends and lovers said much about him.

The coffee bubbled its way to completion behind her. Glad of the distraction, she turned to pour it up. ''So what is this life work that you need a helpmate to accomplish? I mean, if information retrieval is only a hobby?''

"You can't tell from your crystal ball?" Sardonic humor shaded his voice.

"Sometimes it's easier to just ask." She avoided his gaze as she put his cup in front of him and offered cream and sugar with a gesture.

He shook his head at any adulteration of his coffee. "It's nothing in particular, no special plans or projects, since I don't have to work for a living anymore. I don't even care if this dream woman has plans and a career of her own, so long as she's not fanatic about it. What's important here is the attitude of partnership and cooperation."

"Ah."

"Meaning?" He was still, his coffee cup halfway to his lips, as he waited for her answer.

"Nothing."

"You don't believe me, right? Or else you think I should be gainfully employed, even if it takes a job away from someone who needs it worse than I do."

"Not my business. It just seems strange that someone who lives such a privileged life with exemplary expectations should be hunting down my aunt."

"I'm not hunting her down," he said evenly, "only doing a favor for a friend. But if I were after her, it wouldn't be for kicks. Kim Belzoni is wanted for questioning in the death of her husband. Maybe she killed him, maybe she didn't, but it would be to her advantage to talk with my pal Jack Whitaker of the NOPD. He'd like a few answers about her husband's business dealings and Cosa Nostra family connections. If she cooperates, the murder charge may be reduced to manslaughter or even the self-defense that you claim. Either way, she'll be better off in jail than running around where the Belzoni family can get to her.''

"You really think they're after her?''

He gave a slow nod. "So does she, apparently. If she didn't, she wouldn't be hiding out.''

It was a reasonable conclusion. It was also one that had been haunting Lara for twenty-four hours, ever since her aunt had appeared on her doorstep.

Ernesto Belzoni had been the nephew of Don Belzoni, current head of the New Orleans Cosa Nostra. That connection had made Ernesto almost paranoid in the tabs he kept on Aunt Kim, where she went, who she talked to, how she used her credit cards and where. He'd insisted that she drop almost all contact with her own friends and family, had vetted her acquaintances and required that she call in frequently any time she left the house. If she returned home even five minutes later than expected, there had been endless questions about where she'd gone, who she saw, and what they'd discussed. The penalty if he didn't like the answers had been swift and painful.

Aunt Kim hadn't been used to that kind of treatment. She was a free spirit, like all the Kincaid women. As a lounge hostess, sometime singer and blackjack dealer between marriages, she'd worked the casinos of Louisiana and Mississippi for years. Sometimes she struck out for Vegas or Atlantic City or worked a cruise ship for a season, but she always returned to the homier atmosphere of the Southern states.

Lara had fervently admired her mother's younger

sister as a teenager, been incredibly impressed by her vagabond existence, her fancy cocktail rings and evening wear cut down to there, the sophisticated styling of her long auburn hair and her laissez-faire attitude. That had lasted until she watched her aunt have a baby with her perfectly nice second husband, then abandon both while that beautiful little girl was still in diapers. Lara had developed a different philosophy then.

She had changed, but Aunt Kim hadn't. She still went her own way, still refused to be tied down or take any responsibility for her actions. She'd gone through another couple of marriages, then wound up with Belzoni after meeting him at a Shreveport casino. His strict surveillance had come as a shock, though her reaction to it had been silent rebellion in the form of secret escapes and casual affairs rather than outright confrontation. Suspicion of her clandestine activities had only made Belzoni worse, of course, and more determined to dominate her with force. He had put her in the hospital one time too often, however. Aunt Kim had bought a gun and kept it in her purse. It hadn't been long before she was forced to use it.

Lara wondered if her aunt had thought about the consequences before she pointed the gun at Belzoni. Listening to her rant the night before about the unfairness of being blamed for her husband's death, and how unreasonable it was that Don Belzoni might persecute her for it, it was hard to say whether she even realized the trouble she was in. She seemed to have little idea what to do next, few plans for the future.

She'd simply thrown herself on Lara's mercy, then trailed upstairs in her half-destroyed evening gown, dropping sequins all the way. Shedding the dress like a skin she no longer needed, she'd crawled into the guest room bed and gone instantly to sleep.

She was still there.

What Lara was going to do with her aunt or for her, she had no idea. She only knew that it was going to take a miracle to keep her safe, free of prison, and out of Adam Benedict's clutches.

Three

Lara Kincaid wanted something from him, Adam was sure of it. He had an uncomfortable feeling that it might be to pick his brain. Not that he believed she could do that with her so-called psychic powers, but there was always the conventional method. It was the one he was using, after all.

Did she really believe in that ESP nonsense or was it part of some attempt to distract him? He had no idea, but it wasn't exactly a hardship to play along. She was more than easy on the eyes with her silver-blond hair, skin so clear it appeared luminous, and intelligence shining from the crystalline green of her eyes. He wished, suddenly, that he was at the house under simpler circumstances and also less pushed for time.

Most of what she'd said seemed reasonable. He knew from his computer check of telephone records that Kim Belzoni had called Lara from her home shortly after her husband was shot. He'd discovered also that she'd used her credit card to buy discount store purchases that included hair dye and makeup. It looked as if she intended to go into hiding, though he'd got nothing from Lara when he made the suggestion. Did that mean she had no idea where Kim

Belzoni was headed, or only that she'd been fully prepared for the question? Was it possible that the lady was even now on the premises? He listened carefully but could hear nothing from the other rooms of the big house except the distant ticking of a clock and an occasional creak as if the old structure was shifting in its sleep.

He sipped his coffee, a movement that Lara copied almost exactly. His intrusion weighed on him. Forcing himself into people's homes wasn't something he did every day. The fact that Lara Kincaid had allowed it without calling the police was the main reason he didn't get up and leave. If she was nervous of their intervention, there must be a reason. Added to that was the fact he'd agreed to do a job, and his personal code required that he deliver if at all possible. In any case, his absence wasn't going to help Kim Belzoni or the woman across from him.

Adam reached for one of the small, rolled cakes Lara had set out, though more for something to occupy his hands than because he was hungry. It was light and flaky, and as he bit into it, the rich tastes of apricots, almonds, raisins and something more that he couldn't quite identify bloomed on his tongue. "Wow," he said when he'd swallowed. "Where did you find these?"

"I baked them."

"What's the spice?"

"Cardamom. You've probably run across it before in Danish pastries."

"I've never had anything quite like them." He

reached for another small roll. "You could make a fortune in the prepared food market."

"Everything can't be reduced to dollars and cents," she said shortly.

"You're against commercial enterprise?"

"I bake for relaxation and the love of turning flour and yeast into delicious things. Doing it for money would take the joy out of it."

His smile was crooked and his gaze hooded, as he said, "No doubt."

"I know what you're thinking, and yes, my attitude is a lot like the quote about prostitution," she said in cool disdain. "First you do it for love, then for a few friends, and finally for money."

He stared at her a long moment during which he could feel heat gathering under his collar. "Sorry. I didn't intend to be that obvious."

"You weren't, and there's no need to apologize. Your thoughts are your own. You're only responsible for what you actually say out loud."

That was a comfort. Or might have been if he could be sure of keeping his more aberrant fancies to himself. In an effort to change the subject, he asked, "You really make a living with your quilt shop?"

"Of a sort. I teach classes and do machine quilting as well as selling fabric and notions."

"I'd have thought you were too far out of town to have much traffic."

"Quilters don't mind driving to get what they want," she said with humor lighting the green of her eyes like the sun shining through new leaves. "But another project I have in hand is a book using a special design I created called 'Heaven on Earth.'"

An odd look crossed her face as she finished speaking, possibly from surprise that she'd revealed so much. Since he didn't want her having second thoughts about opening up to him, Adam asked immediately, "What? No potions peddled out the back door like your granny?"

"Not much call for potions. I suppose nobody is quite that desperate these days."

"Or they have too many other sources willing to take their money in exchange for a placebo and a promise?"

She tipped her head as she studied him. "You don't think potions work?"

"Sure they work, and always have," he said easily. "Witch doctors used to heal patients, faith healers made the lame walk, and snake oil salesmen cured everything from gout to kidney stones. Positive affirmations and five-year plans are effective, too. The human mind can perform miracles with the right encouragement."

"In other words, it's all in our heads."

"Isn't it?" He waited with more interest than he'd have expected for her answer.

She lowered her lashes. "Maybe, maybe not. Alternative medicine is a viable therapy these days, and many of the compounds used are natural forms of the artificial ingredients found in prescription drugs. But even if they were placebos, what does it matter if the results are the same?"

"Depends on the price," he answered. "Sometimes it's more than people can afford to pay, especially when their lives are at stake.''

"There you have it, the real reason I don't sell potions.'' Her smile was brittle. "It then becomes a question of which does more harm—refraining because the cost is too high or allowing people to go unaided because I refrain.''

It was the problem faced by every person with power to wield. Adam just hadn't expected to come across it in connection with the potions of a back-country psychic. "You'd like to help?''

"Who wouldn't?'' she asked as she looked away from him.

He could relate to that, since a large part of what he did was for the sake of others rather than for a return. "Just what's in these old brews? Do you really know?''

"Oh, the usual eye of newt, frog wart juice and fingernail parings collected from a graveyard at midnight.''

"Funny,'' he said without amusement. A second later, he had to ask, "You can make these concoctions?''

Her lips twisted, perhaps for his obvious skepticism. "I have a recipe book.''

"Ever whipped up something for your own use?''

"Would I tell you if I had?'' she countered.

He couldn't help glancing at his cup, though he'd seen her make the coffee and knew very well that she'd added nothing to it. On the other hand, she could have known he was coming and slipped something into the cup ahead of time if she was truly psychic.

"Don't worry," she said with a low laugh. "You're safe from me."

"That's nice to know." Even as he made that dry comment, he realized that his concern, however brief, was like a crack in the wall of his disbelief. At the same time, he had to wonder just why he was so safe. Was it because she didn't consider him a threat, or that he simply held no appeal for her?

"But come on now," he insisted. "Just what are these magic ingredients?"

"Depends."

"On?"

"What you're interested in, of course. Do you have gout, kidney stones, or the need for a love potion?"

"The potion," he said at once.

"Why are you so interested?" she mused, her gaze steady on his face. "Is it academic, or simply that you'd like to be the stud of New Orleans?"

"You mean I have that choice?"

There was no answering smile for his grin. "It helps if you specify."

What he'd had in mind was finding out what Esther Goodman had fed him all those years ago, but that suddenly didn't seem important. "Let's say I want a special woman to fall so madly in love with me that she worships the ground I walk on and refuses to leave my side, ever."

"You know what they say."

"Be careful what you wish for because you might get it? I'd say the risk is minimal." He watched her while doing his best to ignore the strange trip of excitement in his blood.

"That could be affected by whether you're really serious."

"Now you're saying it's all in my head?" His question carried more than its share of irony.

"Maybe, maybe not," she said, smiling a little to herself. "Let's see, what can I tell you? Chocolate is sometimes added because it's supposed to stimulate love and desire. That's also the reason it's so popular for Valentine's Day."

He gave her a straight look. "I don't think your granny's customers were traipsing out here for chocolate fudge."

"Probably not." She considered a moment, and then an impish glint appeared in the mysterious depths of her eyes. "Olives are said to revive lust and ensure fertility in men, and the same with avocados and bananas, though I'd think that feeding your ladylove a nice, big banana might be more about imagery than..."

"Never mind, there's no problem in that department."

"Yes, well, current wisdom says the results from fruit and veggies have more to do with improved nutrition than any magic effect. However, there's always saw palmetto that was used by Native Americans in this part of the country for prostate and urinary tract problems. It's supposed to have been the Viagra of the eighteenth and nineteenth century."

"Let's skip that part," he suggested in dry reproof, "and get back to the desperate love."

"If you insist. Orrisroot powder is a centuries old attractant. It comes from a type of iris and is used even now as a fixative for potpourri and especially for the sachets that women use to scent their lingerie. While they're enjoying the fragrance, they're turning their men on without realizing it."

"Intriguing," he said dryly, "but still not quite what I had in mind."

"You're left with a choice of sachet or tea. For the sachet, you'll need rose petals and jasmine blossoms. Oh yes, and henbane leaves. Only you have to collect all these yourself, running outside for them just after sunrise and picking them while naked and standing on one foot."

"You're joking."

She sat back in her chair. "Sorry. That's what it takes."

"And after I've caught pneumonia picking this stuff, I slip it into her underwear, right?"

She gave him a repressive stare. "You grind them to a powder along with patchouli leaves and cinnamon bark, then put three tablespoons of the mixture in a little bag that you wear on a leather thong."

"That'll turn her on, seeing some grubby sack hanging around my neck. Not to mention sniffing the manly scent of pumpkin pie spice."

"If you're going to take that attitude, then it certainly won't work."

"Forget the sachet. I suppose the tea tastes like castor oil and I have to force it down her throat?"

"It tastes like mint and licorice with a hint of ginger, actually. And if you can't get her to drink it, then you're hopeless anyway."

"If I could persuade a woman to drink an aphrodisiac, I shouldn't need one," he pointed out with humor curling the corners of his mouth. "Talking her into whatever I want ought to be easy."

Her expression turned jaundiced. "And probably is, too. This won't get it, you know."

"Won't get what? Mad, passionate love?" He kept his gaze as innocent as possible.

"It isn't going to lull me into a nice, comfy state of intimacy so I'll tell you where I think Aunt Kim might have gone."

She had nailed him, Adam thought, even if he'd had friendliness in mind more than intimacy. His main objective was to gain her confidence. Not that he'd mind getting closer. Something about her mesmerized him, so all he wanted to do was watch her and listen to the lilting cadences of her voice. It wasn't a phenomenon he'd run into before, nor was he sure he liked it.

In dry answer, he said, "You underestimate yourself."

"Sure I do," she said in obvious disbelief. "So why is it again that you're so set on finding her?"

"I was asked to do a job, and I agreed. Detective Whitaker and I shook hands on it, which makes it a binding contract in my book. I'm honor bound to fulfill my part of it."

"Honor bound. How quaint."

He made no reply, though his lips tightened at the arch sound of her voice.

"So you said you'd find my aunt and you intend to do it, regardless of right or wrong, what she may or may not have done, or even why?"

"I don't make the laws. I only do my best to abide by them and, now and then, help carry them out."

"What if it's dangerous for her to be found?"

"She'll be better off in police custody."

"That thought might soothe your conscience, but it wouldn't do a thing for mine. Anyway, you're wrong. She's not the kind of woman who can take that in stride."

"Meaning?"

Lara's brows drew together above her eyes in an expression that mirrored his own. "She's used to ease, comfort, a certain standard of living, but it's not just that. She's one of those people who never quite get the hang of living a normal life. She doesn't cope very well, so something is always rising up and slapping her in the face."

It sounded like more mysticism to Adam. "She seems to have coped enough to find a gun and shoot a man dead."

"She had to do it, or he'd have killed her."

"She could have called the police."

"You think she hadn't tried that?" Lara asked with scorn lacing her tone.

The lack of response to domestic disputes was too complicated a question for him to argue just now. Shifting ground, he pointed out, "She can't have been too afraid of Belzoni or she wouldn't have kept going back to him."

"When a man keeps a gun handy at all times and

tells you he'll murder you if you leave, you tend to stick around. She did everything any reasonable person could expect, but was in constant terror of her husband. What was she supposed to do when it came down to killing or being killed?''

"Alternatives exist, always."

"Such as?"

"What she's doing now, maybe? Running? Hiding?"

Her smile was wry. "You think that's any way to live?"

It was a neat trap that she'd closed on him. He had to admire that even as he was irritated by it. "I think she's lucky to have you on her side."

Her features smoothed, becoming expressionless at that return to the personal. "Thank you, I suppose."

He held her gaze, aware at the same time of his fascination in matching wits with her. The urgency of his mission nipped at his heels, but his most basic impulse was to settle more firmly in his seat and refuse to budge until he had learned every single thing there was to know about her. The strength of that need startled him, especially since he wasn't easily distracted under normal circumstances. His ability to close out extraneous thoughts or physical needs like hunger or thirst was legendary among the people who worked with him. He could function with machine-like precision in the middle of a storm, and had once or twice when the outer edges of hurricanes had blown through New Orleans. He wasn't sure what allowed the woman across from him to sneak under his defenses, but he intended to find out.

It was then that a dull thump sounded from somewhere above them. Adam glanced up, then looked at his hostess with a raised brow.

"A squirrel on the roof, maybe," she suggested with a trace of color blooming across her cheekbones.

"At night?"

"It's been known to happen. Or maybe the wind brought down a rotted limb from one of the oaks."

It was just plausible enough that he decided not to push it for the moment. If he was wrong, it would give her too good an opportunity to ask him to leave, and he wasn't ready to do that just yet. Listening for any repeat of the noise, he drank a long sip of his cooling coffee and considered his options.

Lara Kincaid wasn't going to tell him what he needed to know, not of her own free will. He couldn't force her to cooperate, and it was doubtful that he had the time it would take to really win her trust. What was left then except a physical search of the premises? Yet if he tried that and turned up nothing, he'd be worse off than before.

He should let Roan take care of this thing after all. Admitting failure went against the grain however, now that he was here. The best thing he could do, then, was to continue with their cat-and-mouse game and hope for the best. The main problem with that was keeping it clear in his mind just who was the cat and who was the mouse.

"You've met my brother's wife?" he asked, almost at random. "Since she designs quilting fabrics, you should have something in common."

"She's been in a couple of times with her daughter.

I keep her commercial fabrics in stock, as well as some of her special hand-dyes.''

Adam wanted to ask if Janna had ever mentioned him but didn't quite dare. "She's a creative wonder."

"Her work is beautiful," Lara agreed with a nod. "How is Lainey?"

It was obvious the two women had hit it off if she knew about the kidney transplant of his young niece by marriage. "She's fine. You'd never know she'd had a problem."

"I'm glad," she said simply.

"She and Janna have had more than their share of troubles."

"Some people do"

"Clay intends to see that nothing ever touches them again. He's made it his life's mission."

"He's the perfect knight-errant, at least in Janna's eyes," she agreed. "But it seems to be a family trait. I've heard tales of Benedict exploits."

"Greatly exaggerated, I expect."

She gave him an assessing look. "Maybe, though I don't remember any suggestions of sainthood."

Benedict sins weren't something he wanted to get into, Adam thought, but he would like to know how the rest of the family viewed Lara. "Anybody invite you to the family get-together this weekend?"

"I'm not a Benedict," she said, the words abrupt.

That told him nothing, but perhaps it was what she'd intended. He was still thinking about that when another sound came from the upper regions of the house, like water draining in wall pipes. Deliberately, he got to his feet, resting his fingertips on the tabletop as he stared up at the ceiling. Before he could speak, before he could even begin to form the question in his mind, Lara rose with fluid grace and placed her hand on his arm.

"Wait. Please."

Her touch exploded along his nerve endings. The sensation rocketed through him, jolting his heart into an unnatural rhythm then centering just south of his belt buckle. He was no playboy, though he'd been through a few relationships, but he'd spent endless minutes on foreplay without that much reaction. Frowning to cover his amazement, he straightened and turned to face her.

"I know...that is, I'm assuming you provide information for money. I mean, the New Orleans police pay you?"

"As a consultant, yes. I'm no bounty hunter."

She blinked at that. "I didn't think you were."

"Just clearing that up for future reference." As if he'd have any kind of future with this woman after tonight, he thought with derision.

"I've no idea how much you get for something like this," she went on, lowering her gaze to the spot where her fingers burned his forearm, "and my aunt isn't exactly wealthy, but..."

"Stop right there," he said, his voice hardening.

"No, really, I'm sure she could afford to make it worth your while to just..."

He reached to close his hand on her wrist, removing that barrier to sanity. She clenched her hand into a fist, and he could feel her inner strength, as well as the quick throb of her pulse. It helped to know that he wasn't entirely alone in his response to their physical contact. He should release her, he knew, but couldn't find the will on such short notice. "You couldn't actually think I'd agree," he said. "What is this then?"

"Call it a test." Her wide green eyes searched his, perhaps for some sign of what he meant to do next.

"Of what?"

"Whether you're knight-errant material, maybe, like your brother and your cousins."

"Knight-errant is usually an unpaid position. What was I supposed to do, refuse the money and come to your aid—or rather your aunt's—out of pure and noble compassion?"

Her smile was strained. "You're very quick. I'd have had to explain that to most men. But the answer to the question is yes."

"And if that didn't work?"

"Who knows?"

The words were so soft he almost didn't hear, still they seemed plain enough. Regret was a suffocating pain inside him. Still, he forced himself to let her go and step back. "Sorry," he answered. "My allegiance isn't for sale. Not at any price."

Four

He meant it, Lara could see that easily enough. She saluted that integrity in him even as she regretted it. It would have been much easier if he could have been seduced by her small attempt at corruption. He didn't appear susceptible, which meant that she would have to use other means.

Giving up was not an option, of course. She had her own principles that would not permit turning her aunt over to the uncertain mercy of Louisiana's criminal justice system. Family loyalty was not solely a Benedict trait.

"So," he said with a lifted brow. "Who's upstairs? Or would you like me to guess?"

To answer with the truth or stall for time, that was the question. But she was given no chance to answer it. Footsteps approached, then the swinging door between the kitchen and the sitting room flapped open to allow a woman to step through. She paused as she saw them, then moved on toward the sink.

"Sorry to interrupt your little tête-à-tête, Lara love, but I woke up and thought I smelled coffee."

It was Aunt Kim, with a housecoat of heavy white terry cloth wrapped around her, red hair flowing over her shoulders, and sardonic amusement in her face.

Lara stood in frozen consternation for long seconds while possibilities flashed through her mind. Then she gave a resigned sigh.

"Interrupt, by all means," she said. "You may as well, since this man is here to see you."

"Is he really?" Her aunt took a water glass from the cabinet and filled it before turning around. The gaze she rested on Adam held apprehension overlaid by pure female speculation. Then her eyes, lavender blue by grace of tinted contacts, widened a fraction and a slow smile curved her lips. "Well," she said in tones that were abruptly lighter and a shade breathless. "Hello."

Lara hid a grim smile by turning to fill another coffee cup. Aunt Kim could no more prevent herself from coming on to an attractive man than she could stop breathing. Flirtatious speech and body language were simple reflex actions after years of being dependent on male support, male attraction, male assurances of her worth as a female. They were also natural defenses against male danger.

"You're Kim Belzoni?" she heard Adam ask from behind her.

"I suppose I should have introduced you," Lara said, and rectified that lapse as she turned to put the coffee mug on another place mat at the kitchen table. A quick glance at Adam's face told her nothing. His expression was measuring yet closed-in, as if he deliberately suspended judgment. She picked up his cup to refill it. While her back was turned, she considered adding a little something extra to it along the lines of what they'd been discussing a few minutes ago. She wasn't sure she could manage it without attracting attention, however, and did not want to think of the repercussions if that happened. Turning again, she put the coffee in front of him.

"To what do I owe this honor?" Aunt Kim asked as she slid onto a chair then drank from her water glass, watching him over the rim in apparent fascination. She should have appeared haggard, but looked rested and relaxed instead. She had creamed her face and applied moisturizer, so her skin appeared fresh and unlined, not at all that of a woman several years older than the man who held her interest—or one who had shot her husband only twenty-four hours ago.

"Your husband's death," Adam answered. He resumed his seat only after Lara had returned to the table.

"Oh." The animation faded from Aunt Kim's face and she shifted a little in her chair before darting an accusing glance in Lara's direction.

"If you think I sent for him, you're wrong," Lara said at once. "He has police connections."

Aunt Kim glanced at Adam again. She set down her water glass and picked up her coffee cup before she said, "He doesn't look like a policeman."

That was certainly true. "He found you anyway. If he can manage it so quickly, then it's not safe here for you."

"Where would it be? Safe, that is?"

"You could come with me," Adam interjected. "I know a few people who have questions they'd like to ask you."

"And if I don't want to answer?" Aunt Kim asked in querulous disdain.

"You'd rather take your chances with your husband's uncle?"

Her face paled, and she looked suddenly older. "If you really want to know what I'd like, it's to be far, far away from here. All I have to do is figure out where to go."

"Cooperating with the authorities would be much better for you. They can protect you and, if you're telling the truth about what happened, then..."

"If?"

"Then you have nothing to worry about," he finished, ignoring the interruption.

"So you say," Aunt Kim snapped. "But what if Ernesto's family uses its influence to see that I'm convicted? It's all politics you know—favors, money, elections, deals. Truth and justice have little to do with it."

She had a point. Lara looked at Adam to see how he'd respond.

"It's better than being dead," he said flatly.

Lara's aunt grimaced. "I don't look good in prison orange, and the last I heard, there were no manicures or facials available in Angola's hair salon. I'm thinking South America. They appreciate women of a certain age in Rio."

"If you can get there."

She tipped her head. "You could always take me."

The invitation was so bald that Lara was embarrassed. She waited to discover if it was any more successful than her own attempt at influencing the man at the table.

"I don't think so."

Aunt Kim's eyes narrowed. "You're very sure. Why is that, I wonder?" Then her face cleared. "Oh, I see. Your interest is already engaged. How fascinating."

"Don't tell me," Adam drawled, "that you also have the family talent for mind reading?"

"It comes in handy now and then, even when personal involvement prevents it from working as it should."

"Remind me to find out if there are other quirks some time. For now, you have a decision to make."

Aunt Kim stared at him a second. "How can you be so hard? Have you never been in trouble?"

"Not recently, and not when it involves murder."

"It wasn't murder! It wasn't, though I should have killed him ages ago."

Lara cleared her throat as she gave her aunt a warning look.

"I know it isn't smart to say it, but it's the truth," she declared, unrepentant. "He was the kind of man someone was going to kill sooner or later."

"You might have waited until it happened," Lara replied, raking a stray wisp of hair back into her braid.

"I would have, if I'd thought I'd be around to see it," her aunt snapped back.

Lara gave Adam an I-told-you-so look, but he didn't seem to notice. With his gaze on her aunt, he said, "It's a little late to worry about that now. Here's my proposition...."

"Why, Adam, I barely know you," she began.

A flash of irritation was his only reaction to that comment. "Put on some clothes and let me drive you back to New Orleans to talk to Whitaker at the NOPD. Maybe the two of you can work something out."

"What happens if I refuse? Are you going to drag me back kicking and screaming?"

It was a good question, Lara thought. She waited for the answer with almost as much interest as her aunt.

"Not my job," Adam said with a small shake of his head as he reached to unclip his cell phone from his belt. "What I'll do is call Jack. I expect he can arrange to have the local authorities pick you up and hold you until he can send someone after you."

"No, wait. Please." Aunt Kim reached across the corner of the table to touch the firm muscles of his forearm, moving her fingers in a small, distracted caress. "Give me time to think about it a minute? I mean, this is all so…so unbelievable that I can't get my mind straight."

"You don't have long," he warned.

"What do you mean?" She looked from Adam to Lara.

"The Cosa Nostra has computers, too, or so I'd imagine," Lara said in terse explanation.

Her aunt stared at her for long seconds, then a stricken look appeared in her eyes. She dropped her head into her hands with a fiercely whispered imprecation. "If Benedict found me with so little trouble," she said in a muffled whisper, "so can they."

"Exactly."

"They could be here any minute. Oh, my God."

"Never mind," Lara said with as much assurance as she was able. "They aren't here yet."

Aunt Kim raised her face. Her skin seemed suddenly slack and her eyes hot with unshed tears. "I'm sorry, honey, truly. I didn't mean to...to bring this kind of trouble down on you."

"It doesn't matter. We have to decide what to do from this point."

"While you're both thinking, maybe you can tell me who else might be on the property," Adam said. "The police suspect an accomplice in Belzoni's death because both vehicles registered to him were still at the house."

"Meaning?" Lara asked.

"They can't see how you got away, Mrs. Belzoni."

"Call me Kim. Please. As for my so-called escape, it was easy." She gave a short laugh. "I just walked out. When my feet started to hurt, I stopped at a pay phone and called a gypsy cab."

"A gypsy cab," he repeated, as if to be certain he'd heard her correctly.

Lara was almost as amazed. Calling a freelance cab driver with precious little connection to a cab company and lax record-keeping had been a masterstroke.

"I know this great black woman who owns one. She drove me from New Orleans to Baton Rouge, then dropped me at a bar. The barman at this place is a friend. He arranged a rental car for me."

"On his card, I suppose, so your name wouldn't appear in the computer," Adam suggested.

"You've got it."

"No accomplice then, no new boyfriend?"

Aunt Kim looked away. "No help, if that's what you mean."

If there was someone, Lara saw that her aunt wasn't prepared to admit it. Was she shielding him, whoever he might be, or had he only been the catalyst that had persuaded her to finally break free? She half expected Adam to pursue the question, but he took a different tack.

"This rental, I didn't see it out front."

Her aunt gave him a scathing look. "Even I know better than that. It's hidden, of course."

"Because you knew someone would be coming after you." His voice was hard.

"Because I didn't want Lara's quilting customers to know I was on the place. News gets around, and this little community isn't so very far from New Orleans."

It made sense, Lara felt, and was pleased to see Adam's nod of acceptance before he asked, "So where did you hide it?"

Aunt Kim folded her lips and drew her housecoat more tightly around her. Adam stared at her a second. Then he turned his gaze toward Lara with one brow lifted in inquiry.

"The place was a self-sufficient farm until the late nineteen-fifties, with chickens, cows, the works," she said. "Trees have grown up around the old barn out back so it's now in the woods, but it's solid enough to use as a storehouse and garage."

"A bit obvious, don't you think?" he commented with irony in his voice.

"Only if you know it's there."

"And can follow tire tracks?"

"I mowed over them."

He made no reply, but only turned his attention to his coffee.

They seemed to have reached an impasse. Lara tried to think of some way out of it, a way that would allow her aunt to go free while still satisfying Adam Benedict's ethical notions. Nothing came to her.

Aunt Kim seemed to be thinking along the same lines, though with more success. She gave Lara a fixed stare when she glanced in her direction. Immediately Lara's mind was filled with an image of Adam lying in her old brass bed upstairs.

His hands were clasped behind his head on the pillow and smoldering appreciation lay in his eyes. He was watching her undress, following her movements intently as she stepped from her jeans and pulled her T-shirt off over her head. She wore no bra, and her breasts were pale and round in the moonlight that filled the room. She slid her thumbs under the top band of the triangle of white lace that still covered her, then stopped. Smiling, she left that covering in place since she understood that he wanted to strip away that last bit with his own hands. Removing the clasp from her hair, she shook her braid loose, freeing the long, streaming strands. She flung them behind her shoulders, lifted her chin, and then moved toward the bed. Gliding with easy grace, never taking her gaze from the rich, sea-blue eyes of the man who

waited for her, she came nearer, nearer. Then he
raised to one elbow and circled her waist with a hard
arm, drawing her down beside him....

"No," she gasped, her voice choked.

Adam turned a startled glance in her direction.
"What?"

"Really, Lara, would it be such a sacrifice?" her
aunt asked.

"It isn't going to happen," she returned, ignoring
the man across the table. "For one thing, he isn't
interested...."

"Are you sure?" The words had a musing sound.

"For another, I can't. And even if I could, and
managed to sway him, he would resent it later."

Her aunt pursed her lips. "That would bother you,
his resentment?"

"Of course it would."

"I fail to see why, unless you care about the future."

"Do you mind telling me what's going on?" Adam
asked in biting tones. "Especially since I seem to be
a part of it?"

"No, no," Aunt Kim said with the briefest of
glances. "At least you aren't yet."

"Now look," he began.

Lara refused to even turn her head in his direction
for fear of being influenced. "He won't be, either,"
she insisted. "The future has nothing to do with it.
It's an impossible idea."

"Listen," Adam said.

"I don't see that at all," her aunt objected. "A
diversion similar to the one you were practicing be-

fore I came in just now is all that's required, not a lifetime commitment. You needn't pretend to be repulsed by the idea, because I know better.''

''It isn't repulsive at all, just morally corrupt. And though I realize that's not a huge problem for you, it is for me.''

Adam frowned as he cocked his head to one side, staring at the windows. He said again, ''Listen...''

Her aunt sighed. ''Well, if you're going to be that way about it. Heaven knows, I wouldn't want you doing anything that—''

''Listen!'' Adam ordered.

The sudden realization that he had been trying to hear what was happening outside silenced them. As quiet fell, they caught it too, the powerful hum of a car engine as it slowed in front of the house. Then it stopped.

Lara got to her feet so fast that her chair overturned with a hard thump. Aunt Kim sat perfectly still, scarcely breathing. Adam eased to his feet with the lithe movement of well-oiled muscles. They held their places, waiting to see what would happen next.

Five

The chime of the doorbell echoed through the still house. None of the people Lara had met through the quilt shop in recent weeks would show up at this late hour. She could detect no hint of immediate threat, but her nerves were so rattled by the argument with her aunt and reaction to the mental image that had preceded it that her impressions weren't reliable.

She looked at Adam. Keeping her voice low, she asked, "What do you think?"

"Could be Belzoni's goons, but doesn't have to be."

"It seems odd that they'd walk up and ring the doorbell."

"It's what I did, after all."

"That's different," she said shortly. "You only wanted information."

"They could want the same thing. Always assuming that's who it is."

It was them, and she knew it. "What am I going to do?"

"Get the door before they become suspicious," he said, though with apparent reluctance. "Just spin the same story you told me. You've heard from her, know about her husband's death, but she didn't say where she was going.''

"And if they want to look for themselves?"

"Don't let them!" Aunt Kim interjected with a shudder.

Adam spoke to her aunt, though his gaze remained on Lara's face. "Don't worry. I'll be right behind her."

It was amazing, the steadiness she gained from that idea, Lara thought. The feeling stayed with her as the two of them moved back through the sitting room to the foyer. Clicking on the porch light from the switch beside the heavy front door, Lara glanced out through the sheer curtains that covered the sidelights surrounding it.

Only one man stood on the porch, a tall and weedy-looking individual with a narrow face and protuberant eyes. Another one leaned on the fender of the dark Lincoln that sat on the driveway behind Adam's SUV, however, and a driver could be dimly seen behind the steering wheel. Lara was painfully aware that she had not locked the door after admitting Adam since she hadn't expected him to be staying.

Taking a deep breath, she spoke through the door. "Yes?"

"Miss Kincaid?"

Her visitor sounded polite enough, but there was a hard note in his voice that struck a warning chord in her brain. "That's right."

"I know it's late, ma'am, but we need to speak to you concerning a relative of yours, Mrs. Ernesto Belzoni."

"Who are you?" she asked. Though the answer was obvious, she needed to give the impression that she wasn't expecting visitors.

"Business associates of her husband. Could I step inside for a few minutes?"

Adam, standing half hidden by the velvet portiere of the encased opening to parlor, gave a decided shake of his head. Lara signified her understanding, even as she answered the man's question. "I don't think that's a good idea. It really is late, and I can't help you."

"You seen Mrs. Belzoni lately?"

Lara replied as Adam had suggested, then waited with some trepidation for the reaction. From the corners of her eyes, she saw the man who'd been leaning against the Lincoln straighten then walk toward Adam's SUV and open the passenger side door.

"You can't tell me where she might have gone?" her visitor asked without perceptible belief.

"I'm afraid not."

It was quiet on the other side of the door for a second. Finally, the man said, "I'd hate to think you might be lying to me, Miss Kincaid."

"Why would I do that?" She allowed natural irritation to sound in her voice.

"I can't imagine, but it would be a bad move."

A warning laced that comment though it was still fairly civil. Lara had heard that the Cosa Nostra of New Orleans operated with something of the laissez-faire attitude of the Big Easy. That it might possibly be true was counterbalanced by acute awareness of how easy it would be for the man on the other side of the door to simply open it and force his way inside.

The thought was pushed from her mind as the man near the SUV waved a handful of papers at the man on the porch, yelling out something that attracted his attention. She couldn't tell what he said, but didn't like the sound of his voice. Nor did she care for the way the thin man set his feet and squared up to the door again afterward.

"Ma'am?"

"Yes, I'm here," Lara said, much too aware of thudding of her heart in her chest.

"The SUV out front here belongs to an Adam Benedict from New Orleans. You got a visitor?"

Real anger surfaced in her mind as she realized that the papers the second man had brandished had probably been Adam's vehicle registration. "I fail to see how that concerns you."

"You'd be surprised what concerns me. He here on business or pleasure?"

Lara refused to look at Adam as she answered, "Pleasure, of course. Mine."

"You known him long?"

"A while," she answered with swift purpose. "He used to live around here, you know. In fact, Adam's cousin is parish sheriff."

A grunt served as comment. "Let me talk to him."

"Do you know him?" She turned her gaze toward Adam who immediately made a hard, negative gesture with one hand.

"Only by rep. Tell him to step out here where I can see him."

The man's voice carried a warning that he'd accept no excuse. Lara hesitated, uncertain how to reply. Glancing at Adam again, she met and held his dark blue gaze while the mantel clock in the parlor ticked, mindlessly counting down the seconds.

Then he moved from the shadows with near-silent strides. He caught the door's heavy brass handle and jerked it open.

The thin man jumped back before he caught himself. Temper and chagrin were strong in his voice as he spoke. "So it is you, Benedict."

"Demarius. I might have guessed."

"You recognize me. How is that?"

"Your mug shot in the family file. It was pointed out when you became an enforcer."

"Right. I heard you hung out downtown. What're you doing so far out in the boonies?"

"The lady answered that question already. You have anything else to say, spit it out. I have better things to do than stand here talking." Reaching for Lara, he slid an arm around her waist and drew her against him. A shiver ran over her at the warm strength of his hold, the intimation of security in the feel of his hard body against hers, though she hoped he hadn't noticed.

"Can't say I blame you," Demarius offered with his gaze lingering on the front of her T-shirt. "I'd have an idea or two, in your place. But I don't think that's all you've got on your mind."

"Meaning?"

The iron behind Adam's question seemed to amuse

the other man. "We had a tip saying the woman we want was headed up here."

"Can't have been very reliable."

"From a barkeep in Baton Rouge that owed us a favor. You know how it is."

"We'll keep an eye out for her." Adam's tone didn't give an inch.

"Oh, I think you'll do better than that. Fact is, I expect that's the reason you're here. Since I don't want any trouble with you, I'll tell you what. You hand over Mrs. Belzoni and everything will be fine. You can stay right here or take off back to town, no questions asked."

"That's generous of you," he said with an edge of mockery in his voice.

"Ain't it though. You can even have gorgeous here for company."

Lara didn't care to be reduced to the role of mere girlfriend. It was her house, after all. "No thinking, moral person would give up anyone to you," she said in low anger. "You couldn't have my aunt even if she was here."

"Now that's downright noble, ma'am," the thin man said as he shoved his hands into his pockets and rocked back on his heels. "Problem is, nobility can get you killed."

"What do you mean?"

"It gets in the way of self-preservation, you know? What it all boils down to here is a choice. You can stick with your aunt or you can hang out with lover-boy. Benedict can stand between us and the woman we're after or he can stand back and let us have her.

One way you two could get hurt, or worse, and the other way you're okay. Like I said, it's a choice—and I don't care who makes it.''

"That's crazy!"

"I thought it was pretty fair, myself." He shrugged. "We could eliminate all of you, probably save ourselves a lot of trouble."

"Or cause more than you know what to do with," Adam suggested.

The gaze the thin man turned in his direction was as empty as his voice. "There's always that possibility. But sometimes you just have to go with your gut feeling."

"What if my gut says smashing your face in is a fine idea?''

"Adam," Lara said, closing her hand on his arm that still fastened her to him with the strength of a steel cable. The feeling she received now from the skinny Mafioso in front of her, as effortlessly as sound or scent, was of a love of power, especially the power to control by fear. Destruction meant nothing to him, even when it was destroying life.

Adam relaxed a fraction, for she felt it. When she could be reasonably certain he wasn't going to attack the man on the porch, she said to Demarius, "I told you my aunt isn't here."

"I think you're lying, honey, but it doesn't matter a hell of a lot. Tell you what. I never much cared for what I'd heard of Benedict, here, and care even less now that I've met him. If you say you can't put your hand on this aunt of yours, then I'll take him as a substitute. I expect he can be persuaded to find her for us.''

She sent Adam a swift glance, but his set face gave nothing away. ''He could have something to say about that.''

''Makes no difference. You tell me how it's to be and I'll see to it.'' He paused while he glanced at the expensive watch on his wrist. ''You got half an hour to make up your mind.''

''Half an hour!''

He gave her a skeletal smile as he turned to walk back toward the car. Over his shoulder, he said, ''Be glad you got that much. I'd have said ten minutes if I wasn't in such a good mood.''

Lara closed the door and locked it, then moved as if to step away from Adam. He didn't release her, but only stared in front of him with a meditative expression on his face. Putting her spread fingertips against his chest and exerting pressure, she said with some acerbity, ''If you don't mind?''

He looked down at her, then blinked and removed his grasp. ''Sorry.''

Somehow she doubted it, though it didn't seem a good time to press the point. ''What are we going to do?''

''We? Since when did this become a joint effort? The way I heard it, the decision is yours.''

''Divide and conquer tactics. He hopes one of us will let him have what he wants out of fear and self-interest. It only works if we let it.''

''And you don't intend to let it?'' The glance he sent in her direction gave nothing away, though she thought he was probably ahead of her on Demarius's intentions.

"It was bad psychology on his part. Knowing I'd have to live with myself, afterward, makes any bargain impossible."

"You're not tempted, just to be rid of me?"

Her gaze was caustic. "Nothing was said about temptation."

"So it wasn't." A smile tugged one corner of his mouth. "What you really want to know is if I'll turn your aunt over to them?"

"Would you?" Even as she asked, Lara wondered how many men would hesitate more than a few minutes before accepting the trade-off of their life for that of some woman they'd barely met.

"What do you really think?"

For all the mockery in his tone, Lara believed he was still busy with his own thoughts. She was silent, studying his face, weighing her impression until she was sure she had his full attention. "Of course you won't. We're in this together, you and I. Well, and Aunt Kim."

"What makes you so sure?"

"I just know," she said in a voice that dared him to doubt her methods. "It's the way you are. You couldn't hand a female of any kind over to what might be certain death."

"Nothing personal, just a principle, right?"

"Something like that."

"You're only half correct. I'm holding on to your aunt for the same reason that I can't ignore the fact that I found her. I gave my word. That means I'll take her in, no matter who gets in the way.''

"So you'll protect her from one danger in order to turn her over to another?''

"If it comes to it.''

"I think it has,'' she returned succinctly. "But let me get this straight. If you're pledged to shield her in order to keep your word, that must mean you wouldn't be inclined to help Belzoni's uncle locate Aunt Kim, even if I let them have you?''

"No.''

"Regardless of their methods of persuasion?'' She winced mentally at that too-nice euphemism for torture, but she had a point to make.

"There's always that hope.''

"Then giving you up could well buy the time she needs to escape.''

"If you decide that's the best course, after all.''

He seemed so nonchalant about it that she couldn't believe he understood what she was saying. "I could conceivably be as much a danger to you, then, as the men outside.''

"A danger?'' His firm lips curved at one corner.

"You don't think I can be? Especially for good reason?''

"I didn't say that. It's just that I've thought of you in a lot of ways since I got here tonight, but dangerous isn't one of them.''

The need to know just how he'd thought of her was strong. Asking would be like admitting that she was interested, however, and she wasn't ready for that. Besides, there was too much at stake just now to explore it. "The men out there don't change the fact that my aunt doesn't belong in jail."

"Not even for her own safety?"

"You know what the system is like. Once she's caught in it, her motive for killing her husband won't matter because domestic violence is so common it's virtually ignored. The police can close the case, the D.A.'s office can chalk up one more easy conviction, and everybody would be happy. I won't have her become a scapegoat."

"You've seen too many legal dramas," he said shortly.

"Don't patronize me. It can happen and you know it."

"Suppose I said I'd do everything in my power to prevent it?"

She considered that, more aware than she wanted to be of how much she'd like to depend on his word. Every instinct said she could and should, but she dared not rely on them. Her need to believe was too great, and it wasn't her life that hung in the balance, after all. "Not good enough."

"What is? You want a guarantee written in blood? It may come to that before this is over."

He had apparently faced the prospect of being hurt or killed and accepted it without moaning about his fate, without worry over the odds or the fact that this wasn't his fight. He'd made his decision and was prepared to stand by it.

Lara had only just met Adam Benedict, yet the idea of what might happen to him made her feel ill. She didn't want to be responsible for him getting hurt, had no desire to fear his death, despised the idea of needing him. She hated what was happening to them with all its doubts and strains but could see no way to stop it.

It was all very well for the man outside to say she had a choice. There was none that she could see. She could not deliberately abandon her aunt, nor could she use Adam in order to save her. All that was left was a fight against overwhelming odds. The question was whether she and Adam could trust each other enough to join forces, much less to survive the battle.

Six

The kitchen door creaked open beyond the sitting room. Adam whipped around toward the sound, but it was only Lara's aunt who emerged like a ghost from out of the dark in her white housecoat.

"What are you two whispering about?" she asked, her voice sharp. "If you're plotting in here, I think I have a right to be in on it."

Adam left the explanations to Lara, since Kim Belzoni was her aunt. The older woman wasn't going to like them and her objections would be vocal. Not that he blamed her. She had a right to be upset.

He'd noticed a phone in the kitchen. Checking it was probably useless, but something that had to be done. He moved off in that direction, leaving the women talking in low tones behind him.

The line was dead. He stood with the receiver in his hand, weighing it while trenchant thought streamed through his mind. There were three goons out there. No doubt they'd figured that was enough to take care of a couple of women. He'd upset their calculations by getting here ahead of them. Demarius had been put out about that, which was why he'd talked so big in front of Lara.

Now that he'd made his threat, the Mafia enforcer

wouldn't back down. That made for a sticky situation. What would he do when he didn't get the results he wanted, try a frontal assault or opt for stealth in a three-pronged entry? The straightforward approach might have been fine before, but Demarius should realize that he, Adam, would be expecting it now. Would that matter, considering how unlikely it was that they had missed finding his weapon when they rummaged through his glove compartment?

He was an unknown quantity, Adam thought. His presence could make them more cautious or more aggressive, according to how big a threat he appeared to them. It would be nice if he had some of Lara's supposed ESP to guide him, because it was impossible to guess which way they'd jump.

If he were alone, he'd take to the woods. He had hunted and fished the area as a teenager, so remembered its creeks and bayous and how they ran, where the trails crossed side roads, and where those side roads hit the main drag. The guys out there were city dudes who hardly knew which direction was up. He could run circles around them, especially in the dark.

That wouldn't work as long as he had two women dependent on him. He couldn't move as fast or as quietly, and couldn't afford to take chances. The best bet seemed to be to sit tight and call for backup.

Replacing the receiver in its wall cradle, he reached for the cell phone that he'd left lying on the table. He paused for a moment to recall the number for Roan's office, then began to punch it into the lighted panel.

A scream rang out from the sitting room. Adam dropped the phone on the cabinet top and ran.

Kim Belzoni was crouched in a chair with her face in her hands. Lara looked up from where she was bending over her as he skidded to a halt on the center rug. In the dim light from the kitchen, he searched her face for some hint of injury or threat. "What is it?" he demanded. "What happened?"

"Nothing. It's only that—"

"Nothing?" Her aunt lifted her tear-stained face. "You call it nothing that three men are waiting outside to kill me? Nothing, that I've been beaten and abused and hounded from my home, and now have to wait while my niece and an absolute stranger decide whether I live or die? I can't stand it. I can't!"

The last words were spoken on another wail. Adam hovered, feeling helpless, while his heartbeat dropped back to something near a normal pace.

"I told you it's all right," Lara said, rubbing her aunt's shoulder. "Neither of us is going to give you up."

"But he's going to turn me over to the police anyway," Kim said with a stabbing look in Adam's direction. "I might as well be dead!"

"You don't mean that."

"I do mean it. You haven't a clue what prison is like, but I do because I went with Ernesto once to visit his brother. Once was enough to see the crudeness, the ugliness, and complete lack of privacy. Then I'll always be looking over my shoulder for the person Ernesto's uncle will send after me. If I survive, it'll be a miracle."

"You killed a man," Adam said in his most patient tone. "Did you think there'd be no consequences?"

"If I hadn't shot Ernesto he'd have killed me!"

"You won't go to prison unless you're convicted, and you won't be convicted if you're innocent of the intent to commit murder. But you still have to tell it to the judge."

"What if the Belzoni family is a major contributor to this judge's retirement fund? What then?"

"You appeal and ask for a change of venue."

"With what for money? Ernesto's estate will be tied up for years, and I'm not eligible for his life insurance, if he had any, which I doubt. I'd be broke if I hadn't managed to stash a little money away, but it's all I've got to live on. No, no, I have to get away. I just have to!"

"If you manage that, what happens to Lara? Or to me, for that matter?"

"We'll all go. It's the only way."

Kim Belzoni stared at him with such intensity in her red-rimmed eyes that it seemed she willed him to do as she asked. Adam still couldn't agree. "The best thing to do is call Roan. He and his deputies can be here with sirens blasting in ten minutes flat."

"To take me into custody? No thanks."

There was no reasoning with the woman. Stifling an exasperated sigh, he glanced at Lara. She was watching him with waiting stillness in her eyes, as if she expected something more from him. What it might be, he couldn't imagine since he was fresh out of ideas.

It wasn't a comfortable feeling. Swinging around, Adam headed back toward the kitchen and his cell phone.

"Wait!"

It was Lara's aunt who called out to him. As he turned back, she lowered her head, plucking at the pile of her terry housecoat. "I...I don't really mean to be so selfish or cause so much trouble. Neither of you would be in this mess if it weren't for me, and I'm sorry for that. I wouldn't have anything happen to Lara for the world, or to you either, Adam. I'd change things, make them better, it if I could."

"Oh, Aunt Kim," Lara said softly as she rubbed her aunt's shoulder.

Kim gave a quick shake of her head. "It's just that...I don't know. Everything is so mixed up in my mind. Sometimes it seems like a dream. I can still see Ernesto coming at me, still feel it as he hit me so I stumbled against the bedside table. The drawer fell open and the gun was just there. The next thing, I knew, he was clutching at the hole in his chest."

So it had been self-defense, Adam thought. Either that or Kim Belzoni was an extremely good actress. Aloud, he asked, "Why didn't you call 911 for an ambulance?"

"It was no use, I could see that. I...I panicked. At least, I suppose that's what you'd call it. I don't actually remember. I must have just left the house, walked away from the whole mess. Everything is a blank until I came to myself, heading out of New Orleans on Interstate 10 in a gypsy cab. I still had the gun with me, lying on my lap."

Tears overflowed her eyes, and she put her hands to her face as if overcome by emotion. With a gesture of distress and apology, she stood up and moved toward the kitchen as though in search of a tissue or paper towel to wipe her face. When the swinging doors had closed behind her, Adam turned to Lara.

"You believe her?" he asked at once.

"Why wouldn't I?"

"Maybe because her story is so convenient, coming after I hinted just now that a plea of self-defense might help?"

"You have a cynical mind," she said in scathing accusation. "Can't you tell how upset she is about it?"

He shifted the muscles of one shoulder in moody acknowledgment. "She can be upset and still be guilty, can't she?"

"Oh, please."

"I'd like to believe her, since I'd rather not think about what I might be taking her back to face."

"Meaning?"

"Louisiana favors death by lethal injection for capital crimes."

A shudder rippled through Lara, though her face remained composed. "But you aren't convinced?"

"I could be, possibly, if I knew whether she thought I'd turn her in faster if she was innocent than if she was guilty."

Lara gave a mirthless laugh. "I'm not sure her mind is as devious as yours."

"Count on it," he said, barely glancing at her.

"In that case," she told him after a few quiet seconds, "I'd have to say she may have told you what happened to gain sympathy, but probably not to sway your decision. Aunt Kim was never a very forceful personality. She was kind to me while I was growing up, always smiling, always full of things she wanted to see and do. She was special, with the kind of presence actors sometimes have that makes people turn and stare. But whatever life plans she may have had, she never had the drive to reach them. She drifted into situations and out of them again, seemingly without conscious decision. If she murdered Ernesto Belzoni, it was because he gave her no alternative."

The description seemed to fit, for what it was worth. He'd have to consider it later. Right this moment, he had another priority. "This weapon she mentioned, did she still have it when she got here?"

"On the front seat of her car. She wanted me to get rid of it for her, since she couldn't stand to touch it."

"It was a high-caliber pistol I suppose, if she offed Belzoni with a single shot, even if it was at close range. So did you bury it, or just give it a good fling into the bushes?"

"I heard your SUV on the drive when I set out to take care of it," she informed him. "I brought it back inside. It's in my bedroom upstairs."

"Could you bring…"

He stopped as a noise from the kitchen registered in his mind. He'd been hearing the sound of water running into a sink for several minutes, much longer than it should have taken for Kim to splash her face or even to fill a glass to drink. Swinging around on his heel without another word, he headed in that direction.

Lara's aunt had her back turned to him as she stood

at the double sink. White suds mounded one side of it, as if it had been filled for washing dishes. She glanced up, using the dark surface of the big window in front of her as a mirror to check his entry. Then without turning, she reached and picked up his cell phone.

"Don't!" he commanded.

She paid no attention. Holding the phone above the soapy water, she opened her fingers and dropped it.

The phone seemed to fall in slow motion, endlessly plummeting, down through bubbles that fragmented on impact, billowing upward in a froth of tiny, iridescent globules. The gray plastic phone created a white crater that spread in a circular fountain, splashing, hissing. Then the foam closed over it, hiding it from sight.

Adam cursed. Springing to the sink, he plunged his hand into the hot, soapy water. Behind him, he heard Lara enter the kitchen and her sharp exclamation followed by a spate of questions. Kim backed away without attempting to answer.

By the time he fished the phone out of the sink and brought it up, dripping soapsuds, Lara had found a dish towel. She held it out, and he snatched it from her to wrap the phone. With fast, economical moves, he blotted away the water, turned the phone first one way and then another to drain it then flipped open the case and repeated the process. When it was as dry as it was going to get, he stood looking at it.

Waiting was unlikely to help matters. He squared his shoulders and punched the power button.

Nothing.

He tried again, then again, with the same result. He even punched in the numbers that would place his delayed call to Roan, for what good it did him. Snapping the phone shut, he stood with it clenched in his fist while breathing slowly in and out through his nose. Then he turned his gaze to Lara. Indicating the dead device, he asked in deliberate tones, "I don't suppose you have one of these."

"I haven't needed one," she answered.

"We need one now. The regular phone line has been cut." He looked at Kim. "You?"

She sank down on a chair at the table as if destroying the phone had taken the last of her energy. "Not with me. It fell out of my purse while I was looking for my gas card. It's in the car…in the barn."

"Figures." Every ounce of his considerable disgust was in that laconic comment.

Lara moistened her lips, dividing a nervous glance between him and her aunt as if half-afraid he might attack Kim. "What now?"

It was a good question. In a harsh drawl, he asked, "Either of you ladies know how to fire a weapon?"

"If you're thinking of some gung ho commando patrol—"

"Hardly. More like manning the barricades and forcing the goons outside to track us down, room by room."

"I can shoot," Kim said, her voice nearly inaudible. "My third husband loved to hunt. Our honeymoon was spent on safari, though he was in the bush more than he was with me. Our guide thought I should learn to shoot for my own protection so he...taught me.''

''And which one of them wound up with you as his trophy?'' The question popped out before Adam could prevent it.

''Neither,'' Lara's aunt shot back in a flash of spirit. ''Being mounted and stuffed out in the dirt and the flies wasn't my idea of bliss.''

He deserved that, he thought, even as he felt the back of his neck grow hot. A swift glance at the limpid irony in Lara's face informed him that she thought so, too. ''I don't think that story is something you want to tell the judge at your criminal hearing,'' he said in an attempt to regain his lost authority. ''He might jump to the wrong conclusion.''

Kim Belzoni didn't answer, but only looked down at her clasped hands.

It didn't make him feel any better.

''Fine,'' Lara said. ''We have one weapon and they have three—or maybe more, I don't know. Somehow, I don't like the odds.''

''You have a better idea?'' He leaned against the cabinet behind him and crossed his arms over his chest.

''We could slip out the back, make our way through the woods to a neighbor's house to call Roan.''

''If they aren't watching the exits, they're dumber than I think,'' he said with precision.

She pressed her mouth into a straight line and clasped her arms over her diaphragm in an unconscious parody of his stance. At least he hoped it was unconscious. The gesture had a vastly different effect on her feminine curves, one that did nothing to help his thought processes.

"Okay. Here we go." He straightened, clapping his hands together like a coach ready to present a brilliant game plan. "We have only one pistol, but that doesn't mean we don't have weapons. Kitchen cabinets and household junk drawers are packed with them— knives, scissors, hammers, screwdrivers, slicers and dicers. Household chemicals can be turned into lethal weapons. We may be outnumbered, but we aren't out. Lara, I need drain cleaner, for a start, then detergent and gelatin."

She didn't move. "We, Aunt Kim and I, are supposed to stab and slice and fling these explosives or whatever around?"

"You don't think you can do it?"

"Do you?"

"Come on, where's your black widow spider instinct? The female of the species is supposed to be more deadly, and so on? Think of it as preserving your home. Or if that doesn't do it, pretend those jerks out there are me."

The ghost of a smile came and went across her face. "Now there's an incentive."

"Thought so," he said, and was much more aware than he wanted to be of the smooth surfaces of her lips, and the warmth that curled in the pit of his stomach as he watched them. This wasn't the time or the place. Or was it? Libido in the human animal was supposed to be strongest when faced with extinction, wasn't it? On a deep breath, he said, "Right. Time's running out, ladies. Let's get to it."

Lara swung around and left the kitchen, probably to find the drain cleaner. The swinging door squeaked back and forth for a second then was still. In the quiet that descended, Adam looked at Kim. She was staring at him with doubt and dread stamped plainly on her features.

He knew just how she felt.

Seven

Lara slipped through the dark rooms without turning on the lights. She was used to it, for one thing, but she didn't want to advertise the fact that anything unusual was going on. The men outside would expect them to be huddling together in panic mode. They didn't really know Adam Benedict or they'd be a great deal more wary. Still, it would be better not to put them on alert.

What would she and Aunt Kim have done if they'd been alone in the house when the men showed up? It would all be over by now, she suspected. Adam's presence had forced her visitors to rethink their options. The end result might be the same, but at least it gave them a chance.

Courage and fidelity. The colors signifying those qualities had been almost blinding as they stood in the kitchen just now. Even when she had tested Adam, they had not dimmed. Something else had flowed beneath them, however, something as electrifying as it was disturbing. She had felt as well as seen the golden heat of his desire. It had enveloped her, surrounding her with such flowing power that she had been unable to move for long seconds. It was dangerous, she knew, because it would be so easy to become lost in it.

She needed no such complication, not now and not with this man. She was happy on her own. She enjoyed her solitary lifestyle, did not require male companionship or even sex to complete her life. She could take care of herself, under most circumstances anyway.

Black widow spider syndrome, indeed. A small smile curved her mouth as she remembered the amusement and challenge in Adam's face as he'd said those words. He was right, naturally; women were more than capable of violence with good reason. Those reasons were usually self-preservation and protection of their young, rather than posturing for show. That didn't make them better than men, but only indicated that it was nature's way to save female energy for things that mattered.

At the stair landing she paused to glance out the oval window of etched glass that was set into the wall. It looked down on the front drive. She could make out the figure of the driver where he still sat in the car. He was no doubt assigned to watch the front door. The other two were nowhere in sight, which probably meant that Adam was right, and they were covering the back.

Was he correct about there being no way out? Or was staying more risky than trying to leave? Whose instincts should she trust, his or her own?

For the moment, she would accept his judgment. But she reserved the right to change her mind. There were more than two exits to the house.

Continuing toward the upstairs bathroom, she kept her eyes open for possibilities. By the time she'd gathered what she needed and made her way back to the kitchen, she was primed and ready. She waited, however, until Adam was busy with his chemical mixture.

"If you're doing what I think," she said in conversational tones as she stood watching over his shoulder, "I can't say I'm too thrilled. Burning my grandmother's house down around our ears doesn't seem the best way to be rid of our guests."

"It may not be necessary."

"Then again, it may?"

He turned his head to give her a harassed look. "You have a better idea?"

It was the opening she needed. "Old Victorian houses like these often have a couple of side doors for the convenience of the different generations living under the same roof. This one has an extra from the breakfast room and another from an upstairs sitting room with an outside stair that ends in the herb garden."

"You think they aren't watching all exits?"

"They can't be everywhere," she pointed out. "Even if they're watching the doors, there are dozens of man-sized windows in this old pile."

"So I'm to hold the castle while you climb down from the tower and go for help?"

The hint of sarcasm in his voice scraped on her nerves. "I'm not living in a fairy tale just because I'm female, thank you very much. Besides, I have no intention of deserting you."

"And if you get caught? What am I suppose to do if they decide to use you to get to me and your aunt?"

"Exactly what you'd do if I was tied to your side. Nothing, in other words, no negotiation."

"Don't tempt me," he snapped. "Deciding between letting you be hurt or turning your aunt over to those goons isn't something I want to do."

"I don't see..."

"That's because you aren't looking at it from where I stand."

He had a point. While she was mulling it over, Aunt Kim spoke up from where she still sat at the kitchen table. "Does anybody mind if I get dressed? I'm not doing any good sitting here listening to you two argue, and I'd as soon face whatever is going to happen in something besides my nightgown."

"Suit yourself," Adam said without glancing at her.

"I have nothing to put on except the dress I was wearing. Could I borrow a pair of jeans, Lara?"

"Take whatever you need," Lara said at once, and told her where to find them as well as an extra shirt.

"You're a sweetheart, thanks." She hesitated a second, then added, "I'll leave the two of you to it then."

Her departure left an awkward silence. Lara stood watching Adam knead together a gummy mess that bore some slight resemblance to plastic explosive she'd seen on television. After a moment, she asked, "You need something to put that in?"

"Just what I was thinking," he answered. "You have an old margarine bowl or maybe plastic wrap?"

"Doubt it. My grandmother was old-fashioned. She used only butter, drank her cola from glass bottles because she swore it tasted better that way, and stored her leftovers in glass bowls with glass lids that are practically antiques. But I may have a garbage bag lying around." Moving to the big butler's pantry that served as a pass-through from the kitchen to the dining room, she returned with the bag. She also had a couple of glass cola bottles, a quart of scented lamp oil, a package of extra lamp wicks, a box of birthday candles and a box of kitchen matches that she'd searched out.

Adam glanced at the items, then paused in his task with one brow lifted. "That's scary. I was just wondering if..."

"Yes?" Her smile was seraphic.

"Considering that your grandmother was old-fashioned, as you said, and that electric power isn't too reliable around here during storms, an oil lamp or two for emergencies seemed..."

"Logical?" she supplied innocently.

"Right." He watched her for long seconds before taking the items she carried. His lips tightened, especially as he saw the birthday candles, but he went back to what he was doing without further comment.

She leaned on the cabinet, her gaze on the competent movements of his well-formed hands. There was something about watching a man work. It satisfied some kind of internal expectation, she thought, as if women had for millennia found security in that particular signal of proficiency.

To escape the direction of her thoughts, she asked, "Where did you learn about explosives?"

"Chemistry class in engineering college, partly. But my brothers and I experimented one year after reading a manual some of the guys were passing around in grammar school. Wade and I burned down a storehouse and almost caught Grand Point on fire."

"That would have been a shame." The old Benedict place known as Grand Point was an historic landmark, one of several Benedict properties that dated back to before the Civil War.

"Dad thought so, too. He tanned our hides for it, not that we blamed him. Mom thought he'd overreacted, that he was curbing our spirit and discouraging intellectual experimentation. They had a huge blowup about it. She left him, left us, not long afterward."

Lara, listening to what he wasn't saying as much as to the words, said simply, "That wasn't your fault."

He didn't look at her. "I was the oldest. I should have known better."

"I meant you weren't to blame for your mother's leaving. Children aren't, you know. Sometimes people are just too different. They can't make a marriage unless one of them changes beyond recognition in order to fit themselves into the other's life."

"People do it all the time."

"They used to, because women did most of the changing. They did it because it was expected, or because they had no choice, no way to get along without a man. They still do it sometimes because they love that much or have no strong inclination in any other direction. But some can't, or won't, make that sacrifice. They have to leave in order to save themselves.''

Adam was quiet a moment, while carefully wrapping the mixture he'd created in a square of plastic he'd cut from the bag. "My mother was, and is, artistic. She'd forget that dinner was cooking while she painted, make huge messes with dripped and splattered paint. My old man thought she was wasting time better spent cleaning and taking care of her kids, that she was too lenient with us out of carelessness, and didn't care enough about him to keep something edible on the table. Your typical mismatch between an artistic type and a pragmatist."

"And you agreed with your father."

He looked up with surprise in his face. "Why would you think that?"

"Because you're like him, of course." It seemed so clear to her that she couldn't see why he'd even ask.

"You obviously don't know me if you think so."

That was startling enough to give her pause. She was so used to her instinctive understanding of people that she seldom second-guessed herself, almost never had to revise her first impressions. There was a kind of arrogance in that, she realized, since it was impossible to ever fully understand another person.

"You think your mother was right to leave?" she asked with a frown between her brows.

"I didn't at the time. Like all kids, I hated the change, blamed my dad for making her go away and resented her for not taking her kids with her. But I've come to know her better since leaving home, moving to New Orleans.''

''You're close now?''

He glanced at his watch to check the time they had left. ''As long as we don't interfere in each other's lives. She's mighty interested in grandchildren for someone who claims she was never cut out to be a mother.''

''Children don't interest you?'' He needed a funnel for filling the bottles with his explosive liquid. She found one in a drawer and handed it to him just as he picked up a cola bottle.

''They're fine, but first you have to have a wife.''

That sounded as if marriage was the problem, but asking about that was a bit too personal. She made a noncommittal sound and let the subject lapse while she took the bottle that he had filled and handed him an empty one.

''What about you,'' he inquired without looking away from what he was doing.

''What about me?''

He snorted. ''You know what I meant. Why aren't you married with a couple of kids?''

''I make men nervous,'' she said shortly. ''They don't like having their minds read.''

He glanced at the funnel in his hand as he said, ''It seems to have its advantages.''

''Outweighed by the drawbacks, believe me. Imagine having a wife who always knew exactly why you'd overdrawn the checking account—or when you were having impure thoughts about young things in string bikinis.''

"Imagine one who knew exactly when you were in the mood," he countered with the faintest hint of a smile.

"Think of one who could tell when you thought she was being a witch."

"Or one who knew when you wanted her to be one?"

"You don't know what you're saying," she informed him.

"Don't I?" He looked up, the deep blue of his eyes bright with amusement overlaid by understanding. "You think you're different, and maybe you are. But all women's brains are wired differently anyway—the way they work is pretty much a mystery to men. Yours is just a little more mysterious than most."

She held his gaze for long seconds during which she felt enveloped by his rock-solid confidence. What would it be like to be able to depend on that surety, to take what he'd said at face value and abandon the fear of intruding or offending and know only acceptance of both her and her strange gift? The idea brought such fierce longing that she took a step away from him, withdrawing both physically and emotionally.

"What?" he asked, his amusement fading.

"Nothing." She moistened her lips. "It's so quiet outside. What…what do you suppose our visitors are doing?"

He listened for a second, then sent a quick look at the ceiling above them. "It's quiet inside, too, especially upstairs."

She nodded, accepting the chance to escape what

had become an uncomfortable discussion. "I'll see if Aunt Kim's all right."

He made no effort to stop her. Leaving the kitchen, Lara made her way through the sitting room and up the stairs. She tapped on the door of the guest bedroom, then waited. When there was no answer, she knocked again then pushed open the door and stepped inside.

It took only a second to see that the room was empty. The housecoat that Aunt Kim had been wearing was flung across the rumpled bed, her leather purse was gone from where it had sat on the 'thirties dresser, and her high heels that had been kicked off beside the bed were no longer there. Whirling around, Lara walked quickly down the hall to her own bedroom. Here, she found drawers open and the clothing tumbled and left hanging over the sides. Her black jeans and matching T-shirt were missing.

Her aunt was gone.

She should have remembered, Lara thought, that her aunt Kim had been brought up in the old house so knew its many exits as well as she did. Then another idea occurred to her. It took only a quick search to confirm it.

The pistol was gone as well, the weapon her aunt had brought with her and that she'd used to kill her husband.

The only firearm in the house.

Eight

"**W**hy in hell would she do that?" Adam demanded. "Where does she think she's going?"

He didn't really expect an answer, but was only letting off steam. He should have guessed that Kim Belzoni would run since she'd been doing it all her life. It was his fault that the woman was out there now, wandering around in the dark. The thing was that he'd expected self-preservation to keep her from playing hare to the Belzoni family hounds.

"She was afraid, I think, that she might lose in any final test of loyalties," Lara said.

"What? My loyalties? I thought I'd made it clear where those lay."

"You had, but circumstances can change the firmest of intentions."

He didn't have a clue what she was getting at. "I was doing my damnedest to keep her safe."

"She wasn't sure that would hold if—if you were really forced to choose."

"Between?"

"The two of us."

"Because of what I said a few minutes ago,' he said in exasperated understanding.

"She realized how strong your doubts were and so thought it best if she took herself out of the picture."

He was silent while he digested that. Finally, he said, "You're telling me that she could read my mind, too."

"Does that bother you?"

"Hell, yes," he answered, suddenly hot under the collar. "Wouldn't it bother you?"

She only looked at him with that clear, knowing gaze that he was beginning to anticipate, if not appreciate.

"Yes, well, I know what I said about your power, or whatever you call it," he allowed. "But having one woman poking around in a man's head is different from thinking her whole family might be able to do it."

"I do realize."

He was afraid she did, which was the whole trouble, wasn't it? This was getting nowhere, even if they had time for it. "Is this mind-reading thing, assuming it's real, a two-way street? I mean, do you have any idea where she's going?"

"She has no particular destination but is certain that something will turn up."

He stared at the wall behind her while he cursed silently. Then an instant replay of their last exchange flashed through his mind. He set his hands on his hipbones while he gave a slow, disgusted shake of his head. "I can't believe it."

"What?"

"You almost had me believing that stuff." Though

the most irritating thing about it, he thought, was his own ambivalence.

Her face changed, her eyes becoming as opaque as green jade, shutting him out. Turning away from him with an abrupt, jerky movement, she said, "We have to go after her."

That withdrawal felt like a desertion. He wished he'd kept his mouth shut. "I don't think you understand the problem," he said to her back. "The men out there aren't going to let us just walk out, even if your aunt does seem to have managed it."

"What if they discover she's gone? They'll hunt her down like a rabbit."

He clenched his teeth as he realized that she had just used the same image that had flickered through his mind seconds ago. "And five minutes after we're gone, less if we're spotted leaving, they'll find out the house is empty and chase down all three of us. Or do you really think we can outrun them?"

"So we do nothing?"

"I was thinking, rather, of a diversion to delay the discovery that she's gone."

"She could still get lost, maybe wander in a circle so she comes back here. The best thing is to go after her."

He'd known she would find some objection, he'd just known it. "I'd say the chances of both of us slipping out unseen are about a million to one. Suppose I stay put, take care of that diversion."

"While I sneak out like Aunt Kim? I don't think so."

"What do you want from me?" he demanded. "It's the best I can offer."

"Do you really believe that I'd leave you here to chunk pop bottles at men that may be armed with submachine guns? I'm as impressed as all get-out by the heroics, but refuse to accept the sacrifice."

"Not even to save your precious aunt's hide?"

"I don't like the odds," she said, and closed her lips in a tight line.

"If we both get out of here, if we can catch up with your aunt, and if I manage to keep us all alive, I'll still turn her over to the police the first chance I get."

"I know that, but it's better than letting her—"

Shots exploded from the woods just beyond the house. The staccato roar proved that the goons outside were armed to the teeth. It also indicated that Kim Belzoni hadn't got far. Adam said a few choice words even as he made an instant decision.

"Let's go," he snapped as he scooped up the two bottles he'd filled with lamp oil and fixed with trailing, oil-soaked wicks. "If we're going to make it, this is our chance."

"But I don't—"

"Now. While they're busy." He didn't wait to see if she followed, but charged through the swinging door into the darkened sitting room that was on the opposite side of the house from the commotion. He paused with his back to the wall next to a tall window, staring through the glass for any sign of movement.

As Lara arrived at his side, he said, "Clear, I think."

''I'll get the window.''

He didn't argue, since she knew exactly how it unlocked and opened. Still, his chest ached during the few seconds it took her to belly up to the tall glass panes and lift the sash from the low sill. The window went up with only a muted bumping of its iron counterweight inside the old walls, just as it had been designed to do more than a hundred years ago. Lara released the screen, then made a movement as if to skim through the opening. Adam touched her arm, motioning for her to step back. Ladies first was a nice concept, but if anybody was going to get shot at on sight, he'd rather it wasn't her. Ducking out the tall, dark opening in a smooth movement, he dropped to the ground, then turned back to give her a hand. Seconds later, they were easing along the outside wall, searching for the time and place to make a break for the woods.

The bulk of the house was still between them and the hue and cry over Kim. As they eased toward the rear, Adam began to think that the men sent to bring them in had actually been dumb enough to be drawn away after the escapee. Then he put his head around the back corner and caught the smell of cigarette smoke. He spotted the man watching the rear door by the glowing orange tip of his cigarette.

Adam drew back, flattening his spine against the wall. Lara did the same in eerie synchronization with him. He gave her a hard glance even as he whispered, ''Go back. Wait for me at the other end of the house.''

She didn't argue, but only stared at him a second

before moving away. When he could barely see her outline in the darkness, he turned to shield the bottles he carried with his body, then struck a kitchen match with his thumbnail. Lighting one bottle's dangling wick, he immediately stepped out to hurl it at the trunk of a big oak beyond the guard.

The fiery explosion lit up the backyard in a yellow-orange glare that made the surrounding woods appear black. The guard yelled and dived aside, scrambling away from the flames. Immediately, Adam sprinted toward Lara, now out of the guard's direct line of sight. As he reached her, he caught her arm, half directing, half urging her toward the encroaching trees. She understood what he intended without a word, had been waiting only for his direction. Together, they raced for the cover. The wood's dark shadows covered them like a blanket while they pushed deep into it, away from the house.

Behind them lay pandemonium, as men shouted, shots were fired in random bursts and fire crackled toward the night sky. A few seconds of forward progress, and the noise began to fade, replaced by the soft crunch of their footsteps in the leafy mulch of the forest floor and the brush of twigs and branches against their clothing. Adam could hear no pursuit, but he thought it was back there. The question was how long it would last when the real quarry was Kim Belzoni.

He pressed on, circling, keeping his bearings partly by instinct, partly by the distant glow of the brush fire started by his Molotov cocktail. He wound around thickets and deadfalls, crossed dry branches, and found the best spots for three different crossings of the small creek that meandered behind the old house in a channel as crooked as a snake. The night air was tainted with smoke, but still felt fresh and free in his lungs. It was good to be out in it, in spite of everything.

He'd stopped to listen for the third or fourth time. When he started on again, Lara put out a hand to touch his arm as she said softly, "Wait."

"What is it?" he asked, his voice a breath of sound.

"Where are you going?"

"Don't tell me you can't guess?" The question was more caustic than he'd intended, but he let it stand.

"We need to find Aunt Kim."

"Point me in the right direction, and you've got it. That's if she wasn't caught before the excitement started, and if we don't have company on our tail."

"You always have everything figured out, don't you?" she returned with sibilant heat. "Some things have to be done on instinct, because they're right instead of because they're logical."

"Not thinking ahead can get you killed."

"Waiting until you have everything mapped out to the last inch can mean being forever paralyzed by details."

Adam held on to his temper with an effort. "I'm not paralyzed. I'm also not going to run around here without a plan. But if you want to take charge of this little expedition, go right ahead."

"I didn't say I wanted to take charge, and I'm not

criticizing. I just don't intend to follow behind you like a blind monkey. This isn't Me Tarzan, You Jane here. I can help if you'll let me.''

Adam wasn't used to help. He also wasn't used to women who called him on his more macho traits. Except his mother, of course, who sometimes told him in moments of annoyance that he was as overbearing as his father had been. He shoved the bottle he still carried into the back pocket of his jeans, then raked his fingers through his hair. "Look," he said in quieter tones, "we don't know which direction your aunt went, don't know whether the creeps back there are on her trail or on ours. Until we figure it out, we have to keep moving. If we stand still, we become sitting targets and Kim could be getting farther away from us every minute. So I'm taking a circular route that just may bring us to a meeting point if she's moving in a straight line away from where she started. It's the best I can do until we can tell exactly what's happening."

"I see," she said with a slow nod. "All right."

The words signaled understanding, but had a tentative sound that prevented him from moving. "But?"

"But I think...I think she's hurt and hiding."

"Don't tell me," he said in tight control. "You just feel it?"

"In the same way that you're almost sure someone is behind us."

He frowned as he saw what she meant. Whether it was the law of probability, some noise below the level of conscious hearing, or the rising of the hair on the back of his neck, the instinct was there. A small, tight spot inside him eased as her ability began to make sense in a weird sort of way. Staring into the blackness around them, he said deliberately, "I'm also circling around to the barn where your aunt's car is hidden. And where she left her cell phone."

Lara was silent for long seconds. Then she spoke with dry humor that acted like a balm on his too-alert nerves. "That's very…logical."

"Ain't it, though," he said in wry agreement, then added, "Which way, then? Your vote, since you seem to have better information."

She didn't move, but only held his gaze there in the darkness. He couldn't see her eyes yet he could feel them. And he also felt an odd communication of gratitude from her for his acceptance, however reluctantly, of her ability. It embarrassed him since it was such a small thing, a miserly bit of belief. Shaking his head, he looked away.

The night breeze rose, brushing the beard-shadowed planes of his face, sifting through his hair, stirring the treetop above them. Tree leaves whispered, pine straw eddied around their feet, and a swath of cloud covered the face of the moon. It was a perfectly natural change on a night in early summer, but still seemed peculiar, as if time had slowed, taking on a dreamlike Midsummer's Night madness in its headway toward the dawn.

That wind and the weird dislocation it created in his mind were like a replay of that moment when Lara had been caught in his headlights on the drive. He was losing it, Adam thought, if he abandoned logic long enough to even begin to accept a supernatural explanation for that or anything else that had happened tonight. Yet what else was there?

Lara reached out to touch his hand. "Hurry. We have to find Aunt Kim while there's less chance of being seen or heard."

It seemed like a good idea. Before he said or did something he'd regret.

Adam led the way at a half trot, skimming around thickets and through stands of trees, holding limbs aside until Lara passed, then outdistancing her again so he could take the brunt of whatever might show up ahead of them. She held her own, keeping up with him in spite of their twisting, ducking, single-file progress. She was something else. The only problem was, he couldn't quite make up his mind just what.

Abruptly, he felt her absence like a sudden alarm going off in the hollow of his chest. He skidded to a halt in deep pine straw, looked back, to the side, all around. Nothing. He spun to retrace his steps at Mach speed. Fifty feet back down the trail, he leaped a dry branch, then tripped over a crouched figure. Instinct kicked in. He caught the kneeling assailant in a flying tackle as he fell, then rolled to pin him with his full weight.

"Get off, you idiot," Lara exclaimed in muffled anger. "I just stopped to tie my running shoe."

He'd known it was her the instant he touched her, but not in time to stop his forward momentum. The residue of dread that she might have been hurt or picked off by the man who followed them held him rigid.

"You could have warned me," he said. His irritation was not helped by the knowledge that he had lost the extra Molotov cocktail when he jumped her.

"I would have if I'd known you were going to overreact this way."

She had no idea of the extent of his reaction. The sensation of her soft curves, heated from exertion, beneath him was so mind-boggling that he could barely think. It was the effect of a danger-induced testosterone rush, he knew, though it didn't make it any easier to combat. Like an uploading program on a computer, the vision of making love to her there on the bed of pine straw flashed through his mind in a series of images too fast to grasp. Lust, need and an odd, aching pain that had nothing to do with either, gripped him with iron hands. He was consumed by the urge to take her there, to hold her as if the night had no end and he could become a part of her forever. It was a white-hot yearning in his brain, a vital ache at the center of his being.

The main thing that stopped him, other than lack of invitation, was the sure knowledge that the chance of being caught bare-backside-naked in a tangle of briers and discarded clothing would not be a turn-on for most women. And it was definitely no way to die.

Nine

An odd mix of relief and regret shifted through Lara as Adam wrenched away from her and surged upright. She extended her hand, and he caught it and hauled her to her feet with a single hard pull, steadying her until she had her balance.

"You took care of the shoelaces?" he asked in abrupt inquiry.

"Yes." Lara could hear the strain in her clipped response.

"Then stay close. And don't stop again for anything, anything at all, unless I stop first."

It was fear that sounded in his voice, she thought in sudden recognition, the fear that he would lose her in the dark, that something would happen to her that was beyond his control, or that he would fail her in some way. Beyond these things was also consternation that he had come close to being at the mercy of her whim and his hormones. He had wanted her just then, as she knew very well, and was trying to cover it. She felt her annoyance at his commanding tone ease, melting away until it was gone.

With ancient female irony, she answered, "No, I didn't intend to."

He made no reply, but started off again. Smiling a little to herself, she followed.

It was several weary minutes and brier scratches later when the woods began to thin. They had reached an area where the pine timber had been cut over in the not-too-distant past. Through the standing hardwoods, she caught the dim outline of the old barn, mainly because she knew where it was. It was large, as such things went, since it had served a sizeable farm for at least four generations. Down the near side stretched the remains of a toolshed and corn and feed bins, while a milking shed was attached to the other. The center section had once housed animals, plows and wagons, with the level above it used as a hayloft and sometimes a drying area for peanuts. The big double doors stood open, hanging on their hinges. Through the wide opening could be seen Aunt Kim's rental car parked in the ancient ruts of wagons, Model Ts and humpbacked Studebakers.

Lara took a few quick steps to catch up with Adam, then grabbed his elbow to bring him to a halt. "There," she said, indicating the barn's wide shape in the darkness. "You found it."

He put his warm fingers over her hand to draw her deeper into the shade of a large oak. Using its trunk for cover, he stood slowly quartering the night with his gaze, from the deep woods behind them to the lighter area back toward the house that glowed with the fire he'd caused. When he'd scanned every section of the wide area before them, he shook his head.

"No sign of our visitors that I can tell. You?"

He was actually asking for her help and opinion.

The realization brought an odd ache to the back of her throat. However, her answer was still a quiet negative.

"Where the hell are they?" he asked almost to himself.

"Close. I don't think they've given up."

"So much for that hope," he commented in astringent humor. "What about Kim?"

"Close, too."

"You mean—do you think they have her?"

"I don't believe so."

"But you don't know, or can't be sure. That it?"

She didn't reply to that, couldn't for the dread that was building slowly inside her. "What now?"

"Your call."

She tested the sound of that to see if it was on the level. It seemed to be, which left her undecided. Something was coming. They were too far away to stop it, she thought, and she was too involved to see its full outline. But soon, too soon, she and the man beside her would have to face it. Could they? Were they ready? She needed to know beyond doubting.

While she dithered between a safe course and one more risky, the moon emerged from behind trailing clouds. A pale shaft of light fell through the tree limbs above them to gild Adam's hair and face. She turned her head to stare at him, even as he shifted to avoid the light. And suddenly she knew what she needed to do. After all, a man was never more surely himself than when he made love. In that moment of abandon, his reactions, rough or tender, timid or aggressive, considerate or selfish, showed exactly what he was inside.

How to begin? He had given her the clue himself, hadn't he? It had been in his tale of her appearing before him on the drive, naked beneath a cloak of silver space-age silk. If that was his fantasy, then it should be easy enough to carry it to its inevitable conclusion. She had only to join him in it.

Standing in absolute stillness, Lara reached out with her mind to the man who stood so broad and tall beside her. She closed with him in delicate mental probing, seeking his interest, desire or acceptance as an entryway into his imagination. She felt only a barrier, strong and impenetrable. The pain of disappointment was intense, like being physically rejected. It brought a small, unconscious sound of distress to her throat.

Abruptly, the shield he seemed to have raised against her was gone. He turned his head to stare at her, his gaze night-black under the hollows formed by his brows. She had the strange idea that he saw her clearly, both in his mind's eye and in actuality, and offered no resistance to either. It was a stunning feeling, like standing before an abyss with no beginning and no end, one so deep and wide that she could disappear into it forever. Yet she had to take the plunge. She could see no other way.

The tie that held her long braid had caught on some twig and been snatched away. Her hair streamed loose down her back, so that a sudden wind shift lifted its shining filaments around her like wings. And with that sense of freedom and involuntary merging with

Adam's first vision, she summoned the image of a silver cloak and took metaphysical flight.

Her jeans, T-shirt and scant underwear melted away. With the moonlight shimmering on her nakedness and the imaginary cloak swirling around her, she took the few steps that brought her close to him. When the sensitive nipples of her breasts brushed the fabric of his shirt, she lifted her hands, flattening the palms against his chest. She slid them upward, circling his neck, and then exerted gentle pressure to bend his head toward her until his mouth touched hers.

Sweet, warm, tender, the infinite sensory impressions of his kiss filled her mind. She inhaled sharply, taking his scent, the very essence of him, deep inside her. At the same moment, she felt his chest rise with his deep-drawn breath. Then his arms closed around her with warmth and certainty to draw her against him, into him.

It was magic of a superior kind, a fine blending of body, mind and soul. It was grace and generosity so powerful that she wanted to become lost in them. With a soft murmur, she shifted nearer until every possible inch of her skin was pressed to him, as if she could absorb knowledge of him through her pores.

He touched her lips with his tongue in experiment and invitation and she opened to him as naturally as a moonflower to cool lunar rays. That gentle abrasion, the heat of his mouth, glassy edges of his teeth, and taste of him were heady incitements. She wanted more of him, needed to know all that he was or ever could be.

Loosening his hold, he touched her breast, capturing it in the chalice of his hand. Fire licked along her veins, threatening her heart. She shifted her grasp to clutch the hard muscles of his arm, feverishly urging him to greater liberties. He took them, smoothing over her bare skin as if learning its secrets, reveling in its heat and satin resilience. Swinging with her in his arms, he pressed her back to the trunk of the huge oak, then drew away a little to view the gentle hills and hollows that he explored so diligently.

She wanted to see him as well, to feel his bare skin gliding over her own. With trembling fingers, she stripped away buttons, manipulated his zipper, and took the firm, hard length of him into her hand. She felt the throbbing of his heart in the distended flesh and was enchanted by the discovery, filled with such tenderness at that sign of his extreme arousal that she could hardly contain it. At the same time, she was engulfed by bittersweet recognition of how transient was this moment, and how far short of reality it must fall.

Adam's passion, unleashed by her will in this ephemeral encounter, was less introspective. Its surging force banished thought, swept her up in its turbulence. The answering rush of desire inside her was stunning as it swept away doubt, fear, or inhibition, leaving the moist heat of receptivity in its wake.

His entry was a white-hot glide, a vital filling, a merging so incredible that it brought instant completion. Her very being coalesced around him. The glory of it took her breath, turned her muscles to hot stone, shut down the power of thought. Then, supporting her weight against his own body, he moved with her, into her, sending them both spiraling into the darkest, most blood-pounding magic of them all.

One moment they were holding tight, breathing deep, trying to recover in body and mind. The next, they were separated by the exact distance that had been between them when it began. Neither had moved. They had hardly blinked. The entire incident, its delicate, slow-motion unfolding and bright climax, had taken scant seconds.

That small blip of time was enough. Adam had passed her test as he met and blended with her in mental exploration. Lara was satisfied, finally, that he was trustworthy. If there was more to what he was or could be, she dared not consider it, not now, perhaps not ever. Like all human beings, he had his own needs, his own vision of perfect fulfillment that might well involve someone different, a woman less complicated in her approach or requirements.

Yet he was aware. He had felt the same thing she had, known the same momentary bewitchment. It was there in the darkness of his dilated pupils, the stiffness of his neck muscles, the unnerved paleness of his face.

The shot slapped the night, the crack of it tunneling into the darkness with a traveling echo. Adam whipped around toward the sound. Lara stood perfectly still as she followed his line of sight. The breeze that cooled them dropped as suddenly as it had begun.

"There." Lara pointed toward where the old track that led to the barn lay among the trees. In both their minds, she thought, was the memory of Aunt Kim and the missing pistol.

He plunged in that direction at once.

"Adam!" The call, edged with protest and warning, came from pure instinct.

He came to a sliding halt, turned. "Yes?"

"Nothing. I... Wait for me."

Lara joined him with a few quick steps. Then they headed for the place the shot had come from at a fast trot. Seconds later, they caught movement through the trees.

Adam slowed, approaching with caution as he crouched to keep a low silhouette. Lara was on his heels as he slid into a thicket of wild plums at the edge of the old barn track. They shifted positions with silent care until they could see through the thorny branches.

What she'd expected to see, Lara wasn't sure. Some kind of disaster, certainly; Aunt Kim struggling with the two men sent by her dead husband's uncle maybe, or else being frog-marched between them to where they'd left their car. She hadn't anticipated finding her aunt holding two of the goons at gunpoint, one of them, Demarius, clutching his shoulder and the other with his hands stacked on top of his head.

"I'll be damned," Adam said softly.

Lara could only agree.

Ten

Raising her voice, she called, "Aunt Kim!"

"Oh, Lara, thank God."

"Coming out. Don't shoot."

Her aunt sent her a fast glance, then looked beyond her toward the thicket. Her eyes were wild, and her dark lipstick made her mouth appear black in the white mask of her face. The weapon in her hand wobbled for an instant before she steadied it. "Where's Adam?"

"Here," he answered, stepping into the open and moving toward them.

Lara had no time to wonder what kind of reconnaissance or tactic had kept him. Her attention was on her aunt and the despair emanating from her. "Are you okay?" she asked in concern. "You're not hurt?"

"I turned an ankle stumbling around in the dark in these heels, that's all," Aunt Kim said. "But I need to get out of here, and I'm not sure what to do with this trash to keep them from following me."

"What do you mean?"

"I can't just shoot them in cold blood. I mean, I'd rather not. I know they came after me, and all that, but..."

"We didn't want to kill you," the injured man began.

"Shut up," Aunt Kim said, centering the gun on his chest once more so that Demarius cringed away as if trying to present a smaller target. His associate cursed in virulent dislike of his helplessness.

"You're sure this is the same woman you described to me?" Adam asked, his voice dry as he moved to Lara's side. "The misunderstood beauty with little internal fortitude?"

Lara caught from Adam's clothes the scent of smoke and wax, as of a freshly lit birthday candle, along with the caustic odor of drain cleaner. It was a strong hint that a slow-burning fuse in homemade plastic explosive was left somewhere behind him. She frowned even as she began, "I didn't mean—"

"Of course you did," Aunt Kim corrected, her voice strident, "and you were right. But deal with cruelty every day, as I did with Ernesto, and you either die or become mean enough to fight back. Ernesto thought I was weak as well. He underestimated me."

"So did I," Adam said. "Not to mention these two."

"You had other things on your mind," Lara's aunt said with an unsteady laugh. "Besides, I intended it that way."

The two men in front of them cursed. Demarius eased forward a half step as if he thought to use the moment of distraction to try for the gun.

"I wouldn't do that," Adam warned him. "You

don't want to upset Mrs. Belzoni any more than you have already.''

''Oh, hell no. That wouldn't do, would it? She's a crazy woman. Get that piece away from her before she kills somebody with it. Or make that somebody else—'' The hired thug closed his lips abruptly as Adam took a step toward him.

''You see?'' Aunt Kim said. ''What am I going to do? They won't give up. They'll find me wherever I go. I'll never be free.''

''The easiest thing is to call the police,'' Adam said in grim conviction.

Lara's aunt ignored that as if he hadn't spoken. ''I thought about the trunk of their car as a place to put them, only I wasn't sure I could walk them back to the house and make them get in it. But maybe they'll cooperate now that there are three of us.''

''And then what?'' Lara asked. ''Ernesto's uncle will still send someone after you.''

''At least I'll have a head start!''

''Oh, Aunt Kim.''

''Call the Tunica Parish sheriff's office,'' Adam insisted. ''Ask for Roan.''

''And I guess you think I should stick around until he gets here? I won't. I can't stand being locked up. I told you that.''

''It might not come to it.''

''It will! Help me get them to the house. Do you have any duct tape, Lara? We can at least tie them up.''

''What about when it's time to let them go?'' she asked, willing her aunt to meet her eyes.

"What's wrong with you? Are you siding with Benedict against your own flesh and blood?"

"It's not a question of sides but of common sense," she insisted. "I'm afraid of what may happen to you if Belzoni's men run you down some place far away from here."

"You *are* with him. They won't find me, not if you charge them with destruction of property and disturbing the peace." Her aunt's face mirrored triumph as she brought out her solution.

"Charge them? You mean—you're agreeing to let Adam call the police after all?"

"Don't be silly. I dialed 911 ages ago."

The prisoners began to babble again, until Adam silenced them again with a hard gesture. Turning back to Aunt Kim, he demanded, "You called Roan? He's on his way?"

"I couldn't let anything happen to Lara, now could I? I never meant to make trouble for her."

The rich affection and gratitude that rose inside Lara threatened to push tears into her eyes. "Oh, Aunt Kim."

"I could never forgive myself if you were hurt because I came here, honey. I'm not that kind of monster."

"Then you know why I can't stand to see you in trouble. But don't you think…" Lara paused, amazed at what she'd been about to say, uncertain it was the right thing.

"What? Tell me quick, because we don't have much time."

Did she dare? Could she trust Adam that far when

she'd seldom been so dependent on anyone, much less a man? And yet, it seemed the right thing to do. She'd love to see her aunt get away once and for all, see her installed someplace where she could finally relax and be eternally unafraid. But there was no such safe haven, not after what she'd done. If that was anyone's fault, then it was her aunt's, the result of the bad choices made over a lifetime.

"Give Adam the gun," she said, her voice turning firm as she spoke. "Let him hold these men until the police come."

"He'd do that?" She sent him a disbelieving stare. "He'd take over so I can go?"

Lara shook her head. "So you can stay and talk to Adam's cousin and also the police in New Orleans. So you can take advantage of Adam's influence, and his help."

"Lara," Adam began.

She turned toward him, her gaze steady. "You will help, won't you? You'll stand by her, see that she's protected whether it's in prison or out and regardless of the information she may have about the Belzoni crime family? You will do whatever you can so long as it doesn't compromise your word?"

He met her gaze, his own closed in, guarding his thoughts and his feelings. Taking a chance, going once more on instinct, she allowed him to see her acceptance of whatever he might decide. She abandoned all her carefully erected internal defenses while hoping he would do the same. With consummate trust, she gave him what he asked on the chance that he would allow her what she needed. She opened her mind to him like a book that he could read if he only accepted the capability.

The instant expanded, becoming endlessly elastic until it seemed that they were alone in a place far away from the others. Then his gaze cleared, becoming as stunningly transparent as a Caribbean sea. His smile was slow and edged with wry humor as he said, "You should have been a lawyer."

"Will you?" she insisted, needing the words as well as the feeling.

"If I can't, and if there is no guarantee of immunity for your aunt in return for her cooperation, then I give my word that I won't turn her in to the NOPD."

It was more than she'd expected, an enormous concession in return for her own. Turning back to her aunt, she held out her hand. "You heard Adam. Isn't that better than running scared, hiding out, jumping every time a door slams or a truck backfires? Give him the pistol. Please."

"Really, Lara. I can be far, far away by daylight."

"And how much farther will you have to go before you can breathe easy? Tell me something? Why didn't you just divorce Belzoni as you did the others?"

"He said I'd never get away from him, that he'd find me and kill me, no matter how fast or far I ran."

"Out of love?"

Her aunt's face twisted. "Out of obsession, maybe, or else his right to own me. He claimed that if he couldn't have me, then no one else would. I think he really hated me for making him feel inadequate, so that killing me was to be his final revenge."

"Exactly," Lara said, and watched her aunt as her face changed with the realization that nothing was different, that her dead husband's uncle would be just as vengeful. "Where can you go? How long before they find you? You can't kill them all. Even if you could, it's no way to live."

"Oh, Lara," Aunt Kim whispered as her face crumpled into lines of grief. "Then it was for nothing. I might as well have let Ernesto murder me."

"Not if you'll trust Adam now. You have information the police can use. In exchange, they may give you a new life."

Aunt Kim looked at Adam. "Is that true?"

"I can't promise," he answered, looking up from checking his watch by the light of the moon to meet her anxious gaze. "But I'll do everything in my power to see that it happens."

She looked back at Lara. "You believe him?"

Lara met the gaze of the man at her side for interminable seconds while a rich and deep current of something so powerful it had no name flowed between them. "I believe him," she said. "If I didn't, I wouldn't be standing here with him."

From the distance, there came the sound of a siren. Aunt Kim jerked and gave a moan of distress at that audible warning that time was running out. The two men she still covered looked at each other and began to edge into the darkness.

"Aunt Kim?" Lara's voice was sharp.

She whispered a curse, shuddering where she stood. She glanced down at the pistol in her hand.

It was then that the third man emerged from the

darkness and walked forward. He stopped with his legs spread and a snub-nosed assault rifle at the firing position in his hands. "Hold it right there, folks," he said in a thick New Orleans accent that sounded like Brooklynese. "This is my party now."

Aunt Kim turned toward the intruder with the pistol pointed at his midsection. The man bared his teeth and tightened his trigger finger on his assault rifle. Adam turned in the same instant, his muscles tightening as he prepared to lunge.

It was then that the night was blasted apart and the plum thicket behind Adam became a fountain of fire. The concussion rolled toward them. A split second before it struck, Adam slammed into Lara and her aunt, knocking them to the ground and covering them with his body.

The roar passed over them, fading almost as fast as it had begun. Immediately, Adam rolled away and sprang to his feet. In his hand was the pistol that he had retrieved from Aunt Kim.

Demarius and the other thug were scrambling on the ground, trying to crawl away. The man with the assault rifle rolled in the grass, trying to put out the blue flames that licked the sleeve of his shirt. Adam stepped back a pace so he could cover all three. Above the crackle of fire, his voice rang out. "Hold it right there, all of you. On your feet."

The goons struggled upright then turned slowly back to face him with their hands in plain sight. Then they all stood in silence as the police car's siren came ever closer.

Sheriff Roan Benedict was efficiency personified,

Minutes after he and his deputies appeared, the Mafioso trio were disarmed and ensconced in the back of a patrol unit, the two separate fires were out, and Aunt Kim was in protective custody. After closing the passenger side door where her aunt huddled in his patrol unit, he turned and sauntered with rangy grace toward Lara and Adam as they stood near the front steps of her house.

"I should say thank you for coming so quickly," she told him with real gratitude. She tried to smile, but her lips felt stiff and cold. The night's events were beginning to take on a surreal quality that wasn't helped by the flashing blue-and-red lights of the pair of police cars that illuminated the driveway area or the smoke that still drifted in the air.

"No problem. Your aunt told dispatch that Adam was in a spot of trouble. We Benedicts look after our own." He grinned at his cousin as he spoke, and gave him his hand in what looked like a bone-crushing grip.

"I owe you one," Adam said, his smile crooked.

"Nah. Seems to me you had everything pretty much under control."

"Yeah, well, except for not knowing what the devil to do with any of them once I had the drop on them."

"My specialty, putting people away." Roan turned to Lara. "My deputies can stick around to be sure the fires are under control, if you like. No danger to the house that I can see, but somebody needs to keep an eye on them in case they blaze up again."

"I'll take care of it," Adam said.

Roan tipped his head back, giving him a long look

from under the brim of his Stetson. "That's the way it is, huh?"

"Possibly," Adam agreed, though he didn't look at Lara. "So how is Tory?"

"Good, good. She'll be better when this ten-ton kid she's carrying around decides to join the family."

"And maybe you'll get out of the doghouse, too?"

"Literally."

Hearing the wry fervor in the sheriff's voice, Lara had to smile even as she felt a small pang for the strong current of love and concern for his wife that she heard in his voice.

"Shouldn't be so prolific, Cuz, or so competitive. I mean, just because the rest of the guys in the clan got off to a fast start at filling the nursery didn't mean you had to join them."

"Tory's idea," Roan said. "Not that I objected too much."

"I wouldn't think so," Adam said, his voice dry.

"Or that it would have done me any good if I had." Roan cleared his throat with a rasp. "Guess I'll hit the road, since I don't like leaving her alone just now. You'll be all right, here, you two?"

"Fine," Adam said.

It wasn't his assurance Roan was looking for, apparently, since he didn't move but only watched Lara with careful assessment in his eyes.

"I'll be all right, too," she said.

He studied her for a moment longer, then gave a slow nod and touched a finger to his hat brim. "You give me a call if you're not. Okay?"

The warm sense of belonging that his words created inside her was startling but also gratifying. "Yes," she said simply. "I'll do that."

Roan moved around to the driver's side of his vehicle. Lara reached in at the passenger side to hug Aunt Kim, promising to be in constant touch. The doors shut and the patrol cars moved out, leaving her and Adam alone in front of the house.

"I don't think my cousin trusts me," Adam complained when the noise of the departure allowed him to be heard.

Lara gave him an amused glance. "I think he's just a cautious and caring man."

"Another convert to the Sheriff Benedict fan club. I guess you'll be calling him night and day, just like everybody else in the blessed parish."

"Something wrong with that?"

"Not a lot. Except I have a better idea."

"Do you now?" she asked, her voice cool.

"You could come home with me."

She hadn't seen it coming, which was nothing short of amazing. Or maybe it was just that her perceptions had been blunted by everything else that had happened. "Why would I do that?"

"You need protective custody as much as your aunt. Suppose Belzoni's uncle decides he can still get to her through you, maybe kidnap you so she'll think twice before remembering too much about her husband's family?"

He had a point, but that was all she was ready to concede. "Moving into your condo seems like a drastic solution."

"Who said anything about moving in with me?"

She turned her head to frown at him. "My mistake. I thought that was what you meant."

"Not that I'd mind, understand. But I figured you could come with me to Grand Point. There's going to be this big family reunion where you could meet all the Benedicts, Kane and Luke and their wives and offspring, my brother Clay and his wife and daughter, maybe even my other brother, Wade. Roan will be there, too, of course, if that's any incentive."

"Don't be ridiculous. I know very well that he's devoted to his wife, not to mention to his half-grown son, his dad, his home, his dogs, and his job."

"Ah, well. Guess you'll have to settle for me."

Settle? Did he really think any woman would feel she was settling for anything when offered his company? "I suppose," she said judiciously, "that I could get by with that."

He nodded. "Thought so."

"Did you now? You were positive that you had only to suggest and I'd agree?"

"Something like that." The look he gave her was a shade smug, but also carried a wicked glint that made every inch of her skin's surface feel hot.

"Because you're so masterful and irresistible, I suppose?" The sarcasm was sheer self-defense.

"I don't know," he said with a lifted brow. "Am I?"

"Also the most infuriating…"

"Thank you from the bottom of my heart. I think you're the most gorgeous, intelligent, and bravest female I've ever met, too."

"But all wrong."

"Now what makes you say that?" His tone was almost indulgent.

"I'm not a Benedict kind of woman, sweet-tempered, church-going—normal."

"I told you before that you don't know me if you think that's important. And you sure as hell don't know the Benedict women."

She wanted to believe him, which was the problem. "You need somebody different."

"You're about as different as they get."

"I mean different from me," she said in exasperation.

"What, somebody uncomplicated who will believe every word I say, no matter how unreasonable?"

"Well—no."

"A woman who will pout when I'm working without ever trying to find out why it's important to me, or who will expect me to guess what she wants though she can't begin to guess what I need?"

"That isn't fair," she complained.

He moved closer until the muscles of his legs brushed her jean-clad thighs. "Someone who isn't curious at all?"

"Curious, as in crazy, you mean." She refused to look at him, even as he reached to take her hand and draw her toward him, putting her hand on his shoulder and circling her waist before clasping his hands behind her back.

"That isn't what I meant at all. Curious as in wondering, or so I believe. Curious as in expecting. Curious as in anticipating."

"I haven't the faintest idea what you're talking

about.'' She met his gaze for only the briefest of heated seconds before looking quickly away again.

''Oh, I think you do.''

''What in the world would I anticipate?'' She risked a longer glance, and was snared by the tender light in his eyes and the pledge for the future that was backed by the full weight of his strict notions of loyalty and commitment.

''Oh, Lara, you know, you do know,'' he said, his voice warm and freighted with anticipation as great as her own. ''You can't wait to find out if I'm as good as your imagination.''

She studied his face, searching for the final answer. ''You were there, weren't you?'' she asked when she still couldn't be sure. ''You saw, heard, felt everything that I did back there in the woods when I... when we...''

''Only because you let me.''

''But you believe me, about the things I see without being there, feel without touching, know without being able to explain?'' She thought he had more ability than he realized, but only time and use would reveal its extent.

''I believe in you,'' he said simply. ''That means I'll believe in anything you can or will allow me to share.''

He kissed her then, a slow and deep exploration, as if time had no meaning and the world would stand still for them while they communicated on a level that some called primitive but that felt sublime. When he lifted his head, she held his gaze, drowning in its rich, blue depths as in a warm ocean of years and promise.

With a decided catch in her voice, she asked, "So…are you?"

"What? As good as you imagine?"

"Or possibly better?"

"Wait and see, love," he said before he rested his beard-shadowed chin on the top of her head, swinging her gently in the circle of his arms. "Just wait and see."

A NIGHT IN PARADISE

To Kevin Beard
With love and thanks

Prologue

"There is nothing so beautiful as a sunset like this," Michael Wulfson said. Then he turned to the woman at his side and added softly, "Unless it's you."

Mary Beck reached for his hand, and the two entwined their fingers as she replied gently, with just a touch of mischief, "The sunset *is* magnificent, and as to the other, well, I thank God that beauty is in the eye of the beholder."

Michael grinned. "Mary, I tell you, I've never seen more beautiful blue eyes than yours. They're the color of a cloudless day. And you know how partial I am to blue."

"And the sea, of course," Mary said. "Look at the sails out on the horizon."

Michael smiled, squeezing her fingers. "It's so wonderful here. Paradise. And it's incredible to share it with you."

"Ah, well, it's my home," Mary said.

"Once it was my home, too. Well, at least St. Augustine was, all those years when I was out at sea looking for treasure."

"Do you miss the sea?"

He grinned. "I found my treasure on land," he

assured her. "And this place…this place is wonderful. To think you were born here."

"I've always loved it here. Twenty minutes and you're in St. Augustine, an hour and you're in Jacksonville. A few hours' drive and you're in Miami. Theme parks to the west, the hills of Ocala and horse country just above, and here, where we are, the sea, the sand and moss dripping off the old oaks. It *is* paradise."

"You've known it your whole life. As close as I've been, I've really just discovered it," Michael reminded her. "But for all its wonders, it would still be just a place—if it weren't for you."

Mary laughed, reached over and touched his face. "My darling, you are the most incredible romantic. And I thank you."

Michael was serious for a moment, then said, "I want you to marry me."

"What?" Mary said, nearly falling out of her wheelchair.

"I want you to marry me."

A rueful smile crept slowly over his face, still handsome after all these years. "Please, Mary. I'd go down on my knees and be traditional and really romantic—if I could."

"You silly old coot!" Mary said. "You mustn't even think about getting down on your knees."

"I know that. I'd never get up. But the desire is there."

Mary hesitated. "Michael, I love you. I'm grateful for every moment with you. But…well, neither of us knows just how many moments we have left."

"Does it matter, so long as we make the most of them?" he asked. "We could have years, you know. I mean, our bones aren't great—as we've both discovered. And we definitely move slowly."

"Michael, let's face it. We're old. I mean marriage...what sense is it?"

"The best sense in the world, as far as I'm concerned. We love each other. Mary, please, I warn you, if I have to, I *will* try to get down on my knees."

"Don't you dare! You'd wind up breaking one."

"Then...?"

Mary laughed.

"Well?"

"Yes, I will marry you."

Michael smiled. "Then come on, honey. Lay one on these ol' lips before sourpuss comes to take us back in."

They both leaned close. A kiss was still a kiss....

"We're going to have some difficulty explaining this to the kids," Mary said.

"Hmm. What on earth will we tell them?"

"That we're getting married for the only real reason any two people should ever get married, just as you said. We're marrying because we're in love." Now that she had made her decision, she was firm in her resolve. "Besides, Aurora will be delighted. She loves you, too. And, well, you've really only got the grandson I've yet to meet, right?"

"Max," Michael said. "And Max...well, he should understand perfectly. He's always forged out on his own, so he should understand that trait in me. I'd like to tell him in person, and of course, I'd like

him to be my best man. I'm going to have to get him
down from New York.''

Both Mike and Mary had lost their children young,
and both had been mainly instrumental in raising their
grandchildren, Max and Aurora.

"I can't believe it. I'm nervous about meeting
him.''

"Mary…''

"Well, you already know Aurora and Angie. Naturally Aurora will be my maid of honor,'' Mary said.
"I can't wait to tell her. We can do it together, this
afternoon.''

Michael smiled, squeezing her hand. "Here we
are…you and me, in paradise. Mary, in all my years,
I don't think I've ever known such bliss.''

"Michael, you are an incredible man. When should
we have the ceremony?''

"Just as soon as we've got the rabbi and the priest
convinced we haven't got time to mess around with
a lot of interfaith counseling.''

One

Aurora Beck stared at the computer screen before her and hit the backspace key until she had erased an entire paragraph.

She stared at the screen, then wrote: Enter the Witch.

Okay, so the witch was going to enter before the goblin. And say...

The phone started to ring. She should have let it go, but she absently reached for the receiver, still staring at the computer screen.

"Hello?"

"Mom!"

She frowned. It was definitely Angie's voice, but as far as she knew, her daughter was still in the back bedroom, sleeping.

"Angie, where are you?"

"In the shower. Mom, you've got to come quick."

"You're calling me from the *shower?*"

"I'm on the cell phone. You've got to come quick. There's a huge roach in here. I mean a *huge* roach. *Mom!*"

Aurora heard a clatter as Angie apparently dropped the phone.

"Oh, Angie," she muttered, hanging up. "It's not

as if you've never seen a roach before.'' But she armed herself with a can of spray and headed through the living room/office for the back bedroom, and then on through to the back bathroom.

''Mom!'' Angie wailed.

The water was still spraying; the curtain was closed.

''Where is it, Angie?'' she asked with a sigh.

''Crawling over your way.''

''Ah-ha, I see it!'' It was a big one. She'd lived in Florida all her life, kept the place clean and treated for bugs as best she could, but still, it was the nature of the place to get a roach now and then. Spray tended to be her weapon of choice. They would get wet and fall, and then she could pick them up with a large wad of toilet tissue and discard them.

No disgusting smashed creature-bits on the floor that way.

Aurora lifted her can and sprayed.

The roach, instead of falling, crept its way desperately up and over the curtain into the shower.

''Mom!'' Angie shrieked again, leaping from the shower, making a wild grab for a towel and nearly tearing the curtain down.

''It's all right, it's almost dead,'' Aurora assured her. She wrenched back the curtain. The creature had finally fallen. It was lying on its back on the shower floor, wiggling its ugly legs beneath the spray of the shower.

''Get him, get him!'' Angie cried.

''Toilet paper,'' Aurora said, like a surgeon asking for a scalpel.

"Here," Angie said, supplying half a roll.

Aurora leaned forward, forgetting the shower was on.

"Did you get him? Did you?" Angie demanded.

Dripping, Aurora emerged. "Yes," she said dryly. "I got him."

She cast the creature into the toilet and stared at her daughter. Angie stared back and burst out laughing. "Mom, you're soaked."

"Yes, I know—thank you very much."

"Sorry."

"Angie, you're eighteen. You've got to kill your own roaches. It's a responsibility in life. And what on earth were you doing in there with a cell phone?"

"Well, I always bring it in. You said yourself that we need to be available at all times, what with Great-Gran in that place."

"Were you waiting for a call from Great-Gran— or from Douglas?"

Angie flushed. Aurora didn't get it. Yes, she was prejudiced, but her daughter was beautiful. Slim, golden blond, with immense blue eyes and perfect features. And she was in love—with a young idiot with whom she fought constantly.

Before she could say anything more, Angie's cell phone began to ring. Angie retrieved it from the shower, and they both stared at it, amazed the thing was still working.

"Hello?" Angie said. She smiled at her mother. "Hi. Yup, of course. Actually, I was coming by this afternoon. Anyway, she's right here."

With a definite smile of amusement and an I-told-you-so look, Angie handed the phone to her mother. "Great-Gran," she said casually.

"Um, thanks," Aurora said, heading out of the bathroom. "Hi, Gran. Is everything all right?"

"Everything's perfect, dear."

"You're joking, of course." Aurora loathed the place where her grandmother had gone for rehabilitation after breaking her hip, but there had been no choice. And to tell the truth, the place wasn't really that bad. She just didn't like seeing her grandmother there.

"No, darling, it's lovely. I have something important to tell you. I just wanted to make sure you were coming by."

"I am. I was just trying to finish my script."

"Take your time. I'll be here." Her grandmother's soft chuckle amazed Aurora. Mary had been in serious pain after she had broken her hip, though she had never complained. Mary's "incarceration," as they both had termed it, had, in a way, been a good thing. Both Aurora and Angie had been forced to learn that life could be far more difficult than either of them had ever imagined. And Aurora had been able to make up the difference between the cost of the facility and what Mary's insurance and Medicare covered by providing a unique service for the inhabitants—a special theatrical presentation once a week.

"You have good news for me, I take it?" Aurora said.

"The best."

"Tell me now."

"Oh, no, dear. This has to be in person."

"You're cruel."

"I'm trying to be inspiring. Get in there and write."

"All right. I'll see you soon."

Aurora hit the end key and strode back to the bathroom. The shower was still going.

"Angie?"

"Yeah?" Her daughter peeked out from behind the curtain.

"You're still in there?"

"I just got back in. I had to scrub the shower. Hey, there's nothing wrong with Great-Gran, right?"

"No. She says she has good news."

"Cool. I'll run by on my way to class, and then I'll see you later, okay? I won't say goodbye if you're working."

"Okay, but don't forget tonight."

"Yes, yes, I know. I'm the princess. And be on time for rehearsal. Eight o'clock."

"Hey, be glad you get to be the princess."

"I know, I know, you're the witch. Typecasting, if you ask me."

"I didn't."

Aurora hurried back to her computer.

To her amazement, the words began to flow, and the next thing Aurora knew, she was finished and the afternoon was waning. She hit the save key, closed down and hurried out of the house to her car.

"You're going to have to rewrite the scene," Jon Monroe said, staring at Max. His tone implied that Max must have realized that his statement was entirely obvious, since he had just seen Jena Ronson perform. Jon leaned closer to Max. ''Please,'' he said. It wasn't often that Jon had such a note of desperation in his voice.

Max leaned over to Jon. ''There's no way we can replace Jena?''

''Not unless you've suddenly managed to come up with a whole wad of extra millions,'' Jon said quietly.

Max gritted his teeth and lowered his head. The show was being financed by a corporation, a corporation headed by one man. And that one man happened to be the grandfather of one Jena Ronson.

She wasn't a bad dramatic actress, but she was a horrid comedienne. She simply had no sense of timing whatsoever.

''If I rewrite the scene, it won't be the same play anymore,'' he said, but the words weren't argumentative; they were the simple truth. Jon knew. They both knew it.

''Maybe we could turn it into a drama,'' Jon said, looking at the stage.

''All right, we're going to make major changes,'' Max said. They both needed and wanted this show, with the huge money behind it, to be a success. Not that they didn't have their share of successes behind them. But this was different. This was the ticket to ultimate triumph.

And he could rewrite. He could give the actress a true showcase. But it was going to be a whole new play.

He didn't want to compromise on the script he had intended; he would rather do a completely new piece.

"How long…?" Jon queried.

"Not as long as you think," Max said, figuring in his head. "A week. Give me a week, and I'll have what we need."

A week? Max asked himself. He'd lost his mind.

Rather that than their financing.

"I'm going back to my office," Max said.

"Great. What do I do about rehearsal?"

"Hey, you're the director. I've got my own problems."

Despite the distance, Max walked from the theater to his office, which was also his apartment. He had a great two-bedroom apartment in the Village, in a fine old historic building. He did well at his chosen livelihood, and he liked where he lived. Even so, today had been a blow. His work had been critically acclaimed for years, but this was his shot at the real gold. A play that could go on for years and years. And he could make life easier on himself. *Just rewrite the script he already had.*

No.

There would have to be similarities. He knew that. But his comedy lines had been raw and jabbing, the kind that made people think as well as laugh. The actress simply couldn't carry them off.

He reached his apartment, thinking, barely aware of the time he had spent walking and the hordes of people he had passed. When he entered his front door, however, he couldn't ignore Margorie who was his assistant and more.

Margorie had taken it on herself to be girl Friday, mother, mentor and scold, all in one. She'd been with him for ten years. He usually managed to do whatever he wanted to in spite of Margorie, who—with or without being solicited—had an opinion of his decorating, his work and the women in his life. In fact, she could be a royal pain in the butt. But she was also invaluable to him, running the household and his calendar, and intimidating those who didn't toe the line when it came to timeliness—especially in paying him.

Today she was waiting at the front door for him, as if she had a sixth sense that had told her he was on the way. She was small for such an opinionated woman, slim, with a deceptively pretty face. He knew that she was close to sixty, though she could have passed for forty. Once upon a time she had been a dancer, until a broken ankle had ended that dream. She had told him once that she pursued the stage vicariously through him, so he had better be successful.

Closing the door behind him, he groaned. "What is it?"

"Your grandfather."

Max frowned anxiously, his heart skipping a beat. Mike was back home, where he had wanted to be. He hadn't been happy about the decision, but he had respected his grandfather's desire to live where he chose—even though it meant they would no longer have the times together they had once shared. But Mike, despite the fact that he had been nearing ninety, had gotten it into his head to go out on a fishing boat. Not a bad thing in itself, but he'd gone out on high seas, lost his balance, crashed into the hull, and paid for sowing his old oats with a broken femur.

Max had made it down for the surgery. After being

assured that Mike was in good hands, he'd had to hurry back for the opening of a road show that had needed some rewrites. Then, almost immediately, this opportunity had come up. It had been a package negotiated by the corporation. The company would finance a show with Jon directing, Jena starring, and him writing the play.

The only saving grace now was that the play hadn't been specified. But still, he felt his heart sinking. If something was wrong in Florida, he was in trouble time-wise. Mike meant the world to him.

"Has anything happened to him?" he asked, his voice low, not betraying his anxiety.

"No, no, he says he's fine. But he needs you to come to Florida. He says it's important."

"Florida? He's fine—but he wants me to go to Florida? Now? I can't go to Florida," Max said. "Especially not now." Marjorie was staring at him. He walked past her, then turned back. "I'll call Mike. He'll understand."

"I don't think so."

He walked through the entryway and into the room to his left. His office. He sat behind his desk and realized she'd followed him. He stared at her. "He'll understand."

"Good. Because *you* don't."

Max leaned back in his chair, lacing his fingers behind his head. "All right, Marjorie, what is it you know that I don't?"

"Oh, I couldn't possibly tell you," she said. But she didn't leave the doorway.

He waved a hand toward her. "Shoo, then. I've got a lot of work to do."

"You're supposed to be calling Mike."

"I don't need you staring at me while I call him."

"You *do* need me to stare at you until you dial."

He scowled at her. "I'll call him soon."

"You'll forget. Well, too bad. All you'll see then is the announcement."

"What announcement?"

"Better call him."

Max reached over, picked up the phone and punched in his grandfather's number. Marjorie smiled, at last turning and abandoning her post at the doorway.

Max dialed his grandfather's number, wondering if he would catch him in.

Mike liked to be outside. When he wasn't working with his therapist, he liked to get sit in his wheelchair out by the water.

That was one of the great things about the Paradise Senior Care Facility. It was on the water, and if Mike loved anything in life, it was the sea. He could stare at the waves for hours and be happy. Maybe that was natural. In his younger days, Mike had been one of the finest salvage divers on the coast. As a kid, Max had eagerly awaited his summers, the months he spent down in Florida with his grandfather. Usually they went on pretty mundane dives, going down after the personal effects from a yacht sunk by an inexperienced captain. But there were the occasional days when they hunted old galleons and Mike had told Max stories about the days when the pirates had raised all hell along the Atlantic coastline, the islands of the Caribbean and beyond. Mike had been something of a real-life hero to Max. A fun guy with a flair for action. He hadn't given up heading his business until he was well past sixty, and he had captained one of his own ships until that day.

"Hello, Mike Wulfson here."

His grandfather still barked out his name as if he were commanding a fleet of vessels.

"Hey, Mike. It's Max."

"Well, young fellow, did you hear? I've got news for you. When are you coming down here?"

"Mike, I just found out I have to write an entirely new play—in a week."

"You can write in Florida."

"I can't. I won't have the time I have here. I have to get started now. Like right now."

"Max, I know you're a busy man, but I'm going to be sorry. Awful sorry. You're going to miss my wedding."

"Wedding?"

"Yep. I'm getting married."

"To whom? Why? When?"

Max couldn't have been more stunned. And yet of course it was more than possible that Mike had met a woman there in Paradise.

"When? Thursday. And why? I'm in love."

"But, Mike—"

"Oops, I've got to hang up. The beautiful Aurora Beck is coming in. Oh, Max, if only you could see what I see now. She's got short blond hair. Suntouched, like. She's a beauty. Runs in the family.

Blue eyes…Aurora, crank up the bed, will you? Only damned problem with this place. Hundreds of old geezers like me, and the beds all have manual cranks.''

"Mike, you can't go asking an old—older woman to crank up your bed," Max said, frowning.

"Don't worry. Aurora is a spring chicken.''

"What? Seventy instead of eighty? Mike, I'm delighted for you, but you need to think this out carefully.''

"Aurora isn't seventy. What kind of a man do you think I am?'' Max heard his grandfather's soft laughter. "She's thirty-something. Can you imagine that? It's not the years, it's the mileage, though. Max, I have to go now. I really wish you'd come down for the wedding.''

"Mike!'' He couldn't believe what he was hearing. Mike had always been sharp as a tack, but was falling for a hard-up blonde who could crank up his bed?

"I know you can get here if you want. Thursday afternoon. We want to get married on the beach. Isn't that romantic? She's a beauty, Max. I've never been happier. And sweet, too, because at my age, I know there's a lot more than looks to a woman. Don't fail me, Max. You can work here. You can work anywhere. I need you to be my best man. I'm counting on you.''

"Mike, wait. Marriage is a serious step.''

"I have to go. I'll talk to you when you get here. Tell Marjorie to get going on your flight reservations right away. Hell, I'll bet she's already booked you. Can't wait to see you, Max.''

"Mike, take a breath, dammit. Wait! This is insane. You can't go marrying a woman in her thirties without really thinking it through."

His words were wasted. Mike had hung up on him.

Marjorie was standing in the doorway again.

"So? Are you going to Florida for the wedding?"

He looked up at her irritably. "Hell, yes, I'm going to Florida. But not for the wedding."

"Why, then?"

"I'm going to stop the damned thing!"

Two

The young woman was sitting at the desk in what the plaque on the door identified as the Activities Center. She was bent over a computer, deeply engrossed.

She hadn't even noticed that he was standing there, Max thought in irritation. He cleared his throat, and she looked up from the computer, a pleasant, quizzical expression on her face.

She had short-cropped, flyaway blond hair. Lighter at the tips, naturally bleached by the sun. Very blue eyes. Nice features. She was a small woman, but she had a shape. Leave it to Mike. Even if he had been bewitched by a calculating young fortune hunter, she would surely have had the assets with which to bring her scheme to a successful conclusion.

This had to be her. The evil gold digger.

"Yes?"

"I'm Max Wulfson."

She looked him up and down, with apparent disapproval. He felt his temper simmering. He should be the one staring at her and passing judgement. What she was doing was more than shameless, it was disgusting. Like hell she was thirty-something. He doubted she'd made it to her thirtieth birthday yet, while Mike was heading toward ninety at a gallop.

"Well," she said after a moment, "welcome. It was nice of you to come down for the wedding. Spare a few days for your grandfather."

Despite himself, he bristled at the implied insult. "Mike chose to move to Florida. *He* is retired, *I'm* not."

"Ah. A busy man. Of course. He's told me you don't approve." She didn't seem surprised. As well she shouldn't be.

"Of course I'm against it."

"Why?"

"Oh, come on. You know why."

"Quite frankly, I don't. It's what your grandfather wants."

"My grandfather is an old man."

"He isn't senile."

Max felt a tic of anger pulse at his throat. He strode into the room. There was a spare chair near the computer desk. He drew it around backward and straddled it, staring at her flatly. "No, Mike isn't senile. But he is old, so I can see where he would be flattered, wanting to believe that a woman your age was in love with him."

"A woman my age...?" Her eyes widened; then her lashes swept them, and she lowered her head.

He was glad she at least had the grace to be ashamed. The he realized that she wasn't ashamed at all. She was smiling.

She stared up at him again, her countenance serious

once more. "I believe age is irrelevant when two people love each other, Mr. Wulfson."

"Naturally. I'm sure you started practicing that line the minute you became engaged."

She was still smiling, but her eyes had changed. There was something steely and hard in them now. Obviously she had realized that she wasn't going to get away with this whole thing as easily as she'd hoped. Mike might have gotten old and easy, but *he* hadn't.

"Frankly, Mr. Wulfson, I didn't have to practice that line. I really do believe it."

"And you mean to tell me that you love my grandfather?"

"Yes, actually, I do love him. Very much."

"Too bad. I intend to stop this marriage."

"Oh? How?"

One slim sun-browned leg crossed over the other, she stared at him, her hands folded in her lap, her words a challenge.

"Break it to Mike that you're after nothing but his money."

She leaned forward and asked a little breathlessly, "Does he really have that much?"

"Enough, Ms. Beck. Enough to get you out of here, I imagine."

"Well, bless us and save us," she murmured, a Southern accent he hadn't noticed until that moment echoing in her words.

"I'm willing to write you a check," he said.

"How long did *you* have to practice *that* line?" she asked sharply.

Ignoring her, he went on. "Of course, that's a limited-time offer. You call it off now and I write the check. You make me fight you, and...well, then I guarantee, you'll walk away with nothing."

"I'm perfectly willing to take that risk, Mr. Wulfson."

"I'd give you a substantial amount."

She leaned even closer. "But I want the whole ball of wax. And I'm willing to bet that this wedding will give your grandfather far more happiness than you—or he—could ever hope to buy. Now, if you'll excuse me, Mr. Wulfson, I'm busy."

He'd been dismissed.

"Fine. I'll have to talk to Mike, then. The truth now will be better than the pain you intend to cause him later."

A smile curled her lips, and she leaned close. "This wedding will give him nothing but pleasure, I promise you." She almost purred the words.

The woman was incredibly self-assured, Max thought. She was a barracuda, and she had spotted her quarry. Now she didn't intend to let go.

She didn't really look the type. No big bleached-out fall of sexy hair. No implants. A tank top and shorts. She didn't shout sex appeal.

She had it, though.

Maybe they made man-killers differently down here.

She sat back on the chair, folding her legs beneath her. Her feet were bare. Her sandals were on the floor.

"You can't see Mike right now."

"Hey, I came down from New York when I really

shouldn't have left. You can bet I'm going to see Mike.''

"You can't. He's out.''

"Out? At the doctor? Tell me where the office is.''

"He's not at the doctor's.''

"Look, you can't keep me away from him.''

"I'm not trying to keep you away from him. He's going to be delighted that you're here.''

"Then where is he?''

"I don't know, exactly.''

"Then 'not-exactly' where is he?''

"Shopping.''

"Shopping?''

"He's about to be a bridegroom, after all.''

"He's looking for a wedding ring? I'd have thought you'd have picked out the diamond a long time ago.''

"I'm not exactly sure what he's shopping for. Maybe some sexy underwear.''

"Aren't you amusing?''

"Not at all.''

"All right, would he be buying that sexy underwear for you—or for himself?''

"Oh, for himself, of course.'' She smiled innocently at him.

"Where would he be shopping?''

She shook her head and lifted her hands. "I haven't the faintest idea. He's not on a leash, you know. Merely getting married. He had his chauffeur come this morning.''

"Fine.'' He stood. "This isn't the end of this, you know.''

"Naturally not." Her voice had that challenging purr in it once again. "I look forward to having you in our lives—though not too often, of course."

"I'll be in your life, all right. You can just bet I'll be in it," he assured her.

Max turned and walked out, tempted to slam his hand against the wall. He felt ill. He loved Mike, and the old man sure didn't deserve this in the last years of his life.

What the hell had seized hold of his highly intelligent and usually rational grandfather?

One thing was for damned sure. No one was going to use Mike or make a fool out of him, not with Max Wulfson in town.

Even if it meant giving up the biggest break in his career.

It was all Aurora could do to keep from screaming.

That man was a self-righteous asshole. So worried about his own inheritance that he jumped to ridiculous assumptions.

He probably wouldn't like Mary any better.

He wouldn't want Mike marrying anyone. That would compromise his expectations for the future.

She was so angry she couldn't see straight. Time to hit the save button on the computer.

Suddenly the screen went blank.

What had she done? She had finally come up with the right dark, scary lines for her witch, and now…now she couldn't remember even one of them.

"No," she said aloud. "Please, no."

She scrolled up and down, hit every key, but it was futile. The dialogue was gone.

She gave up, trying not to let tears flood her eyes. She stood, then walked down the hall, past Mr. Hollenback, who no longer responded to any stimuli, though she usually spoke to him and patted his cheek anyway. She went on past the bingo room and had almost made it to Mary's room when a voice called out from 157.

"Aurora? Aurora, dear, is that you?"

She took a deep breath and stopped, popping her head into the room.

Daisy Marks was looking at her anxiously. "Sweetheart, they pushed my table to where I can't reach it. Would you be a dear?"

"Of course, Daisy."

She reached for the table, meaning to wheel it closer to Daisy.

It nearly flew through the window instead.

"Oh, dear," Daisy said, snow-white brows raised against her crinkled face.

"I'm so sorry," Aurora murmured, retrieving the table.

"What's the matter, dear? Oh, no...you've fallen in love, haven't you?"

"Of course not."

"Yes you have. I can tell."

Daisy giggled delightedly. "I know who he is."

"Really?"

"Of course. Mike's grandson."

"You've met him before?"

"Of course, dear. He wouldn't have considered letting Mike come here for treatment if he hadn't been down to approve the place.''

"I'm amazed he didn't try to yank Mike back up north with him.''

"Oh, he tried.''

"I dislike him more every second.''

"What a pity. You're about to become step…step somethings. Like cousins. He's very good-looking, I must say.''

"He's an idiot.''

Daisy was once again delighted. Aurora decided she could at least be glad she was creating such vast amusement for Daisy, who would be one-hundred on her next birthday. She had outlived all three of her children. Her grandchildren came to see her, but they lived in different states, and their visits were few and far between. After all, the grandchildren all had little children of their own to care for at home.

Daisy's body might be failing her, but her mind wasn't. "A good-looking idiot,'' she said pertly.

"I don't think so, Daisy. Besides, he's dead set against the marriage.''

"Really? That doesn't sound like Max. He dotes on Mike.''

"He thinks he's marrying me. And don't you go correcting him.''

Daisy cocked her head slightly. "So where were you off to in such a huff?''

"I was going to go tell Mary. I'm not so sure she should marry a man who has such a jerk for a grandson. I mean, think of the genetics.''

"Oh," Daisy said gravely. "Right. They could have two-headed children."

"Daisy, I just mean that…I don't want that Northern great white shark thinking my grandmother would marry Mike for his money."

"But we all know Mary would never marry any man for money. Leave it be, sweetie. Mike and Mary will be as happy as two bugs in a rug. No one should spoil that for them."

Daisy was right, Aurora knew.

"You feeling better now?" Daisy asked.

"Yeah, thanks. Daisy, do you need anything else while I'm here?"

"No, dear. I couldn't reach the remote, but you got me all settled."

"Well, good. I'll see you later then."

Aurora started to leave.

Daisy called her name before she could leave the room.

"Aurora, dear?"

"Yes."

"All men are idiots, you know."

Aurora lifted a brow.

"Trust me. I married three of them."

"You kept going back for more, huh?"

Daisy grinned. "Can't live with them, can't shoot them, as the saying goes. It's the nature of the beast. But you don't throw out a puppy because it tinkles. You teach it to go outside. Men are just the same. But they are trainable."

"Thank you for that wisdom, Daisy."

Aurora left and slipped into Mary's room, next

door. Mary was watching the weather channel. She saw Aurora, and her face brightened. "You finished the script?"

"No."

"What happened?"

"I met Mike's grandson."

"And?"

"He wants to talk Mike out of the marriage."

"Oh?" Mary didn't seem at all alarmed.

"Of course, he does think that Mike is marrying *me*."

Mary burst into laughter. "Well, no wonder he wants to stop the marriage."

"But I'm afraid that's not all of it, Mary. I think he's worried that his grandfather's money is going to go to someone else. He's going to do everything he can to talk Mike out of getting married."

"Don't you worry about that, dear."

"But, Mary—"

"Aurora, if we don't marry, it won't bother me at all." She winked. "We'll simply live in sin."

"I think I'd prefer that."

"I was joking, you know. I'm not sure that either of us is capable of sinning at this moment."

"But there may be moments in the future."

Mary shrugged. "Ah, to be young again."

"I'm hardly young."

"You're in the midst of the best years of your life."

"You said that when I was twenty."

"And I'll say it again when you hit forty, which isn't all that far away. And if I'm blessed, or cursed, with a really long life, I'll say it when you're fifty, too.

"Life gets harder, of course, but it's still what we make of it. And as to Mike and me...we'll be fine. Don't you worry."

"If Max ruins things for you..." Aurora began.

"You'll what? Punch him in the nose?"

"That will be the least of it," Aurora promised.

"It will all work out. Once he finds out I'm as ancient as Mike, we'll be fine."

Aurora shook her head. "I think he's just against Mike getting married at all, and the only reason for that has to be that he's worried about Mike's money."

"Then I'll sign a prenuptial agreement. What could I possibly be after at my age?"

"An inheritance for me. The conniving, scheming granddaughter."

"Don't be silly. We'll just explain the whole thing when Mike gets back."

"Is he out buying sexy underwear?" Aurora murmured.

"Sexy underwear?" Mary said, perplexed. Then she smiled again. "Oh, I do hope so!"

Serena, one of the nurses, popped her head into the room. "Phone call for you, Aurora. You can pick it up on your gram's line."

"Thanks."

She expected her daughter, or one of her players, but it was neither.

"Dinner. It will be your last chance."

She was tempted to instantly tell him what to do

with himself, but a glance at Mary changed the words she had been about to use.

"You must be joking."

"Let me convince you. I'll take you to Adjani's."

She was amazed to find herself hesitating. The restaurant had only been open for a year. Just south of St. Augustine, the town that bordered Paradise, it was run by a world-renowned chef. She hadn't been there, of course. She couldn't afford to go.

She couldn't help being tempted to drag her deception on awhile longer. After all, he had made the assumptions.

"I have work to do," she said, thinking out loud.

"Work?"

"I lost something in the computer today." His fault. That was reason enough to go to dinner and order the most expensive thing on the menu, and their best wine, as well.

"You can't actually lose things in a computer," he said. "Besides, why do you need to worry about work? Won't looking after Mike be your job once you're married?"

"I have a previous commitment."

"Tell you what. I'll find your lost file in the computer. That will be easier than trying to find Mike," he muttered.

"Already tried all the risqué shops, have you?" she inquired sweetly.

"Aurora!" Mary said.

Aurora hushed her with a wave.

"Have dinner with me," he said. His voice had regained its steely quality.

She hesitated. She had to jump before he did find Mike, because then her charade would be over. And she was truly dying to prove to this man just how big an idiot he was.

"Fine."

"Six? I have a few things I need to do first. And I'll get back your lost computer data, too. Let's make it six-thirty."

"All right." She realized she would rather rewrite than have this man at her computer. "Forget the data. It—it really isn't that big a deal."

He was silent.

"Well, is there anything else?"

"Yes. I'll need your address."

"Oh." She hesitated, then gave it to him. She was listed in the phone book after all; her address certainly wasn't any big secret.

"See you then," he said.

"I'll be breathlessly waiting," she assured him and hung up.

Over the years, Max had stayed at every conceivable type of hotel, motel, inn and hostel known to man. From the best in the world to a pup tent.

Nothing had prepared him for the Paradise Motor Lodge.

There were no plastic keys here. They were the real thing. And they were handed out with a warning that they had to be returned—or else a whopping ten dollars would be added to the bill.

Gracie MacIver, a middle-aged, middle-sized woman, with a headful of salt-and-pepper hair, had also warned him sternly that if he came back after ten at night—without his key, he was just way out of luck. She went to bed at ten, and so did her husband, Ned.

Other than that, of course, she had been as gracious as could be, offering him a cold drink or hot tea while he signed the register. Ned—also middle-aged, middle-sized and with the same salt-and-pepper hair—had arrived then and offered him a beer.

Gracie had taken her time allowing him to register. She had been on the phone with someone named Sara when he had first arrived, and had told him to take a seat. Then she had smiled and described him to Sara.

Somehow he had kept his natural impatience and his irritation at the entire situation under control, and had waited for Gracie to finish with the local gossip in a manner that was almost polite.

"We're not in a hurry down here, you know," she said.

He tried not to make his smile too brittle.

"It's not New York," she continued.

"No, it's not New York."

"New York is a great place. But Paradise is better."

"Yes, it's beautiful here," he had managed to say.

Gracie gave him a strange smile.

"Take the time to look around. You'll be able to say that and mean it."

"I know Florida. I spent a lot of time here, growing up."

"You don't know Paradise, though."

Paradise.

They should have named it Purgatory.

The strange thing was that his room was great. It was spacious, with the kind of amenities that belonged on a tropical island. Each room was really a little bungalow, and the rear doors opened out on a deck that led directly to the beach. The units were spaced far apart, with plenty of palm trees and wild grass growing between them. With the doors open, the breeze from the sea wafted in and lifted curtains of some sheer fabric that added another of those island touches to the scene. The furniture was wicker, and there were a kitchenette and bar beyond the half wall against which the bed rested—the better to see the sunrise.

The room did feel a bit like paradise.

He allowed that concession as he dressed for dinner. No tie, but a jacket, despite the heat. Although, he had to admit, stepping out on the lanai that led to the beach, the breeze made it comfortable, even with a jacket over his cotton shirt. He might have been alone in the world, with nothing but sand and the sea stretching before him. The solitude, the sound of the surf, the occasional call of a shore bird...

It *was* almost paradise.

He stepped back inside, thinking about the restaurant, and walked to the phone. He almost made a call to make sure that Aurora was aware that shorts were not allowed.

But she would know that. In fact, he was certain that when he picked her up, she would be impeccably dressed. She hadn't snared Mike by being a fool.

As he stared at the phone, it rang.

He picked it up. It was Mike.

"Max! I'm so glad you came. I have to tell you. I feel like a kid again."

"You're marrying a kid," Max said. "We've got to talk."

"Well, come on over."

"I, uh, I can't come. I'm taking your fiancée to dinner."

"You're taking my fiancée to dinner?"

"Yes. I thought we should talk."

"Mary can't go to dinner with you. She's meeting me in the cafeteria in five minutes."

"She agreed to go with me—wait a minute. Who's Mary?"

"My fiancée. Mary Beck, the sweetest woman ever to draw breath."

Max frowned, staring at the phone.

"Then who the hell is Aurora?"

"Her granddaughter, of course." Mike's gruff laughter suddenly exploded in his ears. "You thought I was marrying Aurora?"

"Well, yeah. You were telling me all about her the other day. Don't you remember?"

"What? Oh, that's because she had just walked into the room. So you came down here thinking some young beauty was marrying me for my money, huh? The bones are old, son. The eyes are going, and, quite frankly, the hearing sucks. They're right when they say getting old isn't for sissies. But the mind is all here, son, though I admit to being confused. Surely Aurora explained that I'm marrying her grandmother."

"Actually, Aurora didn't explain."

"So you're picking her up for dinner?"

"Yes, that's the plan. Though now I have to meet the real fiancée...no, I'm still going to dinner."

"That's fine, Max. We'll spend some time together tomorrow, and you can get to know Mary then. I'll just give Aurora a call—"

"No!"

"What?"

"Mike, she played me for a fool. Give me tonight to pay her back a little."

"Now, Max, you don't know that girl."

"Don't worry. I'll be courteous to a fault," Max assured him.

"Hmph," Mike muttered. "Don't you mess up my marriage."

"Apparently both Aurora and Mary are eager for the wedding."

"And you still have your doubts."

"I just don't understand why you want to marry anyone."

"I love her, boy. I love her. Wait until you meet her. Aurora may be a beautiful young thing, but no one has Mary's eyes. So enjoy dinner, I'll see you in the morning, bright and early. We old folks don't sleep much, you know."

"Bright and early."

"After a night of courtesy."

"You bet."

Max hung up and glanced at his watch. Time to go.

Oh, yeah. He'd be courteous.

Three

Nothing was ever easy, Aurora reflected as she waited for Max to arrive.

She was supposed to be at the playhouse, and she would be, just as soon as Max Wulfson finished making his latest threat against her if she went ahead and married Mike. This opportunity had been just too good to resist.

Aurora had owned the playhouse for over ten years, and she had cause to be proud of her accomplishments. Once, owning the place had been a dream she had shared with Kevin, and his death had almost made her give it up. But they had saved to buy what had once been an old cinema, and though she had almost let the sale fall apart, at the last minute she had decided it was just what she needed to get through her grief after the small plane he had been flying—another of his passions—had crashed.

She had made the theater into a showcase for local talent, young and old. With the multitude of colleges in the area she had been able to hire plenty of young dreamers. She had also been able to give a stage to those who had once dreamed of the grandeur of New York or Hollywood but given in to the reality of small children, spouses, mortgages, aging parents, or other responsibilities. She had never allowed anything to be done in less than a professional manner, though, no matter how young or eccentric her performers or tech people, and in a matter of a few years, she had been stunned to receive offers of work from several well-known professionals.

So the Paradise Playhouse had gained respect and an entry in the "must see" lists of most of the travel guides. None of this had changed the fact that the players also performed for local schools, and now for the rehab and retirement home.

Nor had it changed the fact that she still struggled to stay afloat.

That didn't mean that she wasn't happy. She was. She treaded water carefully, and kept the dream alive. And, she thought wryly, she lived in Paradise.

Of course, at times she felt very alone in Paradise. But even at her lowest points, the theater was her baby. Without her, it floundered.

But as for tonight…

She picked up the phone and called John Smith.

John had been with her for five years. He was an incredible actor, and she wasn't always sure how she had gathered him into her fold. He hadn't come with a résumé, and he seldom talked about his past. He didn't want to give explanations, and she wasn't about to force them. He sometimes served as stage manager, and he was there even when she desperately needed someone to paint scenery. He seemed perfectly happy to be in Paradise, making practically nothing, enjoying the natural beauty and asking little else from life. She didn't know his age—he might have been thirty-something or fifty-something—she only knew that he was there for her, and that she was blessed to have him.

"John?" she said, glad just to hear his voice when he answered the phone.

"Of course it's me. Who were you expecting? I live alone."

"I'm relieved that you're home, that's all."

"What's up? No script, eh?"

"Not that bad. There's a script. Sort of. Just no Act II. But I'm going to be late. Can you open up and get the rehearsal going?"

"Sure I can, but what about you? You're the witch."

"Shelley can stand in."

"Nancy is sick. Shelley will be standing in for her."

"She'll have to stand in for us both."

"That will be great. She'll be giving half her lines to herself."

"Then you can stand in for me."

"I'm the goblin."

"You'll work it out."

"Why are you going to be late?"

"I have a dinner date."

"Oh, great. We haven't got a finished script, and you're going to show up late because you've got a dinner date. Wait. Never mind. This is a good thing. I forgot that I'm the one who's always telling you that you have no life, and that you'd probably be a better writer if you had sex on occasion."

"John, I'm having *dinner,* not sex."

"That's a pity. Your meal scenes are fine. It's the romantic interludes that need fixing."

"John, I'm working on a fairy tale spoof for children and geriatrics. There aren't any sex scenes in the show. Besides, how dare you say I have no life! I have a great life. I have a home, a daughter, a job—"

"Doing what? Waiting on a bunch of senior citizens hand and foot?"

"Someone has to do it. But I wasn't referring to that. The theater is my baby, and it's doing well."

"Sure. You're helping every would-be star in the state. And barely breaking even."

"I have respect."

"You have no money, and no sex."

"But I'm doing what I want to do and making a living at it, at least. That's a lot. And you're delaying us both here. I have to get ready, and you have to open the theater. And you have no life, either, outside of Paradise, so don't you dare lecture me."

"Ah, but you don't know what I do with my off hours."

"And how do you know what I do with mine?"

"You have no off hours. So go have dinner. And if the offer comes up, have some sex, too."

"John, go open the theater."

"I'm out the door, I promise. Oh, by the way. Wear something a little risqué."

"Thanks for the advice, John."

She hung up before he could give her any more. She already intended to dress the part of the young vixen out to snare the old codger.

Angie came in just as she finished dressing. Her

daughter plopped down on the bed and stared at her, frowning.

"Did you write a new role for the show? Is this going to be a dress rehearsal for the wicked-hot witch?"

"I've got a dinner date."

Angie's jaw dropped. "You—you have a date?"

Aurora frowned. "Yes, is that so strange?"

"Uh, no. I mean, *yes*. I don't remember you ever having a date."

Aurora wondered if Angie was upset. If she was thinking about her father. She sat down by her daughter's side, smoothing back the soft shining fall of her hair. "It's not actually a real date. It's Mike's grandson. He thinks I'm the one marrying his grandfather. And he's a regular...jerk. I thought I'd lead him on awhile longer, and maybe then, when he realizes his grandfather is marrying Mary, he won't be such a complete idiot about the whole thing."

"Oh," Angie said. She sounded concerned.

"Oh, Angie, I won't go if it upsets you."

"Upsets me? I just wish it *were* a real date. You need one. You would understand better about...oh, never mind."

"I'd understand better about Josh if I did, is that right?" She hadn't meant to allow her voice to become so tight.

"Yeah," Angie said. The word closed a door.

"Angie, I don't dislike Josh."

"You just don't like me seeing him, just because we've had some fights. Well, we made up. I'm seeing him tonight, after the rehearsal."

"Great," Aurora said. She stood, looking at her hair in the mirror, running a brush through it, not really seeing what she was doing.

"Great? You don't mean that all."

"You're right, I don't. He's going to see you for a few weeks, tell you that you're wonderful and beautiful and that he adores you, and then he's going to call one afternoon with other plans, because you're not worth it to him."

"We've already been back together for weeks now, Mom."

"Oh, good, then the phone call is coming."

"Not this time."

"Not this time, not the last time, or the time before that. Angie, there are other people in the world. Nice people, guys who will realize that you're a beautiful and gifted young woman, and will appreciate you!"

"Mom, I've tried. You don't just go out and see someone, find him attractive, like shopping for groceries. I can't help it. It's idiotic, maybe. But I'm in love with him."

"Then you ought to fall out of love with him."

"Easy for you to say."

"Meaning?"

"You just don't need anyone."

Aurora stared at her daughter, her eyes narrowing.

"Well, you don't. The rest of the world craves companionship. Even Gran. There's nothing so adorable as Mike and Gran. But you...well, you've forgotten what it's like to love someone. To need them in your life."

"Love and need are not the same thing, Angie.

Love shouldn't be based on need. Love is an emotion.''

"Whatever. You've gone without it for too long."

"That's ridiculous. I love you, I love Gran, I have great friends I love...."

"I rest my case," Angie said with a sigh.

"Don't mistake hormones for love," Aurora said, more sharply than she had intended.

"Don't mistake breathing for living," Angie countered.

Aurora was disturbed to feel as if she were on the defensive. "Angie, life is responsibility more than anything else. When your dad died, I had to make a living. I'm really happy in what I do. And I think I've raised a beautiful, intelligent daughter, as well."

"I know, I know, wait until I'm really trying to make it in the world, wait until I have children and a mortgage and all the rest."

"It does change the picture." Aurora felt the tension in her jaw. Then her anger seemed to fall away like a cloak, and she shook her head. "I love you, Angie, and I admit there was a time when you were my whole life, maybe more than was healthy. I don't want to burden you with this now, when you're right at the age when the world will be opening up to you. So trust me when I say, I love what I do, I'm happy and well-adjusted, and I know love isn't something you can order over the Internet, or go out and find just because you've decided you need it in your life. But I don't like to see you hurt—and this guy hurts you all the time. You owe yourself—not me—more."

Angie nodded gravely. "Advice heard. May I give you some?"

"Go on."

"You don't go out looking for someone, but don't shoot him down if he happens to come along."

Aurora stared at her daughter.

"Dad is dead, Mom. And he wasn't perfect. He was a great guy, but he wasn't perfect."

Aurora found herself staring at her daughter.

"Well?"

Aurora nodded. "Advice heard."

The doorbell rang, and they both jumped.

"Damn," Aurora swore.

"That's him?" Angie's eyes widened. "I'll get it!"

Max was startled by the girl who opened the door. She was somewhere between seventeen and twenty years old, in jeans and a T-shirt, with such perfect features that she could have been on the cover of any magazine. Actually, he realized, she was like a copy of Aurora Beck, just a bit younger.

"Hi. Come on in. You're Mike's grandson, right?"

"Max," he said, nodding. "Max Wulfson. Are you...Aurora's sister?"

She smiled. "Mom would like that. She's ready by the way—good old Mom, always punctual." The girl spoke the words with a sniff, as if habitual timeliness was annoying, but there was affection in her tone. "I'm Angie, by the way. Make yourself at home. I'll get my mother."

So Aurora had a child who was more or less

grown-up. Aurora couldn't be quite as young as he had first estimated.

Not that it mattered, since she wasn't really after Mike, just tormenting him for his presumption.

She had done a good job, but now it was his turn. Ah, the taste of revenge.

He smiled at Angie. "Thanks."

The girl disappeared. Max, left in the living room, appreciated the air-conditioning and looked around.

It was pleasantly chaotic. Though it wasn't located on the beach, it had the look of a beach house. The furniture was light pine, the cushions deep and comfortable on the sofa, love seat and armchair. There was an entertainment center that housed hundreds of books, DVDs, CDs and tapes. The draperies were light, in shades of yellow and blue. The floors were hardwood, with area rugs.

It wasn't the home of a sophisticated bloodsucker preying upon an older man. He wondered if he would have realized that when he arrived here, if he hadn't already learned the truth from Mike.

Maybe not. Maybe he'd been so protective and self-righteous that he couldn't see a thing before his own eyes.

He noted a shelf of bound plays and movie scripts. His interest piqued, he walked over to the entertainment center, hunkered down and began to look through them.

"Mom!"

Angie said the word with the same passion she had expressed in her cry for help over the roach.

Aurora spun around to see her daughter standing in the hallway. "What's wrong? Did he do something to you? Was he rude to you? He'd better not have been."

"Mom, he's—he's *hot!*"

"What?"

Angie took a soaring leap onto the bed. "He's handsome. Tall. Dark. Great voice. He's…well, he's hot," she repeated.

"Great vocabulary, Angie."

"Hey, when a word fits… You know, you really shouldn't blow this."

"Blow this? I'm only going because he's a pompous idiot and I want to take him down a peg or two."

"He's still one darned good-looking pompous idiot."

"Looks, my dear, aren't everything." She looked at her watch, "You're supposed to be at rehearsal."

"And you're supposed to be on a date."

"It's not a real date, and it *is* a real rehearsal."

"I'm out of here. You can have the house."

"No, wait, we'll leave together."

Aurora preceded her daughter out of the bedroom. Max Wulfson was seated on the sofa, a pile of her bound plays and scripts at his side as he leafed through one.

He looked up when she came into the room. His smile was pleasant. He really was good-looking, she realized. Dark hair, a little shaggy despite the combing it had obviously been given. Features craggy, but handsomely arranged. A smile that did something to the ebony darkness of his eyes.

"This is great," he told her.

"What?"

"This is yours, right? It has 'by Aurora Beck' written on it."

"Yes, it's mine." She found herself flushing slightly, and without thinking she walked over to retrieve the play, close it and slide it back in place on the shelf.

He stood. "Is that what you do?" he inquired.

"Well, when you're not pursuing old men, of course. Are you a playwright?"

"I own a little theater," she murmured, then noticed that her daughter had come up behind them. "Angie, get to rehearsal."

"I'm going."

"And we have reservations, right?" Aurora asked Max.

"Yes, we do," he agreed. They all walked out together. Angie gave a wave as she headed for a beige Saturn. Aurora waved back and started toward her own little beat-up van, but then she saw the blue sports car in the driveway and altered course. He was right behind her.

She realized—after she'd opened her own door and slid into the passenger seat—that he'd been about to open the door for her. It had been a long time since she'd been out on anything that resembled a date. She was out of practice.

He made no comment but smoothly walked around

to the driver's side. A moment later, he was shifting into gear.

"Great car," she said.

"It's all right for a rental. Actually you're right. It's pretty great for a rental. By the way, you have a really beautiful daughter."

"Thanks."

"How old is she?"

"Young. Eighteen."

He grimaced, inclining his head slightly as he drove. "Well, who knows? Maybe, when I'm in a nursing home, she'll come after me."

Aurora shot him the most contemptuous stare she could manage.

"Well, my grandfather *is* quite a bit older than you are."

"Yes, but it's different."

"How?"

"I'm old, too. At least, I'm not..."

"You're not your daughter?" he said quietly.

"Exactly."

"So, tell me about your theater."

She shrugged. "I own the Paradise Playhouse."

"You own it?"

"Well, the bank and I own it."

"Still, that's quite impressive."

"How do you know? It could be a barn."

He shook his head, a slight smile curving his lips as he drove. "Nope, I've heard of it. Don't know why I didn't think of it right away when I saw your scripts."

"Oh?" Aurora couldn't help but feel a bit pleased.

She looked out the window, though, and said, "You were preoccupied with other matters. Like a younger woman trying to fleece your grandfather."

"Well, at least now I understand."

"What do you mean, you understand?"

"You need the money for the sake of art—to keep your playhouse going. So I have a new proposition for you."

"And that is?"

"My answer will have to wait. There's the restaurant."

She didn't have to make a decision regarding whether she should or shouldn't wait to let him open the door for her; a valet did so, and then Max Wulfson came around to take her arm and escort her into the building.

The décor was beautiful. Chandeliers, deep blue carpeting, soft toned walls, candles, silver and flowers. They were seated at a small table in a little alcove that looked out on a small bubbling fountain. The sommelier was the first to arrive at the table, and Max listened carefully as the man listed the contents of the restaurant's cellar. Max smiled at her across the table. "Do you have a preference?"

She hadn't recognized a thing the man had said, but before she could reply with "White wine"— which would have been her answer—Max made it easier.

"Well, we haven't looked at the menu yet. I think we'll make the decision between meat and fish first, shall we?"

"Lovely," Aurora murmured.

"Well, I can tell you now that if you are fish lovers, we have an excellent broiled dolphin with a shrimp and lobster sauce tonight."

"Are we fish lovers?" Max asked Aurora.

"Absolutely."

"Then the California merlot would be an excellent choice."

"Merlot sounds divine," Aurora said.

The tuxedo-clad waiter hovered behind the tuxedo-clad sommelier. Their dinner order was taken. Water and the wine arrived. Max tasted the wine without appearing affected—she had to grant him that much. He approved the bottle, and their glasses were filled.

Suddenly they were alone.

Max lifted his glass. "To becoming related."

She lifted hers in turn. "I thought you came out tonight to stop the wedding?"

"Ah, yes, of course. Well, then, here's to stopping you from marrying Mike."

"And I'm supposed to drink to that?"

"Okay, then, here's to a night in Paradise."

"We're only out for dinner."

"But it is night, and it is Paradise. Are you always so argumentative?"

She flushed.

"All right, let's toast to dinner. This is an excellent wine, after all."

"Imagine that. In the backwoods of Florida."

"Amazing. Can we toast yet?"

Aurora lifted her glass. The wine was excellent. Probably the best she had ever had. Smooth, crisp, not too dry. It went down like water. She warned herself to slow down.

"What's your proposal? Or proposition. Or whatever."

"That you don't marry Mike."

"That's not a proposal, that's merely a statement of what you want. A proposal would be explaining to me what you can offer that would keep me from marrying Mike."

He leaned close to her across the table. "In the long run, I'm worth more."

She nearly fell off her chair. "What?"

"All right, you need money, so you're marrying Mike. But his money is all tied up. Despite his marriage, it *will* come to me."

"You might want to check Florida law."

He waved a hand in the air. "Trust me. I've had lawyers all over this."

"So…?"

"So I can make it worth your while not to marry Mike."

Aurora delicately trailed her finger around the rim of her wineglass. "That would be the check you offered to write."

"Not exactly."

"Oh?"

He leaned back in his chair, sipping his wine. Aurora felt as if she were being studied as thoroughly as he might study a car he was considering purchasing.

And he was giving away nothing of what he thought of the merchandise.

"Oh?" she repeated.

"Salads."

"What?"

"Our salads are here. I think we should enjoy them first."

Frustrated, she sat back as the waiter appeared, bearing iced salad forks and their salads.

Max seemed inclined to eat without talking. She took a bite herself and was instantly amazed that anyone could make lettuce and a few garden vegetables taste so good. She realized then that she hadn't taken the time to eat all day, and that she was famished. The salad was so good that she had finished the entire thing before she realized he had been watching her for some time, attempting, without much success, to conceal an amused smile.

She set her fork down. "That was very good."

"Yes, it was. This place has gained its reputation through good food and service, rather than pomp and price."

"Oh, I think the prices are up there."

"Maybe. But stick with me on this and it won't matter."

She remembered the role she was playing and leaned forward, fingers drumming lightly on the white tablecloth.

"Well," she said, giving the single word a husky edge. "Just what are you proposing?"

"You turned down my first offer."

"But I haven't heard the second."

"My first offer was flat-out money."

"Yes. But then, at the time, I had no idea that Mike's money was tied up."

"I see. So if I came up with an offer now, just for money, you might accept it?"

"Oh, I don't know. I do love him, you know. And guess what? I never even suggested marriage. Mike was the one insisting on it."

"So I gather. But then again..." He leaned closer. "I can see where he was simply driven to distraction. Willing to do anything for your company."

She felt a frown crease her forehead. His voice had grown as husky as her own. She edged back a little in her seat.

"Just because he's old and I'm young?"

"Just because you're...you." The last word seemed to hang on the air, filled with all kinds of implications.

Those dark eyes could be as cold and hard as an ebony pit. She had learned that already today. She had also learned that he could be calculating and ruthless.

But he could wear many faces. Now he had a better set of bedroom eyes than any soap star she'd ever seen. The wine seemed to burn like a lava fire in her stomach. She felt like a Southern belle of old, as if she might have the vapors. She needed a fan to flutter away the disturbing heat.

It had been far too long since she had dated.

"I really don't understand at all what you're getting at, Mr. Wulfson."

"Max. Please, you've got to call me Max. And

surely you must understand what I'm getting at. Don't you?''

''Just what—''

''Fish.''

''What?''

''Our entrées are coming.''

The man must have had a secret pact with the waiter, who had indeed appeared, the two covered plates balanced expertly on his arm. He set the food down and was joined by a second server so that their entrées were presented as one.

The aroma of the food was another shot-of sensual bliss, and she found herself reaching for her wine.

Max had raised his glass once again. ''To the simple pleasures in life.''

She toasted with him. His fingers brushed hers, and she was again startled by the sensations that swept through her. She really needed to get out more. Wine and a meal and a nasty man out to ruin her grandmother's life were coming together to make her feel orgasmic. She was going to get through this, get through the wedding, then work on her social life.

Not easy when her customary circle contained mainly of geriatrics, devastating males of a different sexual preference, and a few married co-workers.

''I'm still waiting,'' she said.

But he didn't reply right away, because the sommelier had made a smiling reappearance to refill their wineglasses. And because she was nervous, she began sipping again. Not such a bad thing, she assured herself. Wine this good wasn't customarily on her menu.

Since he was being such a grade-A idiot about the wedding, she might as well consume his wine.

"Taste your fish. It's delicious."

"It is," she agreed, taking a bite.

"You don't have a Southern accent," he said. "Not much of one, anyway."

"Florida isn't really known for an accent," she reminded him.

He smiled. The man had a really great smile, she realized. His dark good looks could give him an austere, even dangerous, appearance. His smile was full of pure charm. Unaffected, easy, even rueful.

"Ah, now, that's not true. Perhaps in the big East Coast cities, where there's a blend of immigrants and transplants, along with the natives, there's not much of an accent. But in the center and the north of the state, you can come across a lot of lovely accents deriving from the Deep South."

"You don't sound like a New Yorker."

"And what does a New Yorker sound like? You mean I don't have a Brooklyn or Bronx accent."

"Well, I majored in theater in college. In L.A.," she said. "That's where I lost my accent."

"I see."

"And you?"

He shrugged. "I spent a lot of time right here when I was growing up."

"Right here?" She frowned.

"OK, not right *here*. In St. Augustine."

"With Mike?"

"You got it."

"On the boat? You...went salvage diving with him?"

He nodded. He had finished his fish. She realized she had, too. Cleaned the plate, actually. The food had been divine. And her wineglass was empty again. The sommelier saw to it that it didn't stay that way.

Her head was spinning, but not in a bad way. She felt light-headed, certainly. And...wow. Great. She felt as if she were walking on air, except that she wasn't walking at all. She was sitting. Warm, amazingly relaxed.

"You didn't think a New Yorker could dive?"

"Well...no, not exactly. I mean, there are ski shops all over Florida. They're a very big business down here. I guess people who live in the heat all the time enjoy getting away to the snow. And people who live where there is a real winter..."

"Enjoy getting away to warm water and balmy breezes."

"Exactly. I just didn't realize you had spent so much time with Mike."

"Amazing. You're marrying him, and you know so little about him."

There it was. The subtle attack. But it didn't bother her. She ran a finger over the rim of her wineglass and took another sip as the plates in front of them seemed to magically disappear.

"We feel that we know the important things to know about each other."

"Namely?" he inquired.

"Well, that we're deeply in love. What else is there?"

"Of course, what else?"

She frowned slightly. "The religion thing doesn't bother you, does it? I mean, Mike is Jewish, and M— I mean *I'm* Catholic."

He shook his head. "See, there's just so much you don't know! My grandmother was Catholic, and so was my mom, at least, when she was young. She moved to a place in Florida after my dad died, a special town for spiritualists. 'All paths lead to one place.' That was her belief."

"That's lovely," Aurora said. She was leaning lightly on the table.

He did the same. "You really are lovely, you know."

"Then you shouldn't mind having me for a step-grandmother," she said. "But then again, you've got a...proposal, for me."

Again, he was close. So close. Eyes on her so intently. She could smell his aftershave. Subtle, nice. Almost feel the whisper of his breath.

"Yes. A proposal..."

Four

"Dessert," he said.

"Pardon?"

"The dessert menu is here."

"Oh...sorry. I'm not much on dessert."

"They have Decadent Chocolate Delight."

"I really don't..."

"Listen to the description. 'An amazing hot chocolate shell saturated with sumptuous mousse and sinfully filled with vanilla bean ice cream, crested with decadent chocolate and vanilla sauces.' We can share one." He was watching her across the table. She realized that her ankle was resting against his. She couldn't quite bring herself to move it. His lips weren't moving, but she could swear she heard him talking again. Describing dessert. *An amazingly fit male of the species, hot, sinfully wicked, delectable to the palate, decadent in every move.*

"Shall we?"

"Shall we what?"

"Share dessert?"

"No!"

"You want your own?"

"No, I, uh..."

"I'll try it. I'm sure I can talk you into a small bite."

He ordered the dessert. And some form of ridiculously aged cognac. She fanned herself with her napkin, then caught him watching her again.

"It's a little warm in here," she murmured.

"Perhaps it is a little warm...at this table."

It's hot here next to you.

She nearly jumped, afraid she had said the words out loud. She hadn't. But his eyes hadn't left her face.

"Now...as to this marriage and my proposal..."

"Yes?"

"Where's Angie's dad?"

She frowned and said softly, "Deceased."

"I'm sorry."

"Thank you."

"Recently?"

She shook her head. "Several years now."

"Ah. Good marriage?"

She found herself smiling. "Yes. Realistic. We fought. We had a tendency to dream the same dreams. We always made up. His one dream, though...he wanted to fly. I was against it. I gave him a hard time, but...not hard enough. He crashed."

She fell silent. She had said far more than she had meant to, so she turned the conversation to his past. "What about you? I mean...look at you. It seems as if someone should have caught you by now. Oh, Lord. That was awful. I didn't mean that the way it sounded. What I do mean is that you're not a kid. You're not old...but old enough."

He laughed. "I have come close. Very close. Twice."

"And what…never mind. Not my business."

"Hey, if you do it your way, you'll be my grandmother. That gives you a right to pry. The first time, we'd lived together for years. But we didn't share the same dreams. And the second time…I backed away."

"Why?"

"There wasn't enough there."

"Love," she said sagely.

He lifted a brow.

"Well…" Chocolate sin or decadence or whatever had arrived. She spooned out a morsel. "I've told you, the only reason for marriage is love."

"Of course."

"And you don't believe I love Mike. Well, you're wrong."

He leaned forward. "Want to test it?"

She didn't answer right away. The dessert was unbelievably good. She was on her third mouthful. The plate sat in the middle of the table, and somehow they were leaning together above it. His dark eyes were right on hers. Hard, and yet…

Bedroom eyes. Was it the dessert? The wine?

Or him?

She warned herself to lean back, then spoke at last. "Test it?"

"I give you a great deal of money…"

"Go on."

"And you give me a week."

Her hand and her fourth spoonful of dessert froze halfway to her lips. "A week?" The fingers of her other hand curled around the small snifter of unbelievably stong cognac. She swallowed it in one gulp.

"A week," he repeated.

"A week of what?"

He had leaned back and was summoning the waiter. After a quick word to the man, he turned back to Aurora. "Shall we leave and discuss this further?"

He was already standing, reaching for her elbow to help her from the chair.

"You have to pay the check," she told him.

"I have an account."

He would.

She found herself being escorted out. Not through the front door, though. They ended up out back, where the breeze was good, cooling her flesh, clearing her mind. The beach belonging to the restaurant was pristine, private, surrounded by flowers....

"Why don't you take off your shoes?" he suggested.

He was already taking off his own. Rolling up his perfectly pressed pants. She was playing a role, she reminded herself. She had to hear him out. She could always give him a shove right into the surf if he got too outrageous.

She bent to slip off her shoes. Her balance was not what it should have been. Afraid of falling, she instinctively reached out. He was there. Steadying her.

"Sorry."

"Not at all. My pleasure."

A moment later they were arm in arm, walking along the shoreline. The moon was riding high in the night sky as gentle waves lapped over their feet. The sound of the water, rushing to shore, was lulling.

"Tell me about this week," she pressed.

"Oh, you know, dinners, dancing, walks along the beach."

"I have to work."

"I can help."

"There's Mike."

"We can visit him together."

"The wedding is this week."

"If you love him, what would it hurt to give it a little time?"

"He would wonder what was going on."

"He'd say you were worth waiting for."

"Maybe not."

"Oh, I'm sure he would. What do you say?"

They weren't walking anymore. She didn't remember when they had stopped. It seemed that her dress left a great deal of her flesh bare, and she could feel the breeze wafting across her skin. She was cool on the outside...

Hot inside. She felt his hands on her bare arms and looked up. He was staring down at her intently.

Then his knuckles brushed her check. There was something so startling about the feeling. Something like tenderness. She wanted nothing more than to curl against him. To feel that caress and more. She wanted to know the texture of his shirt against her face, and what it would feel like to be held, really held. It had been such a long time....

His knuckle moved beneath her chin, raising it. He was tall, and so close. She knew she should move, but she couldn't. His lips moved down to hers. Brushed them so lightly at first that it was like being tempted by a glass of water in the desert, feeling the rim and dying for the liquid within....

Then he kissed her. Really kissed her. Lips fully over hers, persuasive, with a seductive pressure that didn't force, only seduced. His kiss was the sustenance she had yearned for, and her lips parted in response.

And then his tongue entered the moist cavern of her mouth, and it was the most sensual thing she had felt in her entire life. It was just a kiss, yet it seemed like a promise. She was curved into his arm. Held, because she might have slipped away into the sand, otherwise, like a castle swept away by the surf.

His lips moved away. She was still held in his arms, he was staring down at her with his ebony eyes. "A week," he said.

"Walks in the sand."

"Dinners," he added.

"Dinners..." she repeated.

"And sex, of course."

She felt as if the sea suddenly surged from the North Atlantic and became a tidal wave of pure ice that slammed against her. This was a charade, she reminded herself, before she could haul off and slap him with all her strength. She forced herself to remain exactly where she was. After all, this was the kind of thing she had intended, just so that later she could tell him what a complete idiot he was.

"Sex?" she asked.

"Of course. How else will you be able to know

how much more a younger man can offer than an octogenarian? I don't believe you find me totally repulsive.''

Her temper burned. She knew that she was as angry with herself as she was with him. *Hell, no, you're not repulsive, you're the best thing I've seen in forever.*

What an idiot she'd been. Not only wasn't she what he thought her to be, she wasn't even sophisticated enough to play her own game without getting burned.

Scorched.

Somehow she managed to stay still and stare at him coolly.

''How much money are we talking?''

''I don't know. What do you think you're worth?''

''What do *you* think I'm worth?''

''Well, there are going rates, of course. And I'll guess along the line of what the highest might be. So we're talking several thousand, at the least.... It's a whole week, and of course the idea is to get you paid off, keep you from marrying Mike. Ten thousand?''

It was finally as far as she could go.

''You asshole! You couldn't buy me for a million dollars!''

''A million? Hey, the kiss was great, so I'm assuming you're good, but—''

She did slap him then. Slap him, and push away. But her exit was marred by the fact that she stumbled in the sand and nearly fell.

She heard a noise behind her. His anger, she thought, and for a moment, she was afraid of physical harm. She swirled around, on the defense, but the movement was too much for her precarious sense of

GET 2

HOW TO GET YOUR
2 FREE BOOKS AND FREE GIFT!

1. Peel off the MIRA sticker on the front cover. Place it in the space provided at right. This automatically entitles you to receive two free books and an exciting surprise gift.

2. Send back this card and you'll get 2 "The Best of the Best™" novels. These books have a combined cover price of $11.98 or more in the U.S. and $13.98 or more in Canada, but they are yours to keep absolutely FREE!

3. There's <u>no</u> catch. You're under <u>no</u> obligation to buy anything. We charge nothing – ZERO – for your first shipment. And you don't have to make any minimum number of purchases – not even one!

4. We call this line "The Best of the Best" because each month you'll receive the best books by some of today's hottest authors. These authors show up time and time again on all the major bestseller lists and their books sell out as soon as they hit the stores. You'll like the convenience of getting them delivered to your home at our special discount prices . . . and you'll love your *Heart to Heart* subscriber newsletter featuring author news, horoscopes, recipes, book reviews and much more!

5. We hope that after receiving your free books you'll want to remain a subscriber. But the choice is yours – to continue or cancel, anytime at all! So why not take us up on our invitation, with no risk of any kind. You'll be glad you did!

6. And remember...we'll send you a surprise gift ABSOLUTELY FREE just for giving "The Best of the Best" a try.

SPECIAL FREE GIFT!

We'll send you a fabulous surprise gift, absolutely FREE, simply for accepting our no-risk offer!

Visit us at
www.mirabooks.com

® and TM are trademarks of Harlequin Enterprises Limited.

BOOKS FREE!

The Best of the Best™ — Here's How it Works:

Accepting your 2 free books and gift places you under no obligation to buy anything. You may keep the books and gift and return the shipping statement marked "cancel." If you do not cancel, about a month later we will send you 4 additional novels and bill you just $4.74 each in the U.S., or $5.24 each in Canada, plus 25¢ shipping & handling per book and applicable taxes if any.* That's the complete price and — compared to cover prices of $5.99 or more each in the U.S. and $6.99 or more each in Canada — it's quite a bargain! You may cancel at any time, but if you choose to continue, every month we'll send you 4 more books, which you may either purchase at the discount price or return to us and cancel your subscription.

*Terms and prices subject to change without notice. Sales tax applicable in N.Y. Canadian residents will be charged applicable provincial taxes and GST.

balance, and she found herself sitting on the sand, staring up at him.

And he was laughing. Bent over, laughing.

"What the hell...?"

"I'm sorry, I'm sorry," he said. But he was still laughing as he approached her, hand outstretched.

She shimmied away from him on the sand.

"Hey, I'm just trying to help you."

"You're laughing at me."

"No, I'm not. Really."

"Yes, you are."

"Okay, maybe I am, but you deserve it."

"I deserve it?"

He stopped, standing over her. He was so tall and imposing that she allowed him to take her hand and help her to feet just so she wouldn't have to look so far up to see his face.

"I know," he told her.

"You know what?"

"That you're not marrying Mike."

She stared at him in silence. The sea breeze felt almost cold suddenly, but her cheeks were on fire.

"Oh?" Perhaps she hadn't really understood him.

"I know it's your grandmother who's marrying Mike."

She spoke slowly. "You...know. Since when have you known?"

"Since I was getting dressed to pick you up."

The ice had come. She was frozen. Absolutely frozen. Here she had thought she was playing him...

And all night long, he had been playing her.

"Bastard," she hissed.

She managed to turn and walk away.

"Wait!"

He matched his strides to hers without even breathing hard. He caught her by the elbow, but she wrenched away.

"Look, Aurora."

"Ms. Beck to you, buddy."

Damn him, he was still laughing.

"What are you so mad about? You started this whole farce."

"You had no right!"

"*I* had no right?"

"You tried to make a complete fool out of me."

He caught her arm again, and she found that she was staring at him again.

"You were the one trying to make a fool out of me!" he declared.

"I didn't have to make a fool out of you," she told him. "You walked into the place like the world's biggest fool."

"Yes, I did."

"What?"

"I acted like an idiot. You have to understand—I really love my grandfather. And I'm sorry I had it all wrong. But how can you say something special didn't happen between us tonight?"

"Because you're horrible."

"You went with me to torment me, and *I'm* horrible?"

"Exactly."

"You're not making any sense."

"I don't have to make sense to you."

"You're just mad that you didn't make me pay enough for being an idiot—but I've apologized."

"And an apology makes everything okay?"

"Well, it should, when you were the one who started this charade."

"Just let me go." She stared at his hand, still wound around her arm. Long fingers, pleasantly tanned.

She was still angry. This charade had been too real. Standing on the beach with a man—this man—had been too real. The wine, the food, the walk in the surf. The feel of his lips. All too real.

He released her. "I'm going to take you home."

"You don't need to."

"I took you out, I'll take you home. I won't touch you. I won't speak to you, if you don't want me to. But I'm going to take you home."

She didn't want him to. She wanted to walk away and take a taxi, though here in Paradise, it could take half an hour—at the best of times—to get a taxi.

"I'm not going with you," she said stubbornly. But he had walked past her. She couldn't see his face to judge his reaction. She walked along the sand in his wake, not quite catching up to him.

He stopped suddenly, swinging back to her.

"I thought you weren't going with me?"

"Excuse me, but my shoes are in the same place as yours."

He didn't reply, just slid his feet easily into his shoes. To her mortification, she fell—into him—while attempting to put on her sling-backed high-heeled sandals.

He steadied her.

She straightened with a curt, "Thank you."

She went through the restaurant, aware that he was following her. She went out the front door, fumbling for her cell phone. She could call a taxi. Or even call the theater. Someone would come for her.

As she dug out the phone, she glanced at her watch. She nearly fell over again. It was after ten o'clock.

"Oh hell," she swore.

"What now?" he demanded.

She stared at him furiously. "It's after ten."

"And that's my fault?"

"Yes. I thought a few hours, but…it's after ten o'clock."

"Time flies when you're having fun, right?"

She was tempted to slap him again. She didn't really intend to, but the threat must have been in her eyes, because his fingers wound in a light grip around her right wrist. "Oh, no. I might have deserved the first one, but I won't take the blame for it a second time."

"I wasn't going to," she said with dignity.

"That's not what your eyes said."

"You don't know how to read my eyes."

"You're the most readable woman I've ever come across."

"If you can read me so easily, why aren't you running away? I have a black belt in karate, and what I really wanted was to break a few bones."

Ignoring that, he asked, "What the hell does the time matter?"

"I had a rehearsal tonight."

"At your theater?"

"Of course. What else?"

"I don't know. Maybe there's some other guy you think you should torment with a made-up story."

His fingers were still around her wrist. No pressure, no pain. But it was a hold she didn't think she should take lightly.

"Look," he said impatiently, "I'm sure the rehearsal went fine without you."

He was probably right, but...

"I'll take you home," he said.

"I can call a cab."

"You really want to wait here for half an hour or more?"

He was too familiar with Paradise.

"Fine. Just take me home. But don't talk to me."

"Ms. Beck, I won't touch you, talk to you or even look at you."

She stared at him. "Your fingers are around my wrist right now."

He let go of her as if he were holding fire, turned and started for his car. His strides were longer than hers, and the passenger door was already open when she reached the vehicle. She gave him another stiff, "Thank you."

He didn't speak as they started out. She did.

"My grandmother and your grandfather love each other very much. You have no right to cause any problems with this wedding."

He didn't reply.

"Did you hear me?"

"I'm sorry. I thought I wasn't supposed to speak to you."

"You're impossible."

"I am?"

He looked her way, a brow arched high. The way he looked at her...

He was impossible. She hated him. Hated the way that just seeing his face could make her remember those few minutes when they were together on the sand. When his lips touched hers.

She turned to look straight ahead. "You should get to know Mary. Don't dislike her because of me."

He didn't answer again. She dared to look back his way. He was watching the road, but a slight smile seemed to be curving his lips.

"If Mike wants to marry your grandmother and they really love each other, I'll be happy to dance at their wedding."

She eased back into the seat, expelling a soft breath. "Which is soon. They want to get married—"

"Thursday. The day after tomorrow. I know."

They pulled into Aurora's driveway. She was ready to exit the car with the speed of lightning and run into the house.

But she stopped, her hand on the door, staring at the front of the house. Angie was there.

She wasn't surprised to see Angie. It was closer to eleven now than it was to ten, and rehearsal would have been over by ten-thirty, at the latest. What dismayed her was that her daughter was sitting on the porch with a wine bottle at her side, smoking.

She had always tried to be a good parent, but she

had realized long ago that the only way to have her
daughter's confidence was to live in the real world.
She didn't smoke; she knew that Angie did, though
the house was off-limits. She just had to pray that her
daughter, who was eighteen and legally able to leave
home at anytime, would one day decide for herself
that she should quit. As to the wine, the legal drinking
age in Florida was twenty-one, but Angie was welcome to a glass of wine at dinner. Kids were going
to drink, and Aurora knew it. Aurora had an agreement with her daughter. If her daughter was going to
drink, she should drink at home. And if she went out
where the kids were drinking, she was to phone home
for a ride. There would be nothing said. She knew
she couldn't stop teenagers from drinking, but she
could certainly try to stop them from driving afterward.

She didn't realize she had groaned aloud until Max
asked, "What's wrong?"

"That wretched boy," Aurora murmured.

"What?"

"He was supposed to see her, but he probably
didn't show up, and now she's...oh, she's an idiot,
on top of everything else. She's the most beautiful
kid in the world, not perfect, but really wonderful,
and I've told her a million times to forget him and
move on, or at least not to call him, not to just be
there all the time...not to just...." She trailed off and
stared at him. "Why am I telling you all this? I'm
sorry. I'll just get out and...well, I'll see you at the
wedding."

"Hey!" He caught her arm when she would have flown out of the car. "Maybe I can help."

"You don't even know her."

"Maybe that's why I can help."

He got out of the car. As Aurora watched, he walked up to the porch. She hesitated, staring after him for a moment, then followed.

"Hi, Mom," Angie said. She'd been crying but she tried to smile. "I went to rehearsal. John Smith had everything under control. Everything was cool. I even remembered to bring the new act with me. Of course, everyone wants the end of the script, even if this is just the weekly show for the people at Paradise." She was talking too quickly. She'd had more than a glass of wine. "Honestly, everything is great."

"Except that Josh didn't show," Aurora said softly.

Angie shrugged, then looked as if she were going to cry again. "Want to have a glass of wine with me?" she asked.

"I think I had too much wine tonight already," Aurora said. "Angie, you should come in."

Angie shook her head stubbornly. "I just need a few more minutes."

"I'll have a glass of wine with you," Max said.

To Aurora's amazement, Angie brightened. "Really?"

"Sure." Max looked at Aurora. Amazingly, the look assured her.

Aurora had gone through this with Angie before. She'd tried to tell her just to let Josh go, that if he cared enough about her, he would be back. He would quit treating her like a yo-yo.

"How about it?" Max asked. "Hey, I'm nearly your step-uncle, or something like that."

Angie started to giggle. "So you know Mom isn't marrying Mike?"

"Yeah. I know. How about that glass?"

Aurora lifted an eyebrow. Max was looking at her. She didn't know why—maybe she was just too damned tired or at a loss for a better way—but she threw up her hands and went into the house, then came back a minute later with a large paper cup. That was the best he was getting for the porch.

He and Angie were already deep in conversation when she came to them. Max was seated by her side on the porch, saying, "Thanks. And I'd love to have some coffee when we go in."

Aurora wanted to tell him that there was a twenty-four-hour doughnut shop just a few blocks down, but somehow, she refrained. She walked back into the house, closed the door and began to pace the living room floor.

She was crazy.

She'd only met him that morning, and a part of her wanted to do him some serious bodily harm. Yet she was trusting him with her psychologically fragile daughter.

The odd thing was that she did trust him.

It felt as if she had known him a very long time.

Angie had indulged in quite a bit to drink. Far more than she had let on to her mother. Now she was ready to talk, at least to a stranger. So far, she'd explained about Josh and that she didn't want to feel the way she did about him. She knew her mother was right. But feelings and logic had very little to do with each other, and her mother didn't understand the way she felt.

"She doesn't understand," Angie said. "She hasn't been out on a date since my father died, and that's been…" She paused, trying to think. The wine did her in. She waved a hand in the air and finished with, "Years. Not that she has many men to choose from in Paradise. The guys in the theater…well, a lot of the time, they've made other life choices, if you know what I mean. They're great guys…just gay. And then, well, what? She's going to find a guy at the old age home? Whoops!" Angie actually laughed. "That's right—you thought she was going to marry your grandfather. But that's my point. She has no life. She's forgotten what it's like to be in love. To need somebody. To want to be with somebody. She just doesn't remember. So she doesn't understand me. I don't want to feel this way. I don't want to make a fool out of myself. I don't even know what it is about him. He isn't the best looking guy who ever drew breath. And he certainly isn't always nice. In fact, he can be a real spoiled brat, probably because his parents have money, or because he's an only child, or…I don't know. But I want to be with him. And I don't find anyone else attractive. I'll never find another guy."

"Angie, you're young, you've got years ahead of you, and there will be other men in your life."

She waved her glass at him, the wine sloshing dangerously. "Now you sound like Mom."

"Because what we're both saying is the truth. Take it from me. You really can't call this guy anymore. He has to come to you. Even if he's been around and behaving great, let him call you."

"You mean...when he's told me how much he cares, then leaves and says 'Call me'...don't?"

"That's exactly what I mean. Angie, you say that one minute things are great. Then he doesn't call, so you call him, and he says that you fight too much, that it's not worth it, and then you wind up crying. So don't call the guy."

"Why do I keep caring?" she asked forlornly.

Max smiled. "If I give you some advice, will you take it?"

"If it's good."

"It will be. I swear it. And I'll even explain every word."

"Shoot."

"The kid is being an asshole. A total asshole."

"You don't even know him."

"I know myself. And trust me, I've been a total asshole at times in my life. He cares about you. He just thinks he has you down pat, just where he wants you. He knows how you feel about him. You're far too honest. He's wonderful, he's great, he adores you. Then his buddies come in from college, and he wants to fool around. He picks a fight and goes out, because he knows you'll be waiting. Don't call him. Whatever you do, don't call him. And when he calls you—"

"What if he doesn't?" she interrupted.

"Then he really doesn't care, and you'll have to get over it. I'm willing to bet that he'll call. But you've got to be firm. You can't wait around while he outgrows being an asshole. Seriously. Make him get over it now. And if he can't, then you have to. That's life. No matter how hard. But things will be far easier for you in the long run if you quit going through this over and over again."

She stared at him, her beautiful blue eyes red-rimmed. "Do you think I had too much wine?"

"Hell, yes."

She grinned. Then her grin faded. "I'm going to be sick."

"Bushes are right there."

Max had to admit, it had been a hell of a long time since he'd helped a drunk throw up.

Thankfully Angie had good aim. She even had tissues in her pocket. He helped her wipe her face.

"Will you get me some water?"

"How about I help you in, let your mom get you to bed and bring you some water?"

She nodded.

He slipped an arm around her. They went into the house. Aurora had been sitting on the couch. She jumped up.

"Angie is ready for bed," he said.

"All right," Aurora said.

"If you point the way, I'll help her."

Aurora lifted a finger and pointed. He walked into Angie's room, a pretty place with more sophistication than frills. A few posters were on the wall. Angie had her own phone, television and stereo, and a comfortable quilt thrown over the bed. Aurora pulled back the quilt and the covers. He set Angie on the bed, and Aurora took off her shoes, then started to leave the room. As he did, he heard Angie tell her mother, "I'm not calling Josh again. Max explained. Men can be assholes. Max knows. He was one."

Aurora shot him a surprised glance. He slipped out of the room and went to sit on the couch. Then he smelled the aroma of freshly brewed coffee, so he went into the kitchen and poured himself a cup. Black. Once upon a time, he'd liked it light. But theatrical assistants, sent out to retrieve coffee, never got it right. He'd given up. Now he liked it black.

He was sipping the hot coffee when Aurora came into the kitchen. She watched him strangely, and for a moment he thought he'd made her even angrier, stepping in where he really had no business.

"Thank you," she said after a minute. She walked to the coffeepot, still looking at him, and poured herself coffee. She drank it black, too, he noticed. She leaned against the counter, her eyes still on him.

"I've talked until I'm blue in the face. I can't begin to imagine what you said to her."

He shrugged. "I can do something that you can't."

"And that is…?"

"Explain guys. Because I am one. You're not."

"It's that simple?"

"Maybe."

"I hope it works." She was reflective, staring at the kitchen floor. Then she looked up at him again suddenly. "By the way, my daughter and I are not customarily…winos."

He laughed. "I didn't think you were." He finished the last of his coffee, set the cup in the sink and started out. "Well, I'll leave you to some peace and quiet."

She followed him out to the living room, where he paused at the front door. "By the way, your scripts are good."

She smiled slowly. Like her daughter, she was beautiful when she smiled.

"Thanks."

He opened the door.

"By the way..." she said.

He paused.

She blushed. "You're not a complete asshole."

"Wow. Thanks."

He closed the door behind him as he left.

Five

Max wasn't sure why he was at Aurora's door the following morning. He didn't really feel apologetic for stringing her along the night before. After all, it had been exactly what she had intended to do to him, whether he deserved it or not. He had decided to come over, he told himself, purely to see that peace was kept in the new almost-family.

It was Angie who opened the door. She had apparently been sleeping, since she was clad in a huge, knee-length sleep shirt with a cartoon character that depicted yawning on the front. She smiled sheepishly when she saw him.

"Hey."

"Do you always open the door to anyone who knocks, young lady?" he asked her.

"Peephole. I checked you out first," she assured him.

"How are you doing this morning?"

"Fine."

"That's too bad. You deserve a hangover."

She grinned. "Sorry. And thanks. I guess I was off the deep end a bit."

"You were fine."

As he spoke, the phone began to ring. Angie in-

dicated that he should come in as she left the front
door and went to the phone. She didn't pick up the
receiver, just stared at the caller ID.

A moment later, after Aurora's message, a young
male voice came on. "Angie, it's me. Josh. Pick up.
Hey, listen, I'm sorry about being a no-show. Give
me a call. Soon."

Angie reached toward the receiver, then drew her
hand back.

"It's the asshole," she said gravely.

"And you didn't pick up. And you're not going to
call back," he reminded her.

She gave him a broad smile. "Right." Then she
said, "Oh! Mom's not here. Actually, I think she was
going to stop by your place before going over to the
home. She was trying to work earlier...I mean really
earlier. Then she got annoyed and said something
about it all being your fault, so she was going to get
you and take off for Paradise." Angie wrinkled her
nose.

"Looks like she missed me. What was she working
on?"

"Just a little skit. She can usually whip something
like that out in an afternoon. And she loves to do the
fairy-tale thing, but we do a lot of improvisation when
we do the shows at the home. Actually it's turned
into quite an event. To make up what Gran's insurance doesn't quite cover, she entertains there on Fridays. Which is cool, because right now it's the off-
season down here."

He pointed across the room to a desk. "Is that
where she works?"

Angie nodded.

"Think she'd mind if I took a look?"

"Yes," Angie said with a grin. "But I think you should go right ahead." She swept a hand in the direction of the computer. "How about some coffee?"

"Sounds good. I'll only be here a minute, though. I just want to take a quick peek."

In a small town like Paradise, there were bound to be good things and bad things, Aurora thought.

A good thing was the fact that she knew the owner of the inn, and he not only walked her along to Max's place, but—when Max didn't answer right away—let her in.

Due to the fact that she was nearly kin, of course.

The bad thing—though that would be only if you were Max—was that the owner let her right in to what should have been his private domain.

"The man is probably out walking on the beach," Ned told her. "Can't have you just waiting outside in the heat, though. Today is going to be a scorcher."

She was amazed herself to find out just how pleasant the place was. Beautiful, really. And Max couldn't have been too concerned about his belongings, because he had left the back door open. Aurora walked through the room. Nice. The bed faced the open windows and the sea breeze, the sand, and the blue glory of the day beyond. Beyond the bed was a counter, with a little kitchenette. The maid had been in, so the place was spotless.

For a few minutes she just sat on the bed, waiting primly. The view from the bed was lulling, mesmerizing. The sun was hot, she knew, but a light breeze was moving the drapes. The water glistened. The sand seemed to stretch before her with a welcoming white-ness and purity. She lived in this town, she reminded herself. But she couldn't remember the last time she had felt so touched by the sight, sound and feel of the sand and the sea. She was dying to stretch out on the cool linen, watch as the sun came up, or just stay and watch the way the water was glimmering and the drapes were drifting.

Then the phone began to ring. She started violently and, without thinking, answered it.

It was Ned, calling from the front office. "Sorry, Aurora, the wife says the Yankee left some time ago. I must have missed him."

"That's okay, Ned. Thanks for calling."

She hung up and stood. She had to get out. He'd rented this place; it was private. One day, though, she would talk to Ned about renting a room just for one night so she could wake up to such an incredible view.

She was appalled as her thoughts suddenly turned to the bed. Clean, cool, linen sheets; plump pillows; sea, sky and sand; a man and woman, making love as the sun fell and the blue of the sky became the mauve of twilight, then the velvet of night. Someone with dark eyes, great hands…

Cool linen sheets. Hot bodies. The senses filled. Things she couldn't even remember.

She groaned aloud and hurried to the door. But as she was walking out, her purse snagged on the closet door, pulling it open. No big deal. She moved to close it.

But she didn't. Not right away.

Max's clothing lined the closet. She was surprised to find herself reaching out, stroking her fingers down the length of a jacket sleeve. Nice duds, as Angie would say. Great, she told herself. The guy has nice clothes. Now, close the door. That's it, get out, leave.

She drew the sleeve to her cheek, alarmed to find herself breathing in a subtle hint of aftershave and something more. She dropped the sleeve as if it could bite, closed the closet door and marched out of the room.

"Do you know it's after twelve o'clock?" Angie asked.

Max looked up, startled, then looked back to the computer. He'd told Mike he'd be in early, but that wasn't going to happen, since he'd sat down a little over three hours ago.

Now Act II was complete. And Aurora was hardly likely to appreciate his butting in on her work.

"Noon," he murmured.

Angie, looking over his shoulder, let out a little cry of delight. "I love it! I love the ending."

"I'm going to start hitting the delete key."

"No! No, you're not."

"Angie, I don't know what the hell I was doing. Your mom doesn't even want me reading her work, much less putting my ideas into it."

"Don't you dare delete that. I play the princess, you know, but I didn't really like the way she was written. And now…like I said, I'm the princess, and I love the ending. Leave it. If she hates it, she'll erase it. You can really write. Do you have any experience?''

Max arched a brow. ''A little. Has Mike said anything at all about me?''

''Of course. He told us you were an important businessman in New York. Is that true?''

''We're all in business, one way or another, aren't we?'' he asked.

''I guess.''

''I'm getting out of here.''

The phone rang again. After a moment Josh's voice came on again. ''Angie, come on, you must be home. It's me. Josh. Pick up the phone.''

Max tilted his head at an angle, challenging her with a lifted brow.

''He's called twice,'' she murmured.

''Yep. If he keeps calling, you could give him a call back—in a day or two. I've got to go.'' He saved his work, then rose and headed out.

Angie called after him, ''Max!''

''Yes.''

''Thanks. Really. Thanks for last night, and…well, I'm awfully glad we're going to be sort of related.''

''So am I, Angie. See you.''

Michael Wulfson was a man who knew how to move once he had made a decision.

Paradise was aglow.

Aurora had arrived in time to join Mike and Mary as they spoke with the priest and rabbi. The bride and groom had been so busy, they hadn't had a chance to grill her about the night before.

They had both stared at her, though. Watched her with speculation.

And Mike had watched her with curious amusement, as well. She had refused to give either of them the satisfaction of an explanation, though, and since so much had been going on, they hadn't really been able to ask. She had been there when the caterer had come—Mike was treating the entire home to his wedding meal. Decorators had even come to fill the place with flowers and arrange the table settings.

She was sitting with Mike and Mary, with the dessert chef on his way out, making a list of the things her grandmother wanted, when Max at last arrived. She greeted him politely, making no reference to their dinner the night before and not mentioning the fact that she had gone by his room hours earlier to make sure that they were on decent terms with each other before seeing their grandparents.

She needn't have worried about his behavior. He was equally polite, brushing her cheek with a friendly kiss, then taking Mary's hand and telling her what a great pleasure it was to meet her. He was sincere; he was charming. He was exceptionally appealing in a light polo shirt that accented his dark good looks.

They were seated at a table in a little garden area surrounded by shade trees. Aurora was sitting between Mike and her grandmother; Max took the seat opposite her. "So..." he said, lifting his hands to indicate their surroundings. "Flowers are coming to Paradise. Everything is moving right along."

"Right along," Mike agreed, his weathered face crinkling with a smile. "Mary and I couldn't be more pleased. That's true, dear, isn't it?"

Aurora was surprised when her grandmother blushed. "Mike has made this place a *real* paradise," she said.

"What time is the ceremony?" Max asked.

"Two o'clock," Mike said. "We've decided to make it an early afternoon affair so our friends can stay awake for it."

"Early," Max murmured.

"Well, my boy, it has to be early. This is an old folks' place, you know. We have to have the ceremony, then eat early. Mrs. Munson gets too much gas to sleep if she doesn't finish eating by four-thirty."

"Charming," Max said with a laugh.

"You think so? If Ida gets gas, the whole floor knows it. We don't want the place bubbling unattractively all evening," Mike said.

"Hey, early is good," Max said. "What else should I know?"

"You've got your tux?"

"I do."

"You're all set, dear, aren't you?" Mary asked Aurora.

"Of course."

"We should have some champagne," Mike said. "Here we are, the bride, the groom, the maid of honor and the best man."

"This isn't exactly a nightclub," Aurora reminded him. "I can get you some ginger ale."

Mike looked at Aurora as if she just didn't get the

point, but then he smiled broadly. "I certainly hope my grandson bought you some champagne last night." Mike Wulfson still had the kind of stare that went right through a body. Aurora was annoyed to realize that she was blushing with greater intensity than her grandmother.

"Dinner was great," Max said lightly, refusing to give in to his grandfather's obvious and gleeful inquiry. "We had the perfect wine and a great meal."

"But," Mike said with a frown, "I thought that…"

"And *I* certainly thought…" Mary began.

"Oh, come on," Max said, looking at Aurora. "Aurora and I did nothing but enjoy a terrific meal."

Mike and Mary both stared at Aurora. "Yes," she said evenly, looking at Max. "We had a wonderful dinner."

"But you thought I meant to marry Aurora," Mike said to Max.

"And you told me, Aurora," Mary said, "that he was the biggest ass—idiot you had ever met."

"Thanks, Gran," Aurora murmured.

"That's okay, she already told me all about her true feelings," Max said. "But we're cool with everything now. We're just both delighted with this wedding."

"Really?" Mary asked anxiously.

"Absolutely." Max squeezed her hand.

"And you're fine with each other? Everything all straightened out between the two of you?" Mike asked with a frown.

"Oh, we're just peachy keen," Aurora murmured.

"So who told who the truth first?" Mike asked.

"Did you tell him that he was an idiot, dear?" Mary asked with a frown.

"Something like that," Max said.

"Max isn't an idiot," Mike said, his voice indignant.

"Well, he thought Aurora was a gold digger," Mary put in.

"Hey, hey," Max protested. "We need peace in Paradise. It's fine. Aurora and I worked it out." He stared at her as if daring her to contradict him.

"We worked it out," she repeated. "We laughed for hours," she went on, trying to keep the sarcasm out of her voice. "I should get going now. Check on a few friends."

"Make sure their beds are cranked?" Mike asked.

"Yes, well, that, too." She stared at Max. "And I lost a file in the computer yesterday, though. I've been assured that I can find it." She looked at Max as she spoke.

"You can't work right now," Mary protested.

"I have to. We put on the show Friday afternoon. I have to give my cast something to rehearse tonight, even if we end up winging a lot of it."

"This show is just for the home?" Max asked politely.

"Yes. But if it's something we really like, we rework it and do it for the schools later," Aurora said.

"You can crank a few beds if you want, but you can't work right now," Mike said.

"I have to."

"Aurora, Mike and I woke up at the crack of dawn to fill out the endless paperwork so we could get permission to take you two out with us for lunch,'' Mary told her.

"I can't go. I'm sorry."

"You two didn't work anything out, did you?" Mary asked with dismay. "Mike, maybe we should put this wedding off a bit."

"Mary, what are you saying?" Mike asked with dismay. "My grandson made a mistake, and Aurora, well, you called my boy an idiot, right?" Mike asked, turning to Aurora.

"Oh, she called me much worse," Max said. "But we've straightened it all out. And the wedding is on." He stood. "Aurora, I'll help you crank beds. And as to the work…I told you, I know computers."

"Even if you can find what I lost, I wasn't done."

"Trust me." Max said, his eyes on her.

"Max has done a little writing here and there," Mike said, eyes twinkling as he looked at his grandson. "Aurora, please. You and Max are the most important people in our lives. Your grandmother will throw me over if she doesn't believe the two of you are happy about the wedding. This is so important to us."

"Mike, I love you, you know that. But I have responsibilities."

"Please," Mary said.

Max had Aurora's arm. "Let's get cranking," he said. He practically dragged her out of her chair, though he managed the act so smoothly that neither Mike nor Mary realized what he was doing.

"I'm screwed," she protested once they were back inside.

"They'll call off this wedding."

"You came to stop it anyway."

"You want to do this to them?"

"No, dammit. You don't understand."

"It will be all right. Trust me. We'll have lunch, we'll get back, I'll play with the computer. The world will not end."

"You may be the hottest thing on Wall Street, but you don't know a thing about writing."

"If that's your opinion, we need to crank those beds quickly."

He started down the hall ahead of her. She swore, then followed.

Max was a good cranker. And he was known around Paradise. She shouldn't have been surprised. She had learned from talking with Daisy the day before that Max had been down here when Mike had first taken up residence. Despite herself, she found it irritating that he should be greeted by so many people with such enthusiasm. And he was never rude, extricating himself from long conversations with the friendly information that his grandfather and his fiancée were waiting for them.

The whole thing was really getting quite annoying. She had spent weeks performing the same service, but as soon as Max walked in, she was barely noticed. Max had spent that one day cranking beds.

Life was certainly ironic.

By the time they were done with their errands of mercy—adjusting telephones, retrieving remote controls, refilling water pitchers, as well as adjusting beds—Mike and Mary were already in the stretch limo Mike had ordered for the day.

Aurora hadn't even been aware that there was a stretch limo to be had in Paradise. He must have ordered the car from St. Augustine.

Mike and Mary were sitting together on the rear seat. The husky nurse's aide who was joining them, Bart Thornby, was seated at the front, his back to the driver. He smiled and greeted Aurora warmly as she lowered herself into the car, but he didn't slide over. Aurora moved across and took the seat along the side, facing the minibar. Max joined her there.

It was a stretch limo. She should have felt as if she had enough room to...stretch, but she was uncomfortably aware of Max beside her. He wasn't the least bit bothered. He was chatting with Mike and Mary. Even Bart was joining in. She felt as if she could hear everyone breathe. No, just Max. She was aware of his every inflection, his every movement. He used his hands a lot. They were good, masculine hands. Tanned. Long fingers, nails blunt cut, clean. She found herself staring at his hands. Then at his mouth as he spoke. She closed her eyes, determined not to watch him. *Think of something else,* she told herself. *Something calming. The sea, the sea breeze lifting the drapes at the Paradise Motor Lodge. Max's bed, the clean white linen sheets, the breeze coming in, Max would look good in that bed, long tanned body against the white sheets.*

"What do you say, Aurora?"

"What?" Her eyes flew open.

Mike had spoken. He frowned, a look of concern

of his weathered face. "Aurora needs to spend more time in bed," he said, shaking his head.

"Bed? No," she murmured, straightening.

"You were dozing, dear," Mary said.

"No...no, I wasn't."

"Dear, you were. Your head was on Max's shoulder."

Aurora stared at Max in pure horror. He looked at her. "It must be the company. I put her right to sleep."

"You work too hard," Mike said sternly. "You need to get to bed earlier."

She definitely didn't want to talk about *bed* anymore. "Where are we eating?" she asked quickly, to change the subject.

"An oyster bar on the outskirts of St. Augustine. And I believe we're almost there."

They had arrived. Getting out of the stretch limo was something of a project, what with the two wheelchairs. For once, though, Aurora found her assistance totally unnecessary; Max and Bart had the situation completely under control.

The garden where they were seated was beautiful, and Mike had preordered the meal of his choice. They were barely seated before the champagne arrived. Aurora tried to demur, but Mike wouldn't have it. They toasted the wedding to come. Mike explained that he and Mary had wanted a private meal with the two of them, the most important people in their lives, since the wedding itself would be a crowd scene, since everyone at Paradise had been invited.

There was nothing to do but lift her glass. The

champagne went down easily, but she knew she should take it easy, because she had rehearsal that night. She tried to go easy, but it didn't seem to matter. Two glasses and she was feeling light-headed. Mike had ordered oysters Rockefeller, clams casino, shrimp cocktail and more. The food was excellent, but somehow eating it seemed to involve more champagne. She knew she was quiet during the meal, but it didn't seem to matter. Mike was talkative, but apparently he was studying her all the while because, when she suppressed a yawn, he announced that the wedding gift Mary had asked for was going to help her, as well.

"You asked for a wedding gift?" she said to Mary.

"Mike insisted."

"New beds," he said.

"New beds?"

"For the home. Beds that don't have to be cranked."

She stared at Mike incredulously. "You're going to buy new beds for the entire home?"

"Aurora, you, of all people, should realize what a great idea it is," Mike said.

"Of course it's a great idea, but—"

"Mary thought of it," Mike said proudly.

Bart, who had been very quiet during the meal, not wasting time on conversation when the food was so good, spoke up. "That has to be one of the greatest wedding gifts I've ever heard of."

"I think so, too," Mike said. He stared straight at Aurora. "You won't have to run around as much. The nurses and the aides will all have more time to actually help people. Besides, Mary and I both be getting out of rehab soon, so we're buying a house.''

"That's wonderful. But as to Paradise...I'll still be running around, Mike. It's not just cranking beds. It's saying hello to people. Some of them don't have families, you know.''

"But saying hello isn't as tiring as cranking beds,'' Max said.

"Maybe you need a new bed,'' Mike said, frowning. "We should get Aurora a new bed, too,'' he told Mary.

"I don't need a new bed,'' she announced defensively. They were all quiet, staring at her. "Thank you, Mike, but really, I don't need a new bed.''

"She likes her old bed,'' Mary said. Then Aurora could have sworn that she said, "She just needs someone new in it.''

"What?'' Aurora gasped, turning crimson.

"I said, you like your bed, you just need some good glue for it,'' Mary said, frowning at Aurora's reaction. "Aurora has a big antique sleigh bed,'' she explained to Max. "Whatever are you so defensive about, dear?''

"I heard you wrong. I'm sorry.''

"What did you think I said?'' Mary asked her, perplexed.

"Nothing. Never mind.''

She could feel Max staring at her, could sense his laughter. She wanted to douse him in the cocktail sauce.

She reached for the bucket to pour herself more champagne, drained her glass, then turned her attention to her plate. Mike began to talk about boats, with Max telling him that he had to be careful. No more broken bones once he got out of Paradise.

Her head was spinning. Mike was still talking. Max's hand was lying on the tablecloth, near her plate. She found herself staring at it. Glancing down, she saw his feet. Big feet. His foot brushed her, and she was certain she could feel the warmth of his flesh through the leather of his shoe.

He murmured, "Excuse me," to her.

"Aurora needs sex more often," Mike said casually.

She dropped her fork.

"Aurora, what is the matter with you?" Mary demanded. "Mike's right. You need to get out on the sea more often. It's a great way to relax."

They were all staring at her. Max even seemed to be smirking, as if he could read her mind.

She prayed for lunch to end.

Finally, a few hours and several cups of coffee later, it did. And she wound up back where she had been when on the drive over: next to Max. By the time they reached Paradise, she was ready to jump out of her own skin. Tempted to shove two octogenarians out of the way so she could get out of the car first. She could have bulldozed her way through wheelchairs, knocked over the aging, pushed past babies, crawled over nuns.

Somehow, she waited her turn.

But once out of the limo, she was ready to run. "It's late," she explained to Mike and Mary. "I've got to get home, then get to rehearsal."

"I'll just walk Aurora to her car," Max said.

"Don't bother."

But he followed her anyway. When she reached her car, she spun on him. "Will you go away? I've got work to do."

"I'm trying to tell you—"

"Don't try to tell me anything. You don't know anything about my life. You live in a cushy apartment in New York City. You have no responsibilities. Your business, whatever the hell it is, just moves along like clockwork. You have no children. You don't usually spend your days cranking beds, something you started doing because you couldn't afford Paradise otherwise." She flung open the door to her car with such energy that the Saturn protested with a groan. She was into the driver's seat with the door slammed again before he could get close.

"Aurora, wait, if you'll let me expl—"

"I have to go." She had turned the key in the ignition. Gunned the engine. She backed out, burning rubber, like a teenager either showing off or just learning to drive.

Didn't matter. She was out; she was gone. The wedding would be tomorrow, and then Max, the big-city businessman, would go away, and she would be at peace again, mentally and physically.

Paradise didn't have much traffic, but since it was summer, they did have a beach contingent. To make matters worse, she caught what rush hour there was in the town.

When she reached the house, Angie was home. She was seated at the dining-room table, doing homework.

Angie loved school, but not math, so she had used the summer break to take two math courses when the community college was slow and the student body small.

She looked up when Aurora came flying into the house.

"Hi, Mom. Are the young lovers ready for the big day tomorrow?"

"Oh, yeah, the young lovers are just about perfect. And I'm in an incredible mess. What time is it now? Almost six. Damn. I'm going to throttle them both." She dropped her purse and headed straight for the computer. "An hour and a half. And then rehearsal. Two days before we perform the stupid thing. And there's no ending. Watch the printer decide to break. That would be it. What am I talking about? I can't print an act I don't have." She sat down at the keyboard, hit the on key, then set her forehead against the monitor as she waited for the machine to boot up.

"Mom—"

"That…jerk. I lost a bunch of stuff yesterday when he came in. 'Anything can be found in a computer!' Like hell. But hey, how was class? How are *you?* No hangover? You haven't talked to that jerk, have you?"

"Chill, Mom. Class was fine, I got some tutoring after, I'm fine, no hangover, and quit trying to knock yourself out on the monitor."

"This computer is too old. Too slow."

"It doesn't matter, Mom. The play is done."

Head still against the monitor, Aurora frowned.

Slowly she straightened and swiveled around in the chair. "What do you mean—the play is done?"

"Max was here."

Had they just changed the subject? Or was Angie losing it, too?

"Here? Max was *here?*" she said slowly.

"Yes, here."

"When?"

"This morning, after you left."

"And you let him in?"

"Of course I let him in. His grandfather is marrying Gran. And he's a great guy. If you don't think so, it's because you haven't gotten to know him yet."

"He's not a great guy. He's a pompous ass who meant to ruin everything for your grandmother."

"No, he just didn't want his grandfather being taken by some gold digger."

"A gold digger? Me?"

"Well, you *were* pretending to be Mike's fiancée, after the big bucks."

"All right, so Max was here. How does that make the play done?"

"Max finished it."

"Finished it. My play. My house, my computer. You let…Max into my computer?"

"He wanted to read the play."

"So you let him?"

"Mom, it's a play. You're going to put it on for a couple hundred people. What did it matter if he read it? He was all excited about your work last night."

"That's not the point. That's an incredible invasion

of privacy. I don't believe this. You let him into my house.''

"My house, too. You've always said I'm welcome to bring my friends in.''

"He's not your friend.''

"He *is* my friend.''

"He waltzed into my house. And he—he went into my computer and finished the play?'' Aurora said incredulously. "The nerve. I'm erasing it immediately.''

"Mom, just read it first.''

"No. It was *my* play.''

"And you were stuck.''

"I would have gotten unstuck. I will get unstuck. What did he think he was doing?'' Aurora whirled the chair around and brought up the file with amazing speed. Apparently even the computer sensed her mood. She began to read, her finger hovering over the delete key.

"It's a great ending,'' Angie said, standing by her shoulder.

"It's all right.''

"It's great,'' Angie repeated.

"It was my play.''

"And you're ticked because someone else came up with a great ending for it.''

"Of course I'm ticked.''

"When were you going to finish it? In between the wedding and the show? When could we have rehearsed it?''

"We could have been spontaneous. We're known for great improv.''

"Or we could have sucked."

Aurora crashed her head down right on the keys. She groaned. "We are going to suck. Dammit! Dammit all to hell. God, I hate that man. It's a good ending." Aurora sat back. "I hate him. I really hate him," she said softly.

"Why?" Angie said with surprise. "I thought you'd like him better. Mom, you write great stuff. But with Gran, working at Paradise, the time you spend at the theater...you had no time, Mom. No time at all."

"There should have been time. I was at the home with the priest, the rabbi, caterers and decorators, when I should have been here, working. Was Max there helping with the details? No, he was here. In my computer. Bonding with my daughter. Who won't listen to a word I say, but when *he* speaks... You haven't called the jerk, have you?"

"Which jerk, Mom? Max? Josh. Never mind. You mean Josh. Max is an asshole, Josh is the jerk."

"Angie, you really shouldn't use that word."

"You use it."

"I should stop."

"So you hate him, because..."

"I don't even know him, and he has more influence with you than I do. *And* he sat down and finished my play. And did a good job of it, damn him."

Angie hugged her shoulders. "He doesn't have more influence. He's just...he's a guy. So he knows how guys think. And he admitted that he'd been an asshole."

"Angie!"

"It's what you called him."

"Idiot fits just as well."

"He can't be an idiot—look how he finished the play."

"So he's an idiot who can write," Aurora said. "I hate him. I hate him. I hate him."

"Methinks thou doth protest too much," Angie said with a laugh.

Aurora gave her daughter the most evil stare she could manage, rose and decided that a shower was in order.

"Where are you going?"

"To take a long shower."

"Cool. I'll just print this out for you and make the copies," Angie said.

Aurora stopped in her tracks and turned back. Somehow, in two days' time, Max Wulfson had cost her her mind.

"Thank you," she said, and marched off, desperate for solitude and the healing effect of cool rushing water.

Six

She was wonderful. Aurora was simply wonderful.

Max should have been working himself, but curiosity had been killing him, so he'd come here instead.

He had slipped into the theater at about nine, using the back door and taking a seat in the rear. It was a small place, seating two hundred, tops, and arranged in a manner that wasn't quite theater in the round, but close to it. The rehearsal was well under way when he entered. The goblin and the witch were on stage when he came in, played by Aurora and a man.

Max realized with definite surprise that he knew the actor. He had disappeared from the Broadway scene maybe five or six years earlier. Jonathan Smith. He had performed in some of the best shows—musicals, dramas, and comedies—of the past few decades.

The story was a fractured fairy tale. The princess of the kingdom was sworn to marry a prince, whom the princess didn't like at all. She was in love with the young minstrel who played at the castle. She had gone to the witch for help, little knowing that the witch was in league with an ogre with a huge crush on the princess, and was plotting to sabotage the wedding, only to steal the princess for himself. There were several very funny short songs, along with a few messages—beauty was in the eye of the beholder, and money and position were not as important as love and emotion and doing the right thing in life. But the show wasn't preachy, just amusing and cute. The ogre, though a monster, became sympathetic, as it became clear in a musical number that he wanted to steal the princess because he had been ugly all his life, never loved for what he was.

His ending was a bit pat, Max thought, but for this show, it fit. As the wedding approached, the ogre and the witch got into a conversation about beauty, grace and coordination. Aurora was an incredible physical comedienne tripping into the ogre's arms as they tried to hide, spilling the wrong ingredients, into her potions and crawling into the cauldron to retrieve them. And when the wedding day came and the witch swooped down to steal the bride, Angie was just as adorably inept. When it came time for the witch to hand the princess over to the ogre, the action stopped. The witch knew how much the princess loved the young minstrel. And then the witch and the ogre stared at one another, realizing that what they had wanted all along was just to find love, and that they had found it with each other.

"Tomorrow night, eight o'clock," Aurora called, after congratulating her cast and crew on a good rehearsal. A young man wearing a T-shirt from the University of Central Florida had come down from the light booth, and the stage manager and a few others had joined them. There was talk and laughter as the cast and crew gathered for a few minutes, then began

to filter out. When even Angie was gone, he started
to rise and join Aurora and Jonathan onstage, but he
stopped in the shadows when he heard Jonathan ask,
"So you didn't write the ending, huh? A 'friend'
named Max did."

"Yes," she said briefly.

"Max who?"

"Mike's grandson. Max Wulfson."

"Ah."

"What does 'ah' mean?" Aurora asked irritably.

"It means you had a nice lunch and you're friends
with Max."

Aurora grunted. "We are *not* friends."

"Oooh, don't we sound witchy tonight."

"Jonathan, lay off."

"Did you have sex?"

"No!"

"Pity."

"Would you quit? He thought I was a gold digger
out to fleece his grandfather. No way would I have
sex with him."

"But he finished your play."

"He finished my play, he straightened out my
daughter and he even had the old folks salivating over
him."

"Gosh. He should be shot."

"You don't understand."

"All that, and no sex?"

"Jonathan, when was the last time you shared your
personal life?"

"I'm not a fool."

"Then, if you don't mind, get out of mine."

"You're a friend. I can't butt out."

"You have no right to preach to me."

"Yes, I do. Because I, unlike other people I know, do indulge. And on occasion I don't look to the future, or bog down in the day-to-day. Go for it. Give yourself one night."

"Great. I'm teaching my daughter to abstain because there are horrible diseases out there, but I should—"

"I didn't suggest you discuss it with her."

Jonathan moved behind her and began to massage her shoulders.

"Think of it…a night completely off. Away from everyone over eighty. Alone, on a deserted beach. In the sand. With a breeze blowing. The sound of the surf—"

"If it was me on that sand, I'd guarantee you there would be chiggers," Aurora said.

"Okay, scratch the sand. A beautiful room, the breeze blowing in, a glass of wine, and he—"

"He? Doesn't 'he' have a name?"

"Just 'he' for right now."

"He'd wind up being gay. Charming, friendly, a great guy, good-looking and wonderful, but gay."

"Max Wulfson isn't gay."

"He'd become gay. One night with me and I guarantee it."

"Why don't you take the chance?"

Aurora pulled away. "Maybe he didn't ask."

"Maybe *you* should ask."

"Great. I should just knock on his door and say, 'Hey, Max, how are you? Thanks for finishing the play. It was a really great ending, and I hate your guts for it. My daughter is acting normal. I hate you for that, too. Mostly I hate you for being a rich asshole. But you are a good-looking rich asshole, and my co-workers seem to think I'm desperate. Want to have sex with me?'''

"Aurora! How have you survived in the theater all these years?''

"By working my ass off.''

"But no romance, no imagination. You knock on his door and waltz into his room. You turn around, strike a pose and say, 'Let's make love.' Make love, Aurora. Not 'have sex.'''

"Jonathan, I really am going to hit you.''

Max decided at that point that it probably wouldn't be wise to let them know he had been there, listening. He quietly left the theater.

Aurora had no intention of following Jonathan's suggestion, but she did know that she had to make herself go see him. She was going to be polite, mature and decent. And the decent thing to do, of course, was thank him for what he had done. That was it. Knock on his door, but not go in, and just say thank-you.

It was late, but not that late. The night had gone like clockwork. Though they'd just received the last act and were working with scripts in hand, the cast had done a beautiful job with the reading. The entire show wasn't much more than an hour, since many of the residents of Paradise were unable to sit for longer, even in their wheelchairs. But it had all gone so

smoothly that they had broken a few minutes before
ten. And there was no traffic to speak of in Paradise
at this time of night.

She made it to the Paradise Motor Lodge in less
than ten minutes. She didn't stop by the office or
call—she would have lost her determination if she
had—just walked straight to Max's door.

But once there, she hesitated, hand raised. No. She
couldn't do it. She would thank him in the morning
and be decent then.

But before she could turn away, the door opened.
She wondered if she was losing her mind, if she had
knocked after all.

Max was in denim cutoffs. That was all. His chest
was as bronzed as his hands. Muscled. Not ridiculously infommercial muscled, but tight and sleek.
He'd showered; his hair was still damp and almost
ebony. She stared at him, her throat suddenly dry, no
words coming to her lips.

"Hi."

"Hi."

"Come in."

"No, no, thanks. I, uh, I just came by to say
thanks."

"You're welcome."

"You shouldn't have done it."

"It was fun."

She didn't know why she was suddenly angry.
"No, I mean you shouldn't have done it. That was
an incredible invasion of privacy."

"Sorry." She could tell from his tone that he didn't
mean the word at all.

He turned around and walked into the room. She followed him. "What if I suddenly decided I was a business genius and took over your office? You have a lot of nerve. That was a horrible thing to do."

He walked past her to the little kitchenette, opened the refrigerator door and pulled out a beer. He popped the top in her direction.

"I'm sorry you were feeling desperate and stressed and I finished your play—and did rather well, I think."

"You really *are* an asshole. You don't get it. You're just a total—Yankee. We don't do things that way in the South. We're polite, we're gracious."

"Wow. Gracious. Yeah, I can see that."

"Fine. Let me just make myself at home here." She flung open the refrigerator and pulled out a beer. "I should just go through your refrigerator. No, maybe I should explore your luggage."

"You were already in here. Didn't you explore my luggage then?"

"What?" She went dead still.

"Harold told me that you waited in my room for me this morning. Did you miss anything?" He walked back out to the bedroom area. There was a desk near the plate-glass window. A laptop sat on it. "There's my computer. And there's the closet. You've seen the kitchen. The bath is over there. Feel free to rummage through the shaving kit."

"I didn't rummage through anything," she told him indignantly. But she had. She'd been in the closet. She slammed her beer down on the counter and strode over to where he stood. She found herself poking his chest. "There's a big difference. A computer is totally...personal."

"A computer is a machine."

"My work was personal."

"I'm sorry I finished your damn play. You're just pissed off because it was good."

"That's not the point." She was still jabbing him. He caught her hand. "Isn't it?"

"It was an invasion of privacy. And you don't understand because you...you don't know what it is to really have to work. To spend days raising beds, going home and writing, arguing with idiotic city officials over permits and praying that tickets will sell, so you can pay the professionals. You don't know what it is to worry about your costuming budget while you're watching someone you've come to care about take their last breath, or calling the nurse, or pouring water, or—"

"Or not really having a life of my own?" he asked.

She wrenched her hand free, suddenly afraid that she was close to getting hysterical. And she'd thought she had it all together. Time for the theater, for Gran, for Angie, for getting by...

"I have a life. I have a great life," she stormed. She started to leave, shoulders straight, strides long, dignity entirely intact.

"Aurora."

He caught her arm, and her own impetus brought her spinning around, smack into his arms.

Against his bare chest.

"Aurora..." His eyes were intense.

Then he said only, "Oh, hell," and kissed her.

Lips over hers. Firm, vital, alive. Tongue slipping between her teeth. The scent of him, the feel of him...

God, it was good.

She meant to protest.

His tongue...

She could feel it everywhere, feel it where it wasn't, feel it where she wanted it.

His hands...

Fingers through her hair, at the small of her back, crushing her against him. His pelvis, crushed to hers, the things she could feel...didn't remember, did remember...longed to experience anew.

His lips broke from hers. Barely. She could still feel the rush of his breath. See his eyes. She moistened her lips. ''I've...I've...''

''What?''

She meant to say, ''I've got to go,'' but the words wouldn't come.

Jonathan's words were hovering in her mind, at the tip of her tongue.

''I—I—''

''Say it.''

Oh, God. His hips. His fingers splayed at the small of her back. His naked flesh. The scent of him.

''I've...'' *I've got to go.*

''Yes?'' Softly, so softly, the words a caress.

''I've been told...''

''Told what, dammit? You've got to...?''

''Have sex.''

The words fell from her lips. She was instantly mortified. But she couldn't move. Didn't want to move. A slight smile was curving his lips, and she found herself babbling once again. "I'm still angry. Furious. And…"

"And I'm still an asshole, but I'm the right sex, have the right inclination and I'm not put together too badly."

She lowered her head. "Oh, Lord, I didn't say that…."

"Shut up, Aurora."

"But—"

"Please shut up, Aurora."

"But—"

"Oh, hell," he said again.

And once again, he kissed her.

She wasn't sure when he turned out the light. She didn't know how her clothing ended up on the floor.

Only that he was kissing her.

And that the breeze was soft, the sheets were cool, and he was bronze against them, just as she had imagined. Moonlight drifted gently in; the sound of the surf seemed amplified. Or was it the sound of her breathing, his breathing…?

It was the fantasy come to life. Sight, sound and touch, all tempered by moonlight, by magic. And more. Beyond the fantasy. His lips…here, there, everywhere. His hands…his tongue. His heat, liquid heat, coursing through her body. Inhibition lost in a sea of sensuality. Touching him, knowing him, being with him on the linen sheets, the air rushing over her where she burned. The feel of his tongue, moving, doing things that had been teased and hinted at in his kiss. Fantasy forgotten in urgency. Binding together, fusing together, moving, writhing, arching…and even thinking, absurdly, that of course it would be this mindless, this fantastic, she'd known he had big feet....

Then a moment of shattering crystal climax, so volatile that she lost the world in an ocean of fire and sensation. There was a cry, her own, and the room faded to black, then came alive again as the breeze caressed her once more, cool against the heat, gentle against the more violent force of nature that had seized her. The scent of the clean salt air returned, the feel of the sheets, the feel of his leg still cast over her own.

Then there was...

Reality.

This was a motor lodge. The rear of the bungalow was open to the beach and the sea. Someone might have walked by. Might have seen them, heard them.

And there was him, of course. Watching her now in the moonlight.

"I've got to go."

His arms tightened around her. "Was that a wham-bam-thank-you-sir?" he asked softly.

"I have to go home. I have an eighteen-year-old daughter."

"She'll be fine for a while longer."

She groaned softly. "I don't even know you."

"I'd say you know me quite well."

She started to move. He rose above her. "Don't go," he said. He lips touched her throat. The brush of his fingers traced the flesh between her breasts.

"I—"

"There's only one way to shut you up," he said. And proceeded to show her.

She awoke, stunned. At first she wasn't even sure where she was. She had been dreaming. A wild, erotic, decadent, unbelievable dream that had left her deliciously sated. But it wasn't dark, and this wasn't her room. The arm around her was real, and windows were open to the sand and sea and the extraordinary sight of the first light of day beginning to break in golds and deep crimson across the sky.

She jumped out of bed and began scrambling for her clothing.

Max was up instantly. "Aurora...?"

"The curtains!"

He drew them immediately, then went to her. She had fumbled her way into her clothing.

"The curtains are drawn. It's all right."

"My God, it's morning."

"It's all right."

"I have a child."

"She's eighteen."

"Aurora, you didn't do anything illegal. It was a great night. A beautiful night."

She dodged his arms, going for her shoes.

When she did, she saw what she hadn't seen the night before. A script, lying next to the computer. A finished, bound play. She missed the title, but she saw his name.

She turned, staring at him in horror. "Maxwell Wulfson. *The* Maxwell Wulfson."

"I don't know about *the* Maxwell Wulfson."

She backed away in horror. "The playwright. The New York playwright who's had more Broadway shows than I can count."

"Yeah. I guess that's me. What difference does it make?"

"What difference? I sat there and said you couldn't write, that you couldn't imagine, that…that…oh, my God! How could you have let me go on?"

"Aurora, it didn't matter."

"Didn't matter? It was just another way for you to let me humiliate myself."

"Stop it. You haven't humiliated yourself in any way. Your plays are wonderful, and if possible, you're an even better actress than you are a writer. Come here, Aurora."

"No! Oh, God, no!"

Before he could reach her, she turned and ran.

She could hear him coming after her. Nude, bronzed, muscled, toned…big-footed.

"Aurora!" He shouted her name, then remembered his state of undress and retreated.

She heard him swearing as she went racing out to the parking lot.

Seven

Max stood next to Mike's wheelchair in the center of the rec hall, which had been transformed. The wedding guests were an interesting assortment, some in chairs at the tables, some in wheelchairs, and then, there was the younger crowd, the nurses, doctors, nurses' aides, kitchen staff, gardeners and everyone else among the working populace of Paradise. Angie was there with three of her college girlfriends and a young man. The kid was tall, with an athletic build, light eyes and dark hair. Max knew he was Josh even before they were introduced. Angie whispered to him that he had left a message, asking if he could please come to the wedding. Since he had visited Mary many times in the hospital, she had decided it was all right to leave him a message back, saying that Mary would certainly welcome him.

Even Mr. Hollenbeck was there. He hadn't responded to anything in more than a month, Max had heard. But Aurora—who had been doing her best to be civil when necessary, ignoring him the rest of the time—had insisted that he be wheeled in, hoping he might enjoy the music and pageantry of the wedding ceremony. Since Max had been handy, Aurora had given him a grudging thank-you when he had taken charge and rolled him in.

A number of Aurora's cast and crew from the theater were there, including Jonathan, who had greeted Max warmly after his initial surprise but hadn't offered an explanation for being there. Max didn't intend to ask him what he was doing in Paradise. If Jonathan chose to tell him, he would do so.

The rabbi and priest were appropriately decked out for the ceremony. The music began, and Aurora entered from the hallway. Her dress was a soft blue knit with spaghetti straps and a softly flaring skirt. She carried flowers and walked with grace, a smile and a solemnity that served the occasion well. He found himself remembering what he had thought of her when he had first seen her. Hair a little short for his taste, yet the natural sun-bleached blond shade was appealing. A nice figure, but nothing extreme. Shorts and casual shirt. Sandals. Those direct blue eyes, that confident, no-nonsense manner. He'd certainly never thought her unattractive—just that she was very low-key for a gold digger.

Things changed.

And quickly. Just one kiss, that night on the sand. One touch.

And one night.

Now he couldn't look at her without remembering the feel of her flesh. Without being tempted to stroke the bareness of her shoulders. He couldn't remember a time when it had felt so good to hold a woman in his arms. Nor could he forget her bewilderment at what she had wanted, the passion and confusion of her outbursts. And those eyes, the way she had looked at him...

She took her position across from him.

Her eyes were on her grandmother as the traditional wedding march began and Mary entered the church. She had apparently been working very hard with her therapist, because she walked in. She was leaning heavily on Bart's arm, but she walked in, and she was beautiful. Like Aurora, she was wearing blue. Soft silk that accented the silver gray of her hair. She came down the aisle slowly—they had to play the march a few times—but when she reached Mike, she was beaming as hard as he was.

Applause suddenly broke out. It was probably the first and last time he would ever witness such a thing at a wedding, Max thought, but it was appropriate and perfect.

Then the rabbi and the priest took turns speaking. The couple had chosen to write their own vows, and they were spoken clearly, and with a certainty that was almost spellbinding. When the priest asked, Max handed over the plain gold bands Mary had chosen.

A moment later they were blessed in English and Hebrew, and pronounced man and wife. Applause rang out again. The bride and groom exited and re-turned—with Mary back in her wheelchair—and another round of applause broke out. The DJ hired for the occasion picked up a mike and welcome the two as Mr. and Mrs. Wulfson. Their first dance would be to "We've Only Just Begun"—Mike's choice—and Max and Aurora took their places behind the wheelchairs, wheeling the newlyweds around to the music as they held hands with each other.

From that point on, the wedding was pure fun. Nurses danced with patients in their chairs, the kids danced with one another, then with the inhabitants of the home, as well. Max was called upon by almost every octogenarian, and though he'd thought himself in pretty good shape, by the time he'd been through thirty or so wheelchair waltzes, he was getting sore. He hadn't been the only one, either. Aurora had been doing the wheelchair fling, as well. As the afternoon wore on, he saw Mary whispering to Aurora, who touched Jonathan Smith on the shoulder. The two of them walked out on the floor, and the DJ played a swing number. The two of them slipped into position as naturally as twins all but joined at birth and danced beautifully.

"She's a looker, eh?"

Max glanced downward. Daisy Marks was at his side. He had promised her the next dance.

"She's a lovely young woman, yes."

"She's Mary, nearly fifty years ago," Daisy said sagely. "She's still breathing fire at you, though, huh?"

"I'm afraid so."

"Well, don't worry too much. I explained that all men were idiots."

"Gee, thanks. I'll try not to take that too personally, Daisy."

"From what I understand, you were a horse's ass."

"Thank you, Daisy. That's just about right."

"The good things in life are worth fighting for,

though. But then, you have that life of yours up in New York City. Starlets throwing themselves at you all the time. You're going back soon, I take it."

"Sunday night."

"You should stay longer."

"Can't. Have to have most of a new play up and going by then."

"You don't direct, do you?"

"No, but a good friend is directing this show, and we're tied into it together financially. If I don't do my part...well, I'm old enough to know that some things you can compromise and others you can't. Now, I believe you promised me this dance."

"No. Aurora is standing over there by Mary. Go get her."

"She may say no, Daisy."

"And you haven't heard the word before in your life? And gotten around it?" Daisy's eyes were twinkling. "Remember, Maxwell Wulfson, anger is a strong emotion. You can't be angry with someone if you're not affected by them. Go dance."

"Just for you, Daisy."

She probably would turn him down, he thought. If he asked.

So he decided not to ask. He walked right up to her and took her arm.

Aurora stared at his hand on her arm, then into his eyes.

"Come on," he said.

"Oh, yes, sweetie," Mary said. "Go and dance with a man who is on his feet and your own age," she commanded.

He whirled Aurora out on the floor. The song ended almost immediately, and as if the DJ were in collusion with him, the next song was slow. Aurora was still in his arms, staring up at him defiantly.

"What are you so damned mad at?"

"You."

"For being me?"

"Why didn't you tell me?"

"What did you want me to say?"

"That you were Maxwell Wulfson."

"You knew I was Max Wulfson."

"Well, somewhere along the line, you might have mentioned that you were a well-known playwright."

"The subject never came up."

"Then you could have brought it up. This whole thing has been so…mortifying."

"It was *all* mortifying?"

"What else could I call it?"

"You could call it good. Or great. I would."

"Oh, really?" She cocked her head, staring up at him. "You swept down here for your grandfather's wedding. Now you'll sweep back up to your black-tie affairs, your celebrity-filled world and the life you were leading. All I did was happen to catch you between actresses."

"I live in New York, I work in New York, and yes, naturally, I have a social life in New York. But I'm telling you the truth when I tell you that I haven't had many nights that meant as much to me as last night."

"Why? Because I'm different? The small town girl?"

He shook his head. "Aurora Beck, you're certainly not the barracuda I first met. You seem to think that everything in my world is easy."

"It's easier than here."

"New York has its benefits. So does Paradise."

"Oh?"

"Aurora, that theater is yours. You have total creative control."

"You get to write whatever you choose."

"Writing and having things staged the way I want are not always the same thing."

"The music has stopped. You can let go of me."

"Not until you admit something."

"And what is that?"

"That it was a damned good night. A great night."

"A stopover on a road show," she said, a slightly desperate note in her voice.

He leaned down, his whisper brushing her ear. "Admit it was a great night."

"All right," she whispered back with passionate anger. "Then morning came. Now let me go!"

"Aurora, why—"

"When are you going back to New York? Tonight?"

"Sunday."

"Well, if I don't see you again, have a great flight. Excuse me. The reception is winding down, and I have a rehearsal I have to get to tonight, but there are a few more things I want to do before I can leave."

She escaped his hold and walked across the floor. Another number had begun. She pulled Mr. Hollenbeck out on the floor. He didn't respond, but he didn't withdraw his hands from hers, either.

From a distance, Max thought he saw the old man smile.

Aurora sat, stage center, legs curled beneath her, and looked at her watch. They were ready to begin the last rehearsal before the performance tomorrow and Jon Smith had still not arrived.

She picked up her cell phone, ready to call him, when the door burst open and Jon entered.

On crutches.

She stood, staring at him. "Jon! What on earth happened?"

"Daisy," he said with a groan.

"Daisy?"

"I crashed into her hospital table when I was trying to help her back into bed. Nothing broken. Major sprain."

She stared at him in dismay. They could find a substitute, but he would never be as good as Jon. "Oh, no. I mean, I'm sorry, of course, I hope you're not in much pain. But…if I pull Scott from the light booth…"

"It's all right. I've found a replacement," Jon said.

Her eyes widened as Max Wulfson walked in behind him. Her heart sank.

"You act?" she asked sharply.

"Only under great duress," Jon answered for him. She stared hard at Jon. So that was where he had come from. The New York stage. Where he had apparently known and worked with Max. "He's willing to take on my role for tomorrow, and at this late date, he's your best option.''

"Look, Aurora," Max said, arms folded over his chest, "if you don't want me to take the role, I won't.''

"Max!" Angie cried out delightedly from the wings. Nancy, Shelley and Tom Long, the prince, emerged behind her, clapping.

Scott hopped down from stage center to the left aisle. "Wow, Max Wulfson—in our play. You're *the* Max Wulfson—right?''

Aurora felt like a fool. Had everyone else recognized the name immediately? But then she had forgotten that Scott's real dream was playwriting.

"Aurora, what are we doing? Time's a-wasting," Jon said. "We need to get in two full run-throughs.''

"Let's go, then," she said, looking at Brandy Dillon, the stage manager.

Brandy nodded. "Places!" she called, heading stage left.

At first Aurora didn't think she would live through it. She was off. Her timing was bad; she missed two lines.

But by the second act, she was back in stride. Because Max was good. He had learned the lines, and he had timing.

By the second run-through, the play clicked, and the cast and crew came out laughing and happy.

She thanked them all. Though it was late, well past ten, they all seemed elated and wanted to go to the coffee shop up on the highway toward St. Augustine. She refused to be coerced into going, then was irritated when Angie agreed to join them—right after Max did.

She had almost made it into her car without a confrontation with him when she realized he had followed her. She couldn't close her door—his body was blocking it.

"What?"

"How about saying thanks?"

She stared out the windshield. "Thanks."

"You owe me."

She looked at him. "I owe you?"

"Sure. I finished your play, now I'm acting in it."

"But you're the all powerful Max Wulfson. Naturally you can act just as well as you do everything else. This is just another piece of cake for you."

"I hate being onstage."

"Why? You're a natural," she found herself saying.

"I like writing and getting involved in production. I'm not an actor."

"Well, you could have fooled all of us."

"Then you owe me."

"Fine. I'll act in one of your plays sometime," she said dryly.

"How about you help me write one of them, instead?"

"Help you write? Yeah, sure."

"Tomorrow night."

"I'm not going to bed with you again."

"I didn't ask you to. Tomorrow night. I know the theater is closed—Jon told me you're not even casting the first show of the season until next week. Tomorrow night, and maybe Saturday, as well. You're going to work for me.''

"Wait a minute. I never made any bargains with you."

"You need an ogre tomorrow, don't you?"

"Are you bribing me? Or threatening me?"

"You figure it out. I need help. And guess what? I know how to ask for help when I need it, and I'm damned glad to get it. So say 'Thanks, Max.' And plan on returning the favor tomorrow night."

Jon and Aurora sat having coffee in the rec room after the stage had been set. They had fifteen minutes before the occupants of the home, and whatever family members were coming, began to pile in for the performance.

As she looked at Jon, he said, "I know what you're thinking."

"You do?"

"You're going to tell me that we're going to keep on doing this. Because you like doing it. Because some of these people, who almost never saw their relatives, get family visits on Fridays now, because their grandkids and even their children like to come see the shows."

"You're good," Aurora admitted.

He shrugged. "You've always known that. Know what else I'm thinking?"

"I'm not sure what I want to know."

"Too bad, because I'm going to tell you anyway. I don't know what approach you decided to take, but you went to see Max.'' He didn't even bother to phrase it as a question.

Aurora wondered how she could be an actress and still give herself away with such a crimson glow. But she wasn't answering. ''Why don't you tell me your story first, Jon? You knew him in New York, right?''

Jon shrugged and took a long swallow of coffee. ''I was the toast of Broadway for many years. Just like old Gus, the theater cat.''

''You're not that old.''

''Pushing sixty.''

''So how was I lucky enough to hire you?''

He laughed. ''Let me not be too immodest. Good things come to good people. I came down on vacation. A hiatus. Hell, I was out of work. They'd given the role I wanted to a younger man. I was actually in St. Augustine. You have to hunt for Paradise, you know—it's not a big star on the average tourist map. I came to one of your productions, saw the ad in the paper the next day, and came in. I know my worth. And I know that being in the arts is risky. But I like this place, and I like you. I like fishing, and I like the water. They say there are no seasons down here, but you can feel it when the air cools just a little and it's fall. And in winter...I love those days when we'd think it was pleasant up north and everyone down here is whipping out their winter coats. I love the fact that I don't have to trudge to work through slush and snow. Sometimes I miss the excitement of Broadway, or the days when the shops on Fifth Avenue are decorated for Christmas and the tree is up at Rockefeller Plaza. So I take a week and go up. And then I come back—to Paradise. But as to Max, yes, I've done several of his plays. I met him when he was a raw kid, pushing his work around town. He's worked hard, I can tell you that. I can tell you more than maybe you need to know. Mike hit it rich with a sunken Spanish galleon twenty years ago. But Max would never take his money to stage a show. Never. So don't go thinking he was worried about his inheritance. Mike tried to float a few of his projects, but Max was determined to make it on his own or not at all. So how was the sex?"

The question, so casually put at the end of his speech, took her off guard. "Great," she murmured without really thinking. Then she stared at him. "You old bastard."

He laughed. "Good news."

"No it's not. He's still an an idiot. He's played me for a fool ever since he's been here. And now he says that I owe him," she added indignantly. "Because he's taking over your part."

"Sorry about the ankle. Of course, he did finish the play for you, too."

"It was his fault it needed finishing. I lost all kinds of stuff in the computer because of him, and I didn't have any time because of him—"

"And life shouldn't be all work. You may owe him, but you owe yourself more, Aurora."

She sat back, staring at him. "So this guy breezes into town, we have a wild fling—and then he goes back north and I'm more aware than ever that my personal life sucks."

"Hey, you've admitted it. That's the first step."

"But it's not true. I love my theater."

"You buried your husband, you raised your daughter, and you made a dream come true. You've been the damned Rock of Gibraltar. Aurora, you have nothing to prove. You're a strong woman, but the best part of being human is that we're social creatures. We need people. Let yourself need someone. And not an old theater cat like me."

Aurora stood up as the door opened and Scott came in, ready to work the lighting. The rest of the cast and crew would be right behind him.

"I needed someone once. He got into a plane and crashed it. Needing people is a luxury. I let myself need this one, and he'll get in a plane and fly away." She kissed his cheek quickly. "I do love you, you old theater cat," she told him. "And I'm incredibly grateful that you didn't get that role you wanted, even if that's selfish of me."

Jon didn't have a chance to respond. The cast began to assemble, and Aurora slipped into the bathroom and changed into her witch costume.

It was the best performance they had ever given at Paradise. In fact, Bart told Aurora, there had been so much fun and pleasure crammed into two days, with the wedding and the show, that he was afraid some of the really old folks might have their hearts give out on them at any time, with so much excitement.

Max might not have cared for being onstage, but he really was one hell of an actor. The ogre had received the most laughs in the entire production, and he had certainly received the best response when he and the witch realized that beauty was, indeed, in the eye of the beholder and walked away, arm in arm.

It was six by the time the props, sets, lights and other paraphernalia had been dismantled, packed and sent back to the Paradise Playhouse. Aurora went into the new room where Mike and Mary were now living together, husband and wife, in their twin hospital beds. Max was there with them, his ogre makeup washed away, his hair damp and glistening the way it was after a shower. He had been in deep conversation with the two of them, and she realized that the discussion had been about the house they'd decided to build. Mary's doctor had already said that he would release her after another week of therapy, though Mike had another couple of weeks left, so they needed to make arrangements for their private lives. She entered the room in time to hear Max explaining that though he did have to go back to New York, he would see to it that construction was started before he left.

"Lovely show, dear," Mary said. "The best yet."

"Aye, me beauty," Mike agreed, using his best pirate accent. "The best. Now, you two get out of here. Mary and I are newlyweds. We need our quality time together before we drift off to sleep."

"Yes, do get going," Mary said. She beamed at Aurora. "I hear that you two have work to do, anyway."

"I'm sorry?" Aurora said, trying not to stare at Max.

"He helped you, so you're helping him. You do know that he has to finish a new play by Monday morning? Well, you must, you're helping out. So go. You two don't have much time left.''

''You two are really all settled in?'' Aurora asked.

''Yes, go,'' Mike said impatiently.

Max, who had been seated in a chair between the two beds, rose. He kissed his grandfather on the forehead and Mary on the cheek.

''We're out of here,'' he told them. Aurora lingered after he had moved, giving Mike a kiss, as well, and fussing over her grandmother.

Max came back into the room and slipped his hand around her elbow. ''Debt time,'' he said softly. ''Let's go.''

He didn't release her elbow. When they were out of the building, she reminded him that she had her own car. ''You don't seem too eager to pay up,'' he told her. ''If you get in your own car, you might drive away. I'll bring you back for it later.''

She gritted her teeth but allowed herself to be seated in his rental car. She found herself irritated to note that he was a very competent driver. He lived in New York. He shouldn't be able to zip around Paradise so easily.

The little five-speed sports car zoomed and roared as he drove. She closed her eyes for a minute as the wind rushed around her. Something of the movement seemed to feed her fantasies. They would get his hotel room, and there would be no script waiting to be written. He'd simply fallen so far in lust with her that he couldn't bear it. He would sweep her into his arms, practically rip her clothes from her body and then they would be all over each other. The light would be dim, the drapes would be closed, and...

"We're here," he said curtly.

She opened her eyes and stared at him.

"You were dozing."

"Sorry."

He walked ahead of her to the room, opened the door and immediately flicked a switch that flooded the room with light. He walked over to the desk, turned on the computer and picked up the bound play next to it. "First, read this. Then I'll explain why I'm not doing it, and you can see what I've started."

He practically thrust the script into her hands, then immediately sat down at the computer. Aurora stared at him for a minute, then took the script and sat down in a chair across the room. Within the first few minutes, she found herself absorbed in the play. It was very dry, and very funny. She twisted on the chair, looked around, and realized he was hard at work. She fidgeted, then got up and sat on the foot of the bed. By the end of Act I, she was completely engrossed in the characters.

By the middle of Act II, she had curled up comfortably on the bed, with a pillow at her side. And Max had stopped. He was staring at her.

"Do you want anything? Coffee, anything to eat?"

"Coffee would be great," she said, straightening to a sitting position. "Do you want me to get it? There's no room service here, you know."

"I'll run out. I'll pick up a pizza, too."

He had started for the door. She called him back. "Max?"

"What? You don't like pizza?"

"I love pizza. No, I…I was going to tell you that this…it's one of the best things I've ever read. Why are you rewriting it?"

"I'm rewriting because a director friend and I were financed in a very big way that I admit, to my great shame, compromised us entirely. We're contracted to use a certain actress for the lead. And though she's a fine dramatic actress, she doesn't have a sense of timing to save her life. I can't give up the production, because too many other people are dependent on it, not to mention that I signed a contract myself. So, for the actress's benefit and my own, there has to be a new play. All right, coffee, pizza…anything else."

"Yes."

"What?"

"Why won't you just let Mike finance the play you want to do?"

He shook his head. "Can't."

"I see. So you don't actually want to *need* anybody."

"What do you like on your pizza?"

"Anything. It doesn't matter."

He went out and shut the door. She went back to reading the play.

She finished quickly, then imagined herself getting to stage a production of it.

Never. It was intended for the big time. Not Paradise.

Where was Max? She rose and stretched, then opened the drapes and the doors to the beach. A huge moon rode high in the sky. The water and the heavens touched. The breeze poured in, mingling with the air-conditioning. She lay back down on the bed, hugged a pillow, then shocked herself with her fantasies. She should just get naked. Crawl beneath the covers. Drape them just so. Wait for him to walk in and…

He'd been all business tonight, though. He hadn't asked her to sleep with him again. Hadn't even hinted at it. Maybe she wasn't that good. That appealing. Maybe she even seemed old to him.

She leaped out of bed. She didn't need any further humiliation at his hands.

She walked over to his computer, went to the beginning of the file and started to read.

She realized immediately why he was such a successful playwright. This piece was entirely different, but just as effective. The first piece had been a sophisticated comedy set in New York City. In this one a family had gathered at a nursing home, where the patriarch was dying. The granddaughter, who truly loved the old man and had been with him for ages while other family members waltzed in and out, couldn't bear his suffering.

At the end of Act I, he was dead. She had given him an overdose of morphine.

In Act II, the other family members realized what had happened, the police were called in, and things went from bad to worse.

He had left off in the middle of a speech the granddaughter, Rebecca, had been giving to one of the police officers. She found herself hesitating, then picking it up. After all, she had spent a great deal of time at the Paradise home. And she had seen the old slip away, some in agony, some peacefully, and she had seen the way loved ones—and heirs who hadn't paid particularly compassionate attention—behaved.

She never heard Max come back into the room. She was too involved in the story, her fingers flying over the keyboard, and though she didn't have the answers to life and death, she certainly had many of the questions, and the arguments.

"Damn."

The word came from behind her, startling her. She spun around, nearly tipping over in the chair. Max caught the chair before she could fall ignominiously to the floor. He righted it, and she leaped up. "Sorry, I just...couldn't stop myself."

He sat in the chair she had just vacated and saved the document, then read through it quickly before standing again. "Finish her lines, then let me back in."

Aurora stared at him, then took her seat again. At first, with Max back in the room, she couldn't so much as remember the character's name. Then she began to write again. She finished the speech, then gave up the chair. Max took it and began to work with the same focused attention she'd been giving the work.

Aurora quietly backed away. The pizza box was on the counter, and she realized she was famished. She helped herself to a piece. Mushrooms, green and red peppers.

She ate her pizza, then drank a cup of coffee, but it didn't really kick in. Max hadn't moved from the keyboard. She curled up on the bed again, waiting.

Maybe she'd paid enough of her debt for the evening. She could tell him that she needed to go home.

She didn't have her car, though, and she didn't want to interrupt him.

If the lights hadn't been so bright, the moonlight would have been streaming in. The breeze was wafting through the room, though, and she could hear the surf, a soft, rhythmic pushing sound. She began to drift.

She opened her eyes, aware that something had changed. The lights had been turned out. The moonlight was streaming in. Max was still at work, hunched over the computer, seeing by the greenish glow of the screen.

She watched the dust motes ride the moonglow for a few minutes. Then she closed her eyes again.

She awoke to a soft touch on her shoulder. He was hunkered down at her side, brushing tendrils of hair from her face. "You've paid your debt," he said softly.

She nodded, still half-asleep. His lips brushed her forehead, then her cheek, and then she was suddenly awake, her arms curling around him when he would have moved. She found his lips with her own before he could straighten. His weight eased down beside her, and the kiss was...

Everything she could have imagined. Her clothes were disheveled. His fingers were brushing bare flesh. The breeze was cool, but she was burning. From the inside out. His touch was as exotic as the breeze, as compelling as the moon, as intimate as...

He was braced on his arms, raised above her.

"Your debt is paid," he said softly. "We owe each other nothing."

"Yes," she whispered. "But I'm known as a very giving person."

"You may not believe this, but so am I. An asshole, of course, but a very giving one."

"I have a proposition," she said. If he moved, she thought she might just go ahead and die right there. "Tonight, let's just give to each other. No payments, no debts. Just a night in Paradise."

She held her breath. He moved. She thought she might sink into the mattress, melt away.

In moments his clothing was gone and she was suddenly next to him, her own clothing quickly following his to the floor. She was standing in the moonlight, and he was doing things to her body, high, low, in between. Where there had been fire, the breeze touched with exquisite coolness, until the liquid fire came again and again, until...

Until she couldn't stand up anymore.

Then they were wound together on the bed, and she thought she must have died and gone to heaven.

But it was only Paradise.

Just a night in Paradise.

Eight

She slept late, since it had been close to 4:00 a.m. when he had brought her back to her car, then followed her home.

She wouldn't even have woken up when she did, except that Angie came in to tell her it was almost noon, and she was supposed to be ready for Max to come by in an hour—they had to finish the play.

When he picked her up, he was all business again. They were going to take an hour to visit the newlyweds, then get started.

Back in his hotel room, they got right to work.

One cousin was determined that Rebecca go to trial for what she had done. The young police officer was falling in love with her. There was a great deal of money at stake, since the patriarch's entire fortune had been left to her.

Rebecca herself was ready to go to prison for what she had done. The young officer wanted her to fight, but she had reminded him that she had helped her grandfather go peacefully, gently.

The play climaxed when the rest of the family slowly turned away from the vengeful cousin, swayed by the policeman's passionate speech about the value of life lying in its quality, not its quantity.

At the end, a courtroom scene, the wait for the verdict, and a moment between the police officer and Rebecca. The belief that there would be a future...

"Is it done?" Aurora asked.

He shrugged. "I'm sure I'll do a little tweaking, but it's probably the most amazing play I've ever written. No, *I* didn't write it. *We* wrote it."

"I wrote a few speeches."

"Don't downplay your contribution."

"I don't. It's still your play."

He shrugged again, looking at his watch. "It's almost six."

She hesitated. "It's all right. Angie is staying with a friend."

He frowned. "Not—"

"Josh? No. He's been calling like crazy, but she's been hanging out with her friends. She even went to a club up in St. Augustine last night."

"Good for her."

He watched her.

She expelled a long breath. "We finished the play. You were supposed to pick me up jubilantly and spin me around, and then you were supposed to ask me— beg me—to stay."

He smiled. The chair fell over as he got to his feet. He swept her up, spun her around, then set her down so slowly that she could feel every inch of him.

"My last night in Paradise. I'm begging you to stay."

He dropped her off at her house at ten the next morning, saying he had some business matters to take

care of for Mike before he left. She reminded him
that it was Sunday, and he assured her that he knew
that, but the things he had to do could be done on a
Sunday.

At twelve she attended the nondenominational service at the home with Mary. At one, she had lunch
with her grandmother and Mike.

At four, one hour before he had to leave for the
airport, Max arrived. She offered to drive him to the
airport, but he declined, saying that he had to return
the rental car.

He said goodbye in the rec room, being incredibly
circumspect, given that they had an audience of se-
niors.

Aurora awkwardly shook his hand.

"Kiss her, you fool," a throaty voice called out.

Aurora turned, astonished. Mr. Hollenbeck had
spoken.

"Thanks," Max called. "I will."

Mary and Mike look astonished as he matched his
actions to his words.

The rest of the room applauded, but then Max was
gone, and she was alone.

In the days that followed, she discovered that Paradise was just a place. The moon continued to ride
the night sky. The breezes blew by. The surf pounded
the white sands of the beach.

But it had only come close to heaven when Max
had been there.

She was busy, though. She had to help Mike and
Mary get ready to move. She had to make her final
choices of plays, cast and crew for the coming season.

Angie needed help, as well, as she finished her summer classes and prepared for her last tests.

Life went on.

Alone in the theater with Jon one day, she found herself asking him just what her splurge with Max had accomplished.

"Happiness," he told her.

"Great. And now he's back in New York. Forgetting all about me."

Jon sighed. "Aurora, Aurora. No one is eternally happy. But we only get to go around once. So we reach out for things that we want, and we savor them while we've got them. And sometimes...well, think about it. Mike and Mary are older, they know they don't have all that much time left, so they're going to make the most of what they do have. That's how we should all live."

She frowned. "Jon, that didn't help me any."

"Ask yourself this, were the moments you had with him worth it?"

"I don't know. Because..."

"Because...?"

"I think I fell in love with him. And now..."

"Now...?"

"I didn't know that I was lonely before. I didn't know that I...needed someone."

Jon didn't have an answer for that one. He stood up and patted her on the shoulder. "Think of it this way. You're going to be a better, stronger person. You'll probably even be a better writer."

That night, she was working on the theater's budget when Angie came rushing in from her bedroom.

She'd been watching television in her room, but had come out to turn on the set in the living room.

Max was on one of the entertainment channels, answering questions about his upcoming show. There had been a preproduction party at Sardi's. Max was pictured with one of the most stunning young women Aurora had ever seen. Jena Ronson. His actress.

The piece was over almost as soon as it had begun.

"Well, there goes Max," Aurora murmured.

"There goes Max." Angie said. "Mom, you missed the beginning. He said he had a co-writer on the play. He said it was you!"

"That was very...decent of him."

"Mom, I bet you're going to get some bucks for this."

"Good. We can always use bucks."

"You should call him right now and thank him."

Aurora hesitated. "I will."

She didn't call him, though. After all, he hadn't called her. She just retired to her room, telling Angie that she was exhausted and trying to remember all the good advice she had ever given her daughter. There was no reason for her to be so hung up on Josh, because there were lots of other men in the world. She was young, with life stretching before her. She was a beautiful woman with a compassionate heart. The world was hers.

Okay, so Aurora wasn't exactly young herself. But neither was she old. She had a life. The world was still there to be conquered.

But that night, she indulged in a fit of tears that might have rivaled her daughter's.

The days marched on.

She went out with a very handsome professor from the community college. There wasn't a thing wrong with the man. She just wasn't the least bit attracted to him. She even avoided a good-night kiss.

She almost asked Angie for advice.

Two weeks after Max had left, she sat cross-legged on the stage of the Paradise Playhouse, the moment of reckoning before her. Plays, plays…plays.

"One Shakespeare. We always need one Shakespeare," Jon insisted.

"*Macbeth* this year," she said.

"My favorite," Jon agreed.

The door opened. Aurora shielded her eyes from the stage lights and looked down the aisle, then jumped awkwardly to her feet.

Max.

She was in cutoffs and an old production T-shirt. He was in perfectly pressed chinos and a polo shirt, his jacket tossed over his shoulder.

"Max," she murmured. "What are you doing here? I saw you on TV. I should have thanked you for the mention."

"You could have called, you know." He didn't sound happy. He paused and stared up at her as he reached the stage.

"I think I left my…my…oh, hell, I didn't leave anything backstage, but I'm getting out of here," Jon said.

Aurora looked at him with a scowl, but he walked away anyway.

"You could have called me, too," she said.

"The hell with that. I have a proposal for you. A proposition."

"Oh?" she said carefully.

He nodded, looking at the stage. "You're making your final choices for the season now, right?"

"Yes."

"Forget one of them. You're doing my comedy."

"Oh?"

"Yes, and you're starring in it."

"Here? In Paradise?"

"Here, in Paradise. Fifty-fifty creative control."

"And what do I get?"

"You get a Max Wulfson play."

"And that's...all that I have to do? Schedule the production and act in it?"

He leaped up on the stage and walked over to her. "No."

"What else?"

"You have to have sex. Lots of it."

"With whom?"

He sighed, throwing his jacket down. "Me, of course. Well?"

"I have to think."

"About what?"

"You're still a Yankee."

"Right. And we won the war. And though I'll grant you the beauty and grace of the South, I want you to learn that the North can be an incredible and vibrant place, as well. Maybe not Paradise, but..."

"Max," she said, backing away slightly. "There's still a lot to think about. We live in separate worlds. And you...well, you have a glamorous, sophisticated and...beautiful actress-filled life. This isn't as easy as you think. I want more.... I..." He was dogging her footsteps, coming closer even as she backed away. "Max, there are some serious issues here. We barely know each other. And there's the distance factor to consider—"

She broke off. He had backed her into the wings.

"Shut up, Aurora," he said. "Because this—" he kissed her, then finished the sentence against her lips "—is all that matters."

Epilogue

"There is nothing as beautiful as a sunset like this. Unless it's you," Max Wulfson said to the woman at his side.

Aurora smiled. "Great line. Where'd you learn it?"

Max grinned. "From Mike."

"Ah."

"He told me it was how he snared Mary."

"I see. So are you snaring me?"

"I rather thought I already had you snared."

"Aren't you the confident one."

He rolled over on the sand, staring up at the sky. "I *am* confident." He propped himself on one elbow, looking down at her where she lay on the beach blanket. "I can conquer the world—when I'm with you."

"Another great line. Mike's?"

He smiled. "My own."

"Yes," she said.

"Yes?" he asked with a frown.

"I'll marry you."

"I haven't asked yet."

"Then you can tell me yes. Since you've given me all this confidence, I'll just go ahead and ask you," Aurora said.

"You didn't get down on your knees. Whoops,

never mind, you're lying down. I think I like that better.''

''You're supposed to do the knee thing.''

''Yes, I know. Mike told me that, too, though he wasn't able to do it himself, because of the wheelchair and all.''

''Well?''

He lifted his brows, rose smoothly, then got down on one knee. ''Marry me, Aurora.''

She got up on her knees to face him. ''Really?''

''Of course, really. A true proposal.''

To his surprise, she frowned slightly. ''Max, you've done everything in the world for me. Life really is wonderful. I opened a smash hit at the Paradise Playhouse.''

''Don't forget, you gave me my real dream. I opened a play with creative control.''

''And the Playhouse prospered for it. I've never been happier than I am with you, but you don't owe me.''

''Aurora, I'm not asking you to marry me because I think I owe you.''

''Then…?''

''I'm asking you for the only reason why two people should ever marry.''

''And that's—''

''Because I love you. Because I believe you love me. I need you. And can't imagine life without you. I want to wake up every morning with you. I want to sleep with you, be with you—love you.''

''Mike's line?'' she asked in a whisper.

"A line as old as time, because it's simple, and true."

"Yes," she said breathlessly.

"Because?"

"I love you."

"We'll have to spend time in New York. Are you okay with that?"

"Of course. Because we can always come home to Paradise."

He shook his head, smiling. "You've put a lot of Deep South in me, you know."

"And that means?"

"Paradise will be wherever we are when we're together. But for right now, I'm glad we're here in the real town of Paradise."

"Why?"

"Because it's where we own a private beach."

"Oh," she said simply.

"No argument?"

She leaned back, shaking her head. "Well, actually, *we* don't own the house. *You* bought it. I love it, of course. I'll be delighted to move into it—"

"Aurora."

"What?"

"Shut up."

He then kissed her.

GARDEN COP

To Joan Johnston.
She and I really did sing with the marines
at a conference we both attended in Atlanta,
but she did it better!

One

The woman was brazen. She couldn't have picked a more public spot to grow those marijuana plants. They were right on the main street in the small north Georgia town, right on a leg of the state highway. It was as if she were daring the police to do something about them.

Little did she know, of course, that Curtis Russell, FBI agent, was visiting his mother right across the street from this brazen woman and her illegal substance. Just because he was on vacation, that pert little blonde shouldn't expect him to look the other way when the law was being broken. He was just off a high-profile murder case in San Antonio, and newly a member of the FBI. He could hardly wait for his first real case.

His dark eyes narrowed as he stared out his mother's picture window across the street, where Marijuana Mary was busily fertilizing her bumper crop. He had to admit, she did look good in those beige shorts and top. She had nicely browned skin, and prettily rounded arms. She lived alone in a small rental house, and drove one of those new VW Beetles, pea-green with a sunroof. He wondered what she did for a living. She'd just moved in three months ago, according to his mother. Just in time to plant marijuana and get it almost to harvest. It was planted in a neat row beside an equally neat row of tall red flowers.

Curtis, no gardener, had no idea what any of it was, except the marijuana. He'd seen that in pictures.

"Curt, I do believe you've got a crush on that lovely young woman across the street," his mother called amusedly as she mashed potatoes in the kitchen.

"Why do you think so?" he asked abruptly.

"For one thing, you've spent the past three days staring out the window at her," came the teasing reply.

"It isn't a crush," he said with pure disgust. He unwound his six-foot frame from the chair he'd been occupying and stretched lazily, taut muscles rippling down his broad chest, before he wandered into the kitchen where his mother was working at the counter. "Do you know her name?" he asked hopefully.

"Mary Ryan," she replied. "I don't know anything else about her."

"Who owns that house?"

"Greg Henry," she told him. "Why?"

"No reason," he murmured, and pulled out a kitchen chair to straddle. He was wearing jeans and a white T-shirt, his dark hair unruly, his brown eyes smiling at his mother. It had been just the two of them since he was six and his father had died of an untimely heart attack. His mother had held down two jobs just to keep food on the table, working full-time as a reporter for a daily newspaper and doing feature material for a regional magazine as a district staff writer.

Curtis took a paper route when he was ten, and he'd done odd jobs to bring in a little extra money. When he was sixteen, he went to work after school to help take some of the financial burden off her. The only thing he hadn't liked about the Secret Service job he'd had before, or the FBI job he had now, was that he had to be so far away from Matilda Russell. But she had her church work and her circle of friends, and she wasn't a clinging parent. In fact, she still did the odd feature for her old newspaper, but no news. Although she did seem to know a lot of things that weren't in the paper. She had contacts everywhere, in the most surprising sort of places, on both sides of the law.

"Are you still hanging out with that convicted gun runner?" he asked suddenly.

His mother, an elfish silver-haired woman with wicked dark eyes, smiled vacantly. "He wasn't convicted," she said pleasantly, transferring potatoes to a bowl. "Besides, he went straight. He's a college professor now."

"Imagine that?" he asked the table. "Teaching what?"

She pursed her lips. "Ethics."

He almost doubled up laughing.

"Just kidding," she added as she put the last bit of her hot, cooked lunch on the table and went to get place settings for the two of them. "He teaches criminal justice."

"That's still ironic."

"Lots of young men get into trouble once," she pointed out and gave him a speaking look as she put plates, silverware and napkins at two places. She went back for coffee cups and the carafe that held the coffee, adding a cream pitcher and sugar bowl to the menagerie on the inexpensive lace tablecloth.

"At least I had the decency to wreck my own house instead of a stranger's," he said with a rueful smile.

"And the good sense to know friends using illegal drugs could lead to trouble," she added. She sighed, studying her only child. "I was never so scared in my life when you were involved in that bust and we went before the judge with your attorney," she added somberly. "I'd covered drug-related stories for ten years. It was terrifying to see it firsthand."

He got up and hugged her warmly. "I never messed up again," he reminded her with a kiss. "I catch guys who do that, now," he added.

"You go after much bigger game than teenagers experimenting with drugs," she replied, holding him by both arms. "I'm very proud of you. That was a first-rate job you did in San Antonio, helping to track down and return that hacker from South America to trial in Texas. Even the state attorney general praised you."

He shrugged. "Shucks, it weren't nothin'," he drawled.

She popped him one on the upper arm and went to sit down. "Just watch your back," she cautioned. "It was bad enough thinking you might have to throw yourself in front of a bullet for some visiting dignitary," she said, referring to his earlier stint in the Secret Service. "It's worse having you working homicide cases."

"Why is it worse?" he teased.

She leaned toward him. "Because I'm retired! Can you think of the scoops I'd have had if you'd done this when I was still an ace reporter?"

He grinned. "You could always come out of retirement and write news instead of little feature articles on some guy's giant pumpkin."

"I like sleeping all night," she mused, pouring coffee into both their cups. "I like not having to spend holidays looking at crime scenes or listening to politicians defend harebrained policies that don't work. Roses," she added, "are much less demanding than editors, and I don't have to pack a laptop and a camera everywhere I go."

"Good point."

"Besides," she added, "I make a lot more money at what I do now."

He couldn't argue with that.

They ate in a companionable silence for several minutes.

"Really, why are you watching the girl across the street?" she asked suddenly. "Do you know something I don't?"

"Not yet," he confessed. "But give me time."

The next day, he went to see Greg Henry at his local realty company. He asked the man about his new renter point-blank.

"Is she in trouble with the law?" Greg asked

sharply, because everybody in town knew what Curt did for a living.

"How would I know?" Curt asked, throwing up his hands. "That's why I'm asking you."

"She's a native of Ashton, a little town south of Atlanta," he replied, thumbing through a file. "She has excellent credit, references from some, uh, odd people, but she checks out."

"What sort of odd people?" came the abrupt reply.

"One of her character witnesses is a former revolutionary from a third world country. Another is the minister of a very large Protestant church in Atlanta—he's on television every Sunday, by the way. And the third is a rather notorious television anchorman in New York City who used to be managing editor for a newspaper in Chicago."

Curt was lost for words. The woman was even more mysterious now that he knew a little about her. Greg wouldn't tell him anything else, although he was grinning outlandishly when he ignored the probing questions about her profession. So Curt thanked him with barely contained sarcasm and wandered downtown to the local police station.

The town's police chief, Jack Mallory, had been in his graduating class in high school. They shook hands and Jack chuckled when he found out what Curt was doing for a living.

"FBI, huh?" the other man said, shaking his head. "I never figured you for a Bureau man. You're too unorthodox."

"They like unorthodox," he returned with a grin. "Ask anybody."

Mallory pursed his lips. "Weren't you with the Secret Service?" he mused aloud. "And wasn't there some sort of scandal about you that got you sent to the Okefenokee Swamp to guard the vice president?"

"I volunteered!" Curt said shortly. "I love swamps!"

Jack grinned. "Really?"

"Never mind about that. Listen, there's a woman across the street from my mother growing illegal plants," he added. "Right on the road, for God's sake!"

Jack was serious now. "What sort of illegal plants?"

"Third world agriculture," came the dry reply.

Jack picked up his hat. "Let's go see."

Curt went along with the police chief in his unmarked squad car. They pulled up in Mary Ryan's driveway. She stood up from her kneeling position, with dirt-covered knees and smears of mud on her face from her weeding. She gave the police car a curious, but not worried, scrutiny.

"You're too late," she called to Jack. "I confessed to speeding only last week and they let me off with a warning."

"It's not about speeding," Jack said. He glanced at the flower bed and gave her a speaking look. "Do I really have to tell you to pull those up, and why?"

"But they're only…!" she began.

"They're illegal. And you know it."

She sighed. "But they're so pretty," she sighed, her big brown eyes poignant. "And I raised them from seed."

"The law is the law. Don't make me send men out here to pull them up for you."

"Okay," she said, saluting. "I'll do the dirty work. But I wouldn't know how to process them," she continued.

"Neither would any of us," he confessed. "But they're still illegal. If you don't believe me, ask Jeanette," he added, nodding toward a house two doors down. "We made her pull hers up, too."

"I'll do it," she said heavily. She stared at Curtis Russell and scowled. "He made you come out here, didn't he? I've noticed him standing at his mother's picture window, glowering at me. Is he the garden police?"

Jack had to bury his face in his hand. Curt wasn't amused.

"You were breaking the law," he said shortly. "And doing it blatantly. I'm with the FBI," he added deliberately.

"Yeah. The Flower Bureau of Investigation." She smiled haughtily.

He wasn't blushing, he wasn't blushing, he wasn't...

He got back into the police car and slammed the door. He refused to even look at her. That didn't faze her. She was still smiling when Jack, choking on laughter, backed out of her driveway.

It didn't take long for the grapevine to serve the encounter up to his mother. She came into the den where he was watching television that night and sat down beside him on the sofa.

"Working for the DEA now, are you?" she asked.

He shot her a glance. "Excuse me?"

"Making women pull up flowers. Honestly!"

"They weren't flowers," he pointed out. "They were marijuana."

"You're sure about that?" she persisted.

"I've seen pictures of it," he shot right back.

"Julie Smith has a little Japanese maple in her front yard. It's almost bald now because some idiot told a friend it was marijuana. Teenagers sneak into her yard at night to rip off leaves to smoke." She grinned. "I'd love to know what effect smoking maple leaves has on them."

He laughed, too. "Okay, maybe mistakes get made. But she didn't deny it, and Jack recognized what it was, too. He told her it was illegal and that she had to pull up every stalk."

She shook her head. "I don't know how I'll ever face Mary again," she said with a sigh.

"You didn't go after her, I did," he reminded her. "Besides, everybody likes you."

"That's because I have a sense of humor," she said, giving him a meaningful look.

"I have a sense of humor," he informed her.

"Right." She got up and left him with his television program.

He got up the next morning, had breakfast, and went barefoot in his jeans and T-shirt to the front door to get the newspaper.

He looked across the street and his temper exploded. Those damned marijuana plants were still there!

He didn't even think. He just marched right across the street and jerked the first plant he came to out of the ground.

"You stop that!" came a furious voice from inside the house.

A minute later, a little blond tornado exploded out the side door in a white bathrobe, rushing straight toward him. She was barefoot, too, and the ground was rough, but she kept coming.

He started to speak. She ran into him at top speed, grabbed for the plant in his hand, and managed to knock them both to the ground. They rolled around in the dirt, fighting for possession of the vegetation.

"You give...me...that!" she exclaimed, and punched him in the stomach, hard.

He jerked her arm behind her and pinned her to the ground, his breath coming as unevenly as hers. She had the most beautiful skin, he thought irrelevantly as he looked down at her. And her mouth was just perfect...

She kicked him. He groaned and while he was helpless, she tore out of his grasp, jerked up her plant and moved back a couple of steps, fuming.

"Don't you touch my plants! This is trespassing. This is vandalism. It's tomato assault! I'll have you up before a circuit judge before you can say 'criminal prosecution'!" she raged.

"I'd like to see that," he said sarcastically as he got to his feet and faced her. His immaculate white T-shirt was now brown and white striped, and his jeans had patches of mud. It had rained the night before.

"Would you? Well, you certainly can!" She grabbed a cell phone from her pocket and dialed a number. "Hello, this is Mary Ryan at 123 Cherry Boulevard. I've got a vandal here. He's destroying my property! I've made a citizen's arrest. I want you to send a squad car to pick him up, right now!"

"Send one for her, too, she's growing marijuana in her front yard!" he yelled at the phone.

She closed it and gave him a shocked stare. "I am not!"

"You've got it in your hand!" he argued.

"This?" She held up the mangled vegetation. "This is one of my prize tomato plants I grew from seed!" She gave him a hot glare. "And if you can't tell the difference between a tomato plant and a marijuana plant, you should leave drug detection to the experts!"

He pulled himself up to his full height. "I belong to the FBI," he reiterated.

"Oh, lucky them," she drawled. "Wait until they see tomorrow's headlines!"

"The police officer told you to pull those plants up yesterday," he continued, hating to lose ground.

"He did, and I have," she almost shouted. "I pulled up poppies. Poppies, Mr. hotshot FBI agent, not marijuana!"

His lips compressed. She sounded as if she was certain that was the truth. He glanced at her garden. Flowers had been pulled up and piled at the end of a row. She said he'd pulled up a tomato plant. It couldn't be true.

"You just wait until I get you into court," she

continued, cradling her broken plant. "My poor tomato plant. I'll have your badge for this!"

"You and whose army? And just what do you do
for a living, if one might ask?" he shot back.

"I'm a deputy district attorney in the county next
door," she said with pure pleasure.

His face went very still. "You're kidding."

"You'll wish I were," she returned. "I came up
here from Ashton where I was with legal aid, to take
up my new job. I expected it to be a step up. Boy,
was I wrong! I think I've moved to Stupidville."

"I am not stupid!"

"Tomato assassin!" she accused.

"It doesn't look like a damned tomato plant!" he
yelled back.

They didn't notice that neighbors were pouring out
their doors into their front yards. They didn't notice
the police car pulling up in the driveway, either.

It would have to be Jack, Curt's old friend, who
answered the call.

"Not again," Jack groaned as he joined the antag-
onists.

"He pulled up one of my tomato plants!" Mary
raged, pointing at him. "He thought it was a marijuana plant! How did he ever get a badge? He must
have stolen it!"

"It looks like a marijuana plant!" Curt defended
himself.

"I want him arrested, for trespassing and vandalism," Mary demanded.

Jack moved closer and lowered his voice, mindful
of the neighbors. "Can the two of you imagine how

Judge Wills would react if this case went to his circuit court?'' he asked them. ''Miss Ryan, you don't want your first term of office to end in public disgrace, now, do you?''

She hesitated.

''And Curt, you don't really want to have to explain to a judge why you were pulling up a neighbor's tomato plants? Frankly, Judge Wills would rather have a tomato sandwich than a steak. I can't imagine how he'd react to a tomato plant killer. He grows prize tomatoes himself.''

Curt grimaced.

''So, suppose we just mark the whole episode down as a learning experience,'' Jack suggested gently, ''and go back to our respective houses and—'' he cleared his throat ''—have a nice, calming shower.''

They were both extremely dirty. Mary's white bathrobe was mostly brown. Curt's white T-shirt was filthy, not to mention splatters of mud on his jeans. His feet were covered in it. So were Mary's.

Curt glared at her through narrowed eyes. She glared back at him.

''We can settle the whole matter right here,'' the officer persisted. ''I'm sure Special Agent Russell would be more than glad to replace the, uh, damaged plant. Right, Curt?'' he added with a deliberate stare.

Curt cleared his throat. ''Certainly.''

''I raised them from seed,'' she said haughtily.

''I'll grow you a replacement from seed and sit on it myself until it hatches,'' Curt volunteered.

The glare got worse.

"The gardening center out on Highway 23 has bedding plants," Jack said quickly. "All sorts, from hybrids to those yummy Rutgers tomatoes that my wife and I always plant."

"I won't be cheap about it, either," Curt assured her. "You can have *two* Rutgers tomato plants. In fact," he added, with a formal bow, "I will plant them for you myself."

"Six feet deep and in somebody else's yard, no doubt," she said with dripping sarcasm.

"You could sit in the dirt with it, since you're so attached to the things," Curt shot back.

"I'll tell you where you can sit...!" she exclaimed.

Jack held out both hands. "Lady and gentleman," he said. "If this escalates any further, I will have no option but to arrest both of you for a domestic disturbance. That will require me to take you both into custody in your present conditions. A reporter comes by my office first thing every morning to check the arrest record," he added with almost visible glee. "What a photo opportunity he would have. Wouldn't he?"

They looked at each other and then at themselves. Mary Ryan bit her lower lip hard.

"Two Rutgers tomato plants. Today," she added firmly.

"Two," Curt replied reluctantly.

"Then I'll settle for that and withdraw my request that you arrest him," she told Jack.

"And I'll withdraw my request that you arrest her for assault with a deadly weapon."

"Assault?" she burst out. "With what deadly weapon?"

"Biological agent," he returned, indicating the mangled tomato plant in her hands.

"It's a tomato plant!" she almost screamed.

Curt drew himself up to his full height. "And how can I be assured of that?" he demanded. "God knows what sort of things are crawling around inside that thing. We all know that genetically altered plants are popping up everywhere today! There could be biological weapons concealed in its stem!"

Jack clapped him on the shoulder. "Quit while you're ahead," he advised urgently.

Mary Ryan was fuming quietly.

Curt shrugged. "Okay."

Mary didn't say another word. She carried her tomato plant into the house and slammed the door.

Curt went back across the street, past his staring, shocked mother, and straight into his own house.

Jack got back into his police car and closed the door quietly. And he'd expected a dull routine morning on the job. He had a feeling dull was not a word he would be using often while Curt Russell was on vacation.

After delivering two tomato plants to Mary's yard, and planting them himself, Curt showered and dressed and came back out into the living room, in clean jeans, a clean shirt, a sports coat and nicely polished black shoes. But he didn't get past his mother.

"All right, let's have it," Matilda said at once. "What happened?"

He groaned inwardly, but there was no way out except through her. He'd never make it.

"I pulled up a tomato plant and she attacked me."

She eyed him warily. "Why did you pull up a tomato plant?"

"I thought it was marijuana."

"A tomato plant?" she asked.

"Well, how should I be able to tell the difference without a photo to compare to it?" he defended himself uncomfortably. "Anyway, Jack was with me yesterday and he told her to pull up the illegal plants and she said she would. Neither of them mentioned that they were talking about opium poppies."

She grinned, because he sounded absolutely disgusted. "Opium poppies? Imagine that! Well, they are very pretty," she added. "But they're illegal, just the same." She gave him a long look. "Tomato plants aren't."

"Oh, rub it in!" he groaned.

"Okay, I'll stop. What else happened?"

"I had to go and buy her two Rutgers tomato plants," he muttered. "I just planted them. This way she drops the vandalism charge and I drop the assault charges."

"She assaulted you?" she exclaimed.

He straightened indignantly. "She assaulted me with the tomato plant," he replied.

She turned away, apparently about to choke. "I have a, uh, committee meeting later. Can you get lunch out?"

"Sure. You okay?"

"Yes. Just a cough." She made coughing noises.

They didn't really sound convincing. "A bad cough!" She sounded as if she were choking instead of coughing.

"Well, I'll be in later. I have to check in with the district FBI office anyway."

"I'll see you for supper, then."

"Sure. Have a good day."

"You, too, son." She spared him a glance and looked quickly away before he could see how amused she really was.

He left, climbing into his sedate gray sedan with panache and without glancing across the street, just in case the garden commando opposite happened to be watching. He started the car and whizzed backward down the driveway, whipping out into the street.

There was a screeching of tires and a loudly blown horn behind him. He looked in the rearview window. There she sat, Mary Ryan, in her pea-green little VW glaring at him for all she was worth, where he'd stopped about an inch shy of her front bumper.

He waved at her in the rearview window and smiled brightly. She blew her horn again.

He took off slowly, not burning rubber because he belonged to the justice department. He made sure he did the speed limit right out onto the main highway.

She passed him like a shot when they reached the divided four-lane that led to the large city about twenty miles down the road. It was the seat of the three-county district court and apparently where Ms. Ryan worked. It was also headquarters for the district office of the FBI. Curt had a terrible feeling that both offices were going to be under the same roof.

* * *

And, sure enough, they were. He had to go through a metal detector, a nitrate scanner, and put the contents of his pockets in a tray before he got into the courthouse at all.

He had to check his sidearm. This required him to display his FBI badge. As he was doing it, the Tomato Plant Empress in a trendy gray suit with a short skirt and high heels passed him by with a haughty smile. The security guard grinned at her and let her right through. Curt bristled from head to toe as he watched her sail right by.

He finished with the search and seizure guy and wandered on down the hall to the local FBI office. The secretary had him sit down and wait because the special agent in charge was taking a long-distance phone call.

He didn't have to wait long, though. Barely two minutes later, the woman smiled and told him he could go in.

The special agent in charge gave him a grin that made him feel as if his feet were melting. He didn't even have to ask if news of the tomato raid had reached here.

Two

The special agent in charge, a pleasant-looking bald man with a little light blond hair named Hardy Vicks, offered him a seat. After his vacation, Curt would be reporting to Hardy. The agent in charge outlined a case they were working on in the county where Curt's mother lived.

"It's a real pain," Hardy told him irritably. "This guy—" he tossed a photo across the desk to Curt "—Abe Hunt, is a government witness for a big media circus trial in Atlanta. They prosecuted the owner of a strip joint and he turned out to be a funnel for illegal drugs. Worse, he's got ties to organized crime bosses in Miami."

"Why is that a problem?" Curt asked as he stared at the photo of a hefty man with curly black hair, dark eyes, and a broad face.

"We can't find him," Vicks said drolly. "He's hiding out, because he doesn't believe we can protect him from retribution. He is afraid of a hit man named Daniels. The hit man is one of the best in operation. Anyway, Hunt knows everything about the operation, and we're willing to give him immunity and a new identity if he'll just finger the bosses. He was in protective custody in Doraville in a safe house. The agents with him were watching that new game show on television, and while they were shouting out answers, the guy walked out the door and vanished.''

Curt grimaced. ''Poor guys.''

''Oh, they'll get over it,'' Vicks said. ''We've got them on surveillance watching counterfeiters eat hamburgers at fast-food joints.''

''Why is that a punishment?''

Vicks grinned. ''They're both on diets.''

''Ouch!''

''Anyway, you're officially on vacation, but if you could keep an eye out for Abe Hunt, we'd appreciate it,'' Vicks told him. ''We know he's got two cousins up in your neck of the woods. In fact, one of them lives just two doors down from your mother.'' He grinned again.

''A deputy district attorney lives just across the street from her,'' he pointed out with a cold glare. ''Why don't you ask her to watch for your escaped witness?''

''We already have,'' came the laconic reply. ''She said she'd be delighted and then she asked if you were armed.''

His eyebrows lifted. ''Excuse me?''

Vicks was trying very hard not to laugh. ''She wanted to know if we let you have more than one bullet.''

Curt's mouth made a thin line. ''She's a real pain,'' he stated.

Vicks's eyebrows lifted. ''Gee, you're the only man in twenty miles who could say that. She likes the rest of us.'' He indicated a small baggie full of cookies on his desk. "She baked those and brought some in for us and the D.A. as well. She sure can cook!"

Curt thought he was going to choke. "Is there anything else?" he asked.

Vicks shrugged. "Not while you're off duty. Enjoy your vacation." The older man shot him a wicked glance as he headed for the door. "By the way, the DEA says if you ever lose this job, don't ask them to hire you." He was biting back laughter. "They don't want an agent who can't tell a tomato plant from a...hey, where are you going?"

Curt was already down the hall, and he left the office door open on purpose, gripping the photo so tightly in his hand that he almost crushed it.

"Russell!"

He stopped just past the metal detector and turned. A deputy sheriff was holding out his pistol in its holster. "You going to give this to me?" the deputy drawled. "That's real neighborly. I didn't get you anything."

Curt took the holster and the pistol and snapped it on his belt next to his badge. He didn't answer the deputy, but his eyes did.

He stalked out of the courthouse with invisible flames coming off his hair. This had been a real bust of a day.

It didn't get better when he got back to his mother's house. There was a big, rawboned red-coated hound dog sitting in the middle of the driveway. He blew the horn and kept blowing it, but the dog wouldn't budge.

His mother came running out the door, with her finger to her lips. She motioned for Curt to let his window down.

"Don't do that!" she groaned. "The man next door works nights. He's trying to sleep."

"I can't park the car," Curt told her. "The dog's in the way!"

"I don't have a dog."

Curt pointed to the big animal, which was now lying down in the driveway.

"Now, where did he come from?" she asked dimly.

"Why don't you go and ask him?"

She glared at him and went to coax the dog off the driveway. It still wouldn't budge. She gave Curt a "just a minute" sign with her fingers and ran inside. She came back out with a cube of meat. The dog sniffed and licked and then followed right along with her while Curt got the car under the carport and parked it, turning off the engine.

The dog was now sitting on the porch, looking as if it belonged there.

"You can't have a hound dog in the city," Curt told her with a glare at the dog.

"Oh, he isn't a hound dog, dear, he's a blood-hound. Don't you see how long his ears are? Now how do you suppose he got here?"

"Hitchhiked, maybe?"

She gave her son another hard look. "There's a government witness loose in this county somewhere, hiding out," she told Curt, keeping her voice down. "His cousin lives in the white house right down there."

"How do you know that?" he exclaimed. "I've only just been told by the special agent in charge of the local FBI branch. The man I'll be reporting to."

She put her hands on her hips and gave him a long-suffering look. "I worked for newspapers. I'm an experienced journalist. We know everything."

"You're retired."

She shrugged. "I saw his wife in the grocery store this morning. She told me she can't stand the guy, but her husband thinks his cousin is the berries because he knows everybody in the rackets, and he's best friends with one or two sports stars." She studied her tall son. "I hate sports."

"Me, too. She had no idea where Abe Hunt might be?"

She shook her head. "But she said she'd tell me if she heard anything. They are leaving town for a vacation somewhere. She didn't give me any details."

He looked at the dog. "Maybe we should call somebody. Have you got a dog pound?"

"Sure, it's right out back…of course there's a dog pound! But it's being renovated right now, and there's no place for strays. Besides, he's got a collar." She reached down to look at it. The dog wagged its tail and hassled while she looked for an inscription. "Maybe he belongs to the prison. The correctional institute," she corrected herself. "I wonder how he got here? I'll just go phone and see if they know anything about him. Don't let him leave," she instructed her son as she went inside.

Curt hitched up his trousers and sat down on the steps, pulling his jacket away from his belt. "See this?" he asked the dog, indicating his pistol. "You try to leave, I'll shoot you."

The dog licked Curt's cheek.

Minutes later, his mother was back with a worried look. "They aren't missing a bloodhound," she said worriedly. "In fact, they don't know of anybody who is. I phoned the sheriff's office, but they don't have any reports of missing animals. Nobody seems to have any idea where it came from."

"It probably belongs to a neighbor," Curt told her.

"Do you think so?" she asked absently.

Curt glanced across the street and scowled. "It's probably Marijuana Mary's," he said gruffly.

"Mary? Oh, no, it's not hers. She doesn't have a dog, although she certainly has a place to keep one," she added, nodding toward the old barn on the lower end of her property.

Curt stared at it thoughtfully. "Maybe our fugitive is hiding in there. Maybe it's his bloodhound. He had it come over to throw us off the track."

She chuckled. "Great thinking. Well, I'll phone the radio station and ask them to put it on the local bulletin board. Whoever owns it can come get it."

"And meanwhile?" he asked uncomfortably.

"It can live here, dear," she said easily. "Come on, boy!"

She opened the door to let the dog in.

"You can't have a dog in the house!" he exclaimed. "Not a filthy, flea and tick infested bag of bones like that! What if it decides to get on the sofa?"

She studied him curiously. "We never had pets when you were a boy because your father was allergic to fur," she recalled. "What a shame."

"I'm too old for a dog," he pointed out.

"Oh, I don't know about that," she said, turning to follow the dog into the kitchen. "Every boy should have one."

"Then I'll go to a pet shop and get a German shepherd!" he called after her.

"Too big, dear. He'd never fit in this small house."

"And you think that big red horse will?"

"He's not a horse."

The kitchen door closed. He sighed and went to his room to change back into his leisure clothing. He took the photograph of the fugitive out of the inside pocket of his jacket and put it on the bureau.

The dog, christened "Big Red," had been thoroughly washed and groomed by suppertime. His presence was announced on the radio, but nobody came rushing over to claim him.

That evening, he parked himself on the sofa beside Curt, despite the man's heated objections, and lay down to watch the evening news as if he were really interested in hearing incessantly about the latest political scandal.

"I'm going to leave the country," Curt announced disgustedly. "That way, maybe I won't have to hear this congressman's name five hundred times a day."

"It won't save you. They have our news everywhere now."

"Humor me." He glanced down at the dog, who had his big paws crossed, his muzzle lying on them as he watched television. "This is interesting to you, huh? Don't have dog scandals, I guess?"

The big dog raised its sad brown eyes to his. It wagged its tail and went back to watching television.

"He's very intelligent," his mother remarked.

"How did you arrive at that conclusion?" Curt asked.

"He's not bounding around the house trying to tear up stuff, and he isn't barking."

About that time, the local newscaster came back on and there was an interview with the man in the photograph Curt had been given, Abe Hunt. The dog perked up its ears and barked, once, loudly.

"Hush!" Curt muttered, leaning forward to hear better.

The sound bite was brief and uninformative. The missing government witness had only said that he knew nothing and refused to testify. The newscaster added the information that the witness had since disappeared and foul play was suspected.

"He's probably lying at the bottom of Lake Lanier," Curt muttered.

"If he is, dear, he won't come up again," his mother offered nonchalantly, working on a piece of embroidery while she spoke. "The water's so cold that even spring heating won't send him to the surface."

"You always come up with these fascinating little

tidbits about dead bodies,'' Curt remarked. ''How do you know so much?''

''I used to date a coroner.''

He shook his head and went back to watching the news.

The dog suddenly lifted its muzzle and howled.

''Stop that!'' Curt muttered. ''What's the matter with you?''

The dog looked up at him and wagged its tail.

''He's probably hungry,'' Curt's mother said, putting down her handiwork. ''I'll feed him some leftover macaroni. Come on, Big Red.''

The dog answered easily to his new name. He leaped down from the sofa with fumbling grace and trotted off after his new master.

Curt gave him a long glare. This was getting to be one miserable vacation. First Marijuana Mary, now the Hound from Hell had moved in with his mother.

After they went to bed, the bloodhound padded softly into the living room, sat in front of the picture window, and let out a howl that would have awakened people in the cemetery.

The doorbell ringing insistently dragged Curt out of bed, in silk pajama bottoms and no T-shirt. His mother could be heard snoring peacefully right through the closed door as he passed her room.

He shouted at the howling dog before he opened the wooden door. There was Marijuana Mary in an oversize navy-blue T-shirt. She was wearing bedroom slippers, pink fuzzy ones, and her blond hair was standing out all over her head. She looked half-asleep and furious.

"Could you please put some tape around the mouth of the Hound of the Baskervilles so that those of us who have *jobs* could get some *sleep?*" she asked with venom.

"I have a job," he pointed out.

"You're on vacation," she returned. She had her hands on her rounded hips, and the posture brought Curt's appreciative eyes to the firm thrust of her breasts against the fabric. She cleared her throat and unobtrusively crossed her arms over her bosom.

He lifted an eyebrow and searched her eyes for longer than he meant to, his eyelids narrowing as he registered her sudden flush.

"Why do you have a dog all of a sudden, anyway?" she asked jerkily.

"My mother fed him and now he won't leave. Besides, he's interested in the evening news."

"So?"

"It's Mom's favorite show. She's given him a name. She never gives up things she names," he added with a grin. "She's had me for thirty-four years."

"She should get a medal."

"Look here, why are you prowling around the neighborhood in a nightgown at midnight?" he demanded.

"It isn't a nightgown!"

She glared at him, but her eyes fell helplessly to his broad, hair-roughened chest, and she couldn't seem to stop staring at him.

"Don't leer at me," he said outrageously. "Sexual harassment of men is a misdemeanor. I could arrest you."

"You son of a...!"

"Foul language is a misdemeanor," he continued, enjoying himself. "I could arrest you."

"That dog—" she pointed to the picture window where the dog had begun to howl again "—is a public nuisance and he's creating a disturbance and disturbing my peace. I could arrest *you*. I am an officer of the court!"

He put his hands on his own hips and stared down at her with renewed interest. She was very pretty. Not only that, she had a temper that was easily the equal of his own. It had been a long time since he'd been involved with a woman. He considered that he wouldn't mind getting involved with this one. She had potential.

"Can't you make him stop?" she wailed, dropping her pose and appealing to his better nature.

"I could, if I knew why he's howling in the first place," he agreed. "Why don't you come in and have a cup of coffee and we can discuss strategy?" He started to open the door.

As if it were an invitation, the dog suddenly made a dash for the open screen door and shot through it like a bullet, barking hoarsely.

"Come back here!" Curt yelled, worried at what his mother was going to say when she found out he'd let her new pet escape. "Oh, hell, I'll have to go chase him!"

He started out the door barefoot, without thinking how he was dressed, and shot off after the dog.

Mary hesitated, then threw up her hands and ran after him. She couldn't sleep. She might as well assist.

Lights went on in the neighborhood as the scantily clad man and woman ran along the pavement calling after the baying dog. When he left the sidewalk and ran into the woods behind Mary's house, she kept going, but Curt hit a low-lying rose branch and yelled in pain.

"Watch out for snakes!" he called after her furiously.

"Snakes?"

It was comical to watch her stop suddenly in place with one foot raised. *"Snakes?"* she repeated, looking around in every direction.

Curt was standing on one foot holding the other and trying to pick out thorns in the streetlit darkness. Not that it was easy. The damned streetlight was temperamental. It stayed on for all of a minute and then began to flicker and suddenly went out. Two minutes later it flickered again and tried to come on. The power company had been called and called, but they insisted it was natural, despite the fact that none of the other streetlights acted similarly. It was something the neighbors had learned to live with. Curt hadn't.

"If I had my pistol, I'd blow you away!" he raged at the light.

Doors had opened. The hound was baying wildly. Mary was jumping from one foot to the other trying to feel her way back out of the tall grass and talking to herself, loudly. Curt was groaning and threatening the light.

A police car came careening down the street, screeched to a halt in front of Curt, and the doors of the car flew open. Two young officers appeared with leveled pistols.

"Hands up!" they yelled.

"I've got thorns in my foot!" Curt yelled back, still holding one foot. "I'm FBI!"

"And I'm Princess Don," came the drawled reply. "Get 'em up!"

"Go ahead and shoot!" Curt told them, exasperated. "But shoot that damned streetlight first, and I'll go happily!"

Just at that moment, it went out, leaving the street in total darkness. There were quick commands, doors opened. A spotlight came on at once, but it not only caught Curt, it also caught Mary and the hound dog, both of whom were suddenly standing beside Curt.

"Is it Halloween?" one officer asked the other.

"No," came the reply. "But I'm calling for backup!" He did, pushing the mike on his shoulder and requesting assistance.

"What's going on out there?" came a furtive yell from the houses behind them.

Curt looked at Mary and they both looked at the dog. It was going to be a long night.

They were taken into custody and transported to the police station. The two of them were temporarily lodged in a cell while the watch commander phoned Curt's friend at home. It would be no use to phone his mother. He knew from long experience that nothing short of a bombing would wake her once she went to sleep. But he had asked them to phone his friend, the chief, Jack Mallory, and ask him to come down and identify them.

They had, at least, given Mary a blanket to wrap over her long T-shirt. She sat glaring at Curt from accusing dark eyes as they occupied opposite ends of a long bunk.

"It smells like people threw up in here," she remarked angrily.

"No doubt," he replied. "This is the drunk tank."

"I'm not drunk!"

"Neither am I, but why else would we be running around the neighborhood in the dark in our pajamas?"

"Because of your dog!" she exclaimed.

"He isn't mine. He's my mother's dog."

"She can explain to the police," she began.

"She sleeps like the dead. She won't wake up until nine, and then she'll wonder why I'm not in the house."

"Maybe your dog," she emphasized gleefully, "will go and howl in her ear."

"Not unless he can open doors," he said with a sigh. He looked down at himself. "This is not going to look good on my record."

Her eyes were gleaming thoughtfully. "I'm going to tell them you were looking for a flying saucer," she said sweetly. "I'm going to tell them you saw an alien and were chasing it!"

"You wouldn't dare!" he exclaimed.

"Stand and watch me, Russell!" she shot back, pulling her blanket closer. "First you accuse me of raising marijuana and then you try to back into my car, and then you have your dog howl all night so I can't sleep the night before the most important case of my...career.... Oh, no!" She put a hand to her mouth and her eyes opened wider. "I have to be in court at nine, to prosecute a drug trafficker. The judge will level contempt charges if I don't show up! And here I sit. With you," she added with absolute disgust.

"It's a minor misunderstanding," he pointed out. "As soon as Jack arrives, we'll get out of here and everything will be fine."

"What if he doesn't show up?" she groaned.

"Just be patient," he admonished. "He'll be here soon."

Jack did arrive shortly, smiling blissfully, and he had company. The local newspaper had an ace photographer with a maniacal sense of humor. He'd been working late in the darkroom at the newspaper office and Jack picked him up on the way, along with his camera. And before either of the perpetrators could open their mouths, they were photographed in their indecent state.

"There," the photographer said with a grin. "Recorded for posterity. How will I caption this? Let's see, ace FBI agent and rising prosecutor frolic in suburban neighborhood at midnight with mysterious red dog!"

"You can say it must be some sort of Druid ritual,'' the police chief said helpfully. ''They could be part of a cult...''

''Get me the hell out of here!'' Curt demanded.

Mary stood up beside him, disheveled hair and flaming eyes. ''That goes double for me! I've got a case in court in Lanier County at nine! An important case!''

The chief studied her bare legs and fluffy slippers thoughtfully. ''Gosh, what an impression you're going to make on Judge Wills.''

''I'll promise him a basket of tomatoes!'' she said haughtily.

''He'll throw them at you, if you turn up in his courtroom looking like that,'' he pointed out with a chuckle. ''Okay, Harry,'' he told the photographer. ''We've had our fun. You can show them your camera now.''

The photographer opened the back of the camera. It wasn't loaded. Curt and Mary gave him a vicious glare as the jailer opened the cell with a grin and let them out.

''But no more midnight flits,'' the chief admonished. ''I hate being hauled out of bed when I've only been asleep two hours.''

''I'm sorry,'' Curt muttered. ''The dog was howling and then she came over—'' he pointed an accusing finger at Mary ''—and flaunted her body at me. While I was staring at her, the dog escaped, and we had to run him down...''

The chief held up a hand. ''I've heard it all before,'' he said with a bored expression. ''Just don't

do it again.'' He glanced at Mary. ''Flaunting yourself at FBI agents again, huh, Mary?''

She kicked him in the shin, turned, and stormed
out into the main part of the station, where several
officers were drinking coffee. They turned and stared.

''It's a T-shirt!'' she raged.

They only shrugged.

She was out the door when she realized that it was
a long walk home and she didn't have transportation.
In her present state, she wasn't going to get far without trouble.

Curt, who was thinking the same thing, strode past
the officers with a superior grin. He had a great phy-
sique, and he knew it. Some of the officers standing
around were long married and had what was affec-
tionately and colloquially called ''dunlap's disease''
(short for the rural Southern phrase, ''his belly done
lapped over his britches''). He marched out the front
door just ahead of Jack, looking as if he'd won a
contest.

''Going somewhere?'' Curt asked Mary.

''Home, when I can thumb a ride.'' She gave him
a hard look. ''At least they gave me a blanket,'' she
added, pulling it closer.

He chuckled. ''I don't want one.'' He stood taller.
''With a body like this, why hide my obvious assets?''

She lifted her foot, and he moved quickly out of
range. Thorns were painful enough, without an angry
foot in his shin to add to his discomfort. But she was
a delight to tease.

"You'll still have to hunt down your dog asset," she said wickedly.

"With any luck," he told her, "he'll be back in his own home by the time I get to the house."

"If you two want a ride, hurry up," Jack called to them from his car. "I'm sleepy!"

They were somewhat discouraged to discover that the photographer was also hitching a ride, but he sat in the front seat and didn't say a word the whole way home.

"Here you are," Jack told them, pulling up in the street between their respective houses. "From now on, stay off the streets at midnight. My men only followed regulations by arresting you." He gave them both a long look and shook his head. "This used to be such a peaceful little town," he lamented, and powered up his window before they could reply.

They watched him drive off. It was light against the horizon. They'd spent hours at the police station.

"I don't suppose there's much use in trying to go back to sleep," Mary said on a sigh. She glared at Curt. "Thanks to you, I'll probably fall asleep in the middle of my summation."

"If you can wrap up that sort of prosecution in one day, I'll eat your blanket," Curt assured her.

She grimaced. "It will take three or four," she agreed. She studied him for a minute and then smiled helplessly. "I guess we did look odd."

He grinned. "Druidic rituals," he murmured. "I'll have to remember and tell the guys about that one."

"No need. I'm sure Hardy Vicks will tell everybody the minute he hears about it." She frowned.

"Why do you have a dog? Your mother says she's never had pets. Aren't you allergic?"

"No, my father was. The dog parked itself in the driveway and refused to move. She adopted it."

"Yes, but where did it come from?" she asked.

He shook his head. "I have no idea." He looked toward his house. The lights were on. He frowned.

Just as he was wondering why the lights were on, the front door opened, and there stood his mother with the dog.

"So there you are!" she exclaimed. "What are you doing in the middle of the street in your pajamas with Mary? Come to think of it, Mary, why are you in the middle of the street in a blanket?"

Mary turned without another word and darted across the street and into her house, which she'd left unlocked. Curt sighed and went up the driveway to try to explain the night to his mother. The dog watched him the whole way, wagging its tail.

Three

The next afternoon, Curt waited for Mary to come home and get comfortable before he left his mother—and the dog—and went over to talk to her.

She answered the front door when he rang, but she looked disturbed.

"Something wrong? Besides the obvious?" he added.

"Come on in." She led him to the kitchen and poured him a cup of coffee. "Your mother says you like it black," she added when she put it down and sat down to her own cup lightened with cream. "Listen, when I got home last night, somebody had gone through my kitchen and carried off a loaf of bread and some luncheon meat."

"Didn't you lock your door?"

She glared at him.

He held up a hand and smiled sheepishly.

"Anyway," she continued, "I was too tired to call the police again, so I checked the house and locked up and went back to sleep for a couple of hours. I was going to go out back and look for sign when you came up just now."

"I'll go with you," he offered. He sipped coffee. "When I was in the Secret Service, I worked a federal case in cooperation with other government agencies. One had an agent who was Lakota. He taught me to read sign and speak sign language. It was interesting."

"Lakota?" she asked curiously.

"Sioux."

"Oh." She studied his lean face. "Don't you have Cherokee blood?" she asked abruptly.

He nodded. "My grandfather is on the Dawes Roll—one of the numbered records of all the Cherokee people on the reservation in North Carolina."

"So you're one-quarter Cherokee?" she persisted.

"Thereabouts." He lifted an eyebrow. "You?"

She smiled and shook her head. "Danish and Scotch," she said.

"That explains the blond hair."

"You should see my dad," she told him. "He's six foot four and blond and blue-eyed!" She studied him covertly. "How long ago did your father die?" she asked suddenly.

"I was six. My mother woke up and found him dead in the bed beside her," he said matter-of-factly. "I don't remember him very well."

"That must have been hard on her, raising you alone," Mary commented.

He toyed with his coffee cup. "It was, but she did a good job. She was a newspaperwoman. I always knew who the bad guys were, where they lived, what they did. She was a fountain of information. She seemed to know everybody, and there were always law enforcement people around. I guess that's why I majored in criminal justice in college."

''She's quite a lady.''

''Yes. She is.''

She finished her coffee. ''Well, let's see how well you track.''

He gave her an amused glance, because she didn't seem to believe he could. He was disposed to prove it.

They went to the back of the lot and he became another person. He stood very still, just observing the lay of the land, the possible paths from the kitchen, the dryness of the soil from lack of rain. He interposed memories of where the police chief had walked, where he'd walked, where Mary had walked when she'd pulled up the poppies.

''I, uh, noticed the new tomato plants,'' she said, disturbing his concentration. ''Thanks.''

''No problem. Stay here.''

He moved forward at a slow pace, his eyes narrowed as he stopped now and again to stoop or squat and study the ground and the plants. He moved steadily toward the outbuilding at the back of the lot, but he stopped and made a sudden turn toward the street a minute later.

''Someone went through there!'' he called to her. ''Back toward the street!''

She went to join him and they moved onto the pavement and went back up the road toward her house with Curt obviously studying the grass on both sides of the sidewalk.

He motioned to her to stoop down beside him while he pointed at the ground.

''That's an ant,'' she pointed out. ''Is he speaking to you?''

''Keep your voice down. Nod, as if you're agreeing with me. I think we're being watched.''

She nodded.

''There's someone who has been staying in your outbuilding,'' he said under his breath, ''and he's been there for several days. There are paths so obvious that even that haywire photographer could follow them.''

''That explains the raid on my kitchen,'' she said, equally low-voiced. ''We should call the police!''

He gave her a hard glare. ''I *am* the police. Federal police.''

''Yes, but it's not your jurisdiction,'' she argued.

''I'm now assigned to this district,'' he retorted. ''Why do you think I was reporting to the district office in Lanier County in the first place? I'm starting there after my vacation.''

She whistled softly. ''What a comedown from Austin, Texas,'' she taunted. ''Whose feet did you step on?''

''Never mind,'' he muttered. ''I've got to go see Jack. You can come, too.'' He had an idea of who was hiding in the barn. It was the government witness. They were in no danger, but it was better to get Mary out of the thick of things, anyway.

''I've got notes to prepare. I'm in the middle of a trial,'' she began.

''I'm not leaving you here by yourself with some fugitive hanging around!'' he told her firmly, with flashing dark eyes. ''If you don't like that, tough!''

She was torn between protesting that she could take care of herself and agreeing that she wasn't equipped to handle a lawbreaker—she didn't even have a firearm.

"If I were in your position, Mary," he said, using her given name for the first time, "I wouldn't argue. Attorneys represent the law, they don't enforce it."

She gave in gracefully. "Okay. You win. But I'll need my briefcase and my laptop."

"We'll go in and get them." He stood up and walked back the way they'd come.

"Hadn't we'd better search the barn for clues first?" Mary asked.

"No," he said after a minute. "I'm in no position to apprehend him, if he is in there now. And I don't want to disturb anything or mess up clues. I tracked him to the street, I'm sure he's gone. Come on. You can ride into town with me. I'll come back with the police later to search for clues."

They went to Mary's house, where she packed up her gear and changed into neat gray slacks and a white sleeveless turtleneck knit shirt before she joined Curt in the living room.

"He'll get away, and we'll be blamed," she pointed out.

He shook his head. "I think he was watching us. He'll assume we're brainless and clear up his trail until the police search the barn. Then he'll come back, feeling safe."

"You'd better hope you're right," she muttered.

"You don't know how I'm hoping," he replied with a smile.

The smile startled her. It made her feel giddy inside. She smiled back, feeling stupid.

"How old are you?" he asked.

"Twenty-seven." She looked at him curiously. "Ever been married?"

He shook his head. "Too busy. You?"

"Yes," she said surprisingly. "When I was eighteen. My folks couldn't talk any sense into me, so they gave in. He was eighteen, too, very mature for his age. I was spoiled and stubborn and I never gave an inch. I drove him nuts. We hadn't been married six months when he filed for divorce. We're still friends," she added quickly. "He's married and has a nice little family."

"What does he do?" he asked, unaccountably jealous.

She looked sheepish. "He's a football coach at his local high school."

"I hate football," he remarked.

She laughed. "So do I. That was part of the problem. It was his whole life."

He shook his head. "How about winter sports?" he asked as they went out the front door.

"Ice skating and downhill racing," she volunteered.

"Great! I love winter sports!"

She grinned at him. It was like a beginning.

They told Jack what they'd found out at Mary's house.

"Any idea who the fugitive is?" he asked Curt.

"Gee, let me think," Curt said facetiously. "There's a federal witness hiding out up here, his cousin lives two doors down from Mary, and somebody's living in Mary's barn. Who could it be?"

Jack gave him a look of disgust.

"He's with the FBI," Mary reminded Jack. "You have to make allowances."

"The problem is, I didn't rush him," Curt continued. "I don't know that he's armed, but his connections usually are, and he comes from a shady background. Mary was with me."

That was enough to give Jack the impression that Curt wasn't putting the woman at risk.

"We don't risk civilians, Miss Ryan," Jack told her, just to make the point.

"I'm not exactly a civilian," she pointed out.

"You are as far as I'm concerned," Curt interjected. "Why don't you go and work on your case?" He turned to Jack. "Have you got a place where she can plug in her laptop while we talk?"

"Sure. Hey, Ben!"

One of the policemen stuck his head in the door. "Yes, Chief?"

"Take Miss Ryan to Don's office and let her use his desk. He won't be in today."

"Yes, sir. Come with me, Miss Ryan."

Curt wanted to ask if Ryan was her married name, but he didn't have the opportunity. She went with the policeman and they were talking about computers all the way out the door.

Curt waited until Ben closed the door behind them before he leaned forward.

"The guy's name is Abe Hunt," Curt told the police chief. "He's got a rap sheet as long as my arm. Mary's got guts, but she's no match for a guy the size of Hunt should he pull some stunt. He's built like a professional wrestler. In fact, he did some wrestling in his past. We've got to get this guy out of her barn."

"The trick is, if we chase him out of there, where will he go? Not to his cousin's. He's not that stupid, is he?"

Curt shook his head. "His cousin took a powder out of town. But, even though the house is empty now, no, he's not stupid. But he is desperate. He doesn't want the mob to find him any more than he wants us to. It's going to be a cat and mouse game all the way."

"I can get the Georgia Bureau of Investigation to assist us with the stakeout," Jack said.

Curt nodded. "That would be a help. I can get some assistance as well, but FBI agents would stick out like sore thumbs around here. I've got a reason, I'm visiting my mother, so I won't arouse suspicion if I hang out in her yard or even if I spend time at Mary's house."

"We'll get right over there and search the barn," Jack added. "That will give Hunt the feeling that, if we don't find anything, he's in a safe place."

"Good point. That's what I thought."

Jack got up. "I'll go over and do a thorough search. You and Mary can hang out in Don's office until I get back."

"Thanks, Jack."

He shrugged. "It's my job. Have you thought ahead to what you'll do when we catch this guy? He can't be forced to testify."

"He can if he's facing a life sentence for being an accessory to murder," Curt told him. "Didn't I mention that another potential witness in this case was found floating in the Chattahoochee River with a bullet to the back of his head?" he added.

"I'll bet he'd rather rat on a friend than go down for murder," Jack said.

"The friend is one of the big bosses, and he's going to the chair if Hunt tells what he knows. So our witness isn't doing himself any favors by hiding out in Mary's barn," Curt said quietly. "At least we won't shoot him on sight. The mob will."

"You could almost feel sorry for the guy."

"Almost," Curt chuckled.

"I'll be back as soon as I can. There's coffee in the coffeemaker. Just put a quarter in the box and help yourself."

"No, thanks. Mary already filled me full of coffee before we came here," Curt recalled with a grin.

Jack pursed his lips. "Well, well, fraternizing with the enemy are you?"

Curt shrugged. "She's a pretty enemy."

"No argument there. See you later."

Curt sat down in the chair across from the desk where Mary was working. She peered over her laptop screen at him.

"You're very quiet," she remarked.

"I didn't want to disturb you while you were working," he replied.

"I'm just rechecking my notes, so that I'll have them in order for court."

"What did this guy do, that you're prosecuting?" he asked.

"He smuggled a bale of marijuana into the county on a truck in between bales of real hay," she said. "He was distributing it to a dozen high school kids for resale when we tipped the DEA boys and they took him down."

"High school kids," he muttered. "Selling drugs, shooting classmates…we live in a crazy world."

"Everybody can tell you why," she said simply. "Too much time unsupervised, too unconnected from their parents, too little natural sunlight, too much time spent at a computer keyboard, video game violence, and the list goes on and on. But nobody has a solution."

He leaned back in the chair and studied her. "Make your kids tell you where they are every minute," he suggested. "Be home when they get home from school. Know who their friends are."

"How many kids do you have?" she asked sarcastically.

"That was my mother's recipe," he said with a smile.

"Obviously, it worked," she had to admit.

"Not really. I found ways to get around her and do what I liked. She was a sound sleeper. I could go out the window after she went to bed, and she never knew. Until I got arrested. I was in the wrong place, at the wrong time—with a group of kids using drugs, that is.'' He grimaced. ''You know what was worse than being arrested? It was having her come to bail me out, and the disappointment in her eyes when she looked at me. I'd let her down. It really hurt her. I never quite got over it.'' He smiled. ''Needless to say, I kept my nose clean forever afterward.''

''I guess so. Your mother's a really nice person,'' she added slowly.

''And you think a bad kid has bad parents, right?''

''Oh, no,'' she said at once. ''That's a naive opinion. Some of the worst lawbreakers have the nicest, most decent parents alive. If a child is inclined to break the law, there really isn't any way to stop him or her. And once they see the consequences, a lot of times they are scared to death and become model citizens.''

''I am living proof that it works,'' he told her with a chuckle.

She grinned. ''I got pulled over for speeding once,'' she volunteered.

''You bad girl.''

''It was the only time I broke the law. My dad grounded me for two months. I missed the junior prom and a date that I wanted more than food. I really learned my lesson.''

''You don't talk about your mother,'' he noted.

Her face grew taut. ''She and I don't speak.''

''Why?''

She stared at her computer screen. ''She left my dad and ran away with her aerobics instructor.''

''Tough.''

"He was one of those health nuts who don't eat real food and spend every spare second exercising. I guess he drove her crazy, because she left him two months later and tried to come back to Dad." Her face hardened. "He wouldn't let her in the door. Neither would I. She moved to California. Last we heard, she was living with a martial arts teacher."

"I'm sorry."

"She wasn't ever much of a mother," she replied coolly. "It was Dad who took me to parties and school dances and track meets. She was never around. She was playing bridge with her friends or working out or traveling somewhere."

"She didn't work?"

"She didn't have to, her parents left her a small fortune," she said coldly. "Dad was never interested in money, although he works hard," she added with obvious pride.

"Do you look like him?"

"Well, I'm not tall, but we have similar coloring," she confessed.

"Is he college-educated?"

She grinned. "Yes, he is. He got his degree about seven years ago. I was so proud of him!"

"I expect you were," he said with a smile.

"She didn't even graduate from high school," she added coldly.

"Maybe education wasn't important to her. It isn't, to some people."

She cocked her head. "It was to you."

He nodded. "My mother worked hard just to get me through school and make sure I had clothes to wear and a house that I wouldn't be ashamed to ask my friends into. When I started college, she helped as much as she could, but I earned most of my tuition by myself. I never failed a course," he added proudly. "Money was hard to come by."

"I felt the same," she said. "Dad helped, of course, but I put myself through college on scholarships and working as an assistant manager at a fast-food place at night."

"Hard work."

"Yes," she said, sharing memories with him. "But I graduated in the top ten percent of my graduating class. Dad was very proud. She didn't even come."

"Did you invite her?" he asked.

She averted her eyes. "Well, no. Because I knew she wouldn't come," she added belligerently.

"How about your ex?" he added.

She chuckled. "We're not *that* friendly," she replied. "I don't think his wife would like it. She's very nice, though."

"Lucky him."

"I'm nice, too," she said. "I can cook. I can even sew a little."

His eyebrows lifted. "Are you auditioning?"

Her eyes slid down to his chest. "You look very good without a shirt," she said outrageously. "And you aren't as stuffy and by-the-book as I thought to begin with. You might have potential."

"As what?" he asked, stonewalled.

"I'll have to think about that," she assured him, and with a secretive little smile, she went back to her laptop.

Curtis Russell, FBI agent, folded his arms across his chest and felt vaguely threatened. In a nice way, of course.

An hour later, Jack was back. He walked into the office, looking disturbed.

"There wasn't a sign of entry or occupation in your barn at all," he said. "Are you sure you saw evidence of a vagrant?" he asked Curt.

Curt didn't protest the question. He just nodded.

"I had the guys go over the place with magnifying glasses. There wasn't a thing. Considering the lack of evidence, how do I justify a stakeout?"

"Good question," Curt had to admit. He stood up with a sigh. "I guess that leaves me. I'll get my black ops outfit out of storage and sit in the woods with the chiggers all night."

"You could have been mistaken," Jack persisted.

"I could. But I'm not," Curt said simply, on the defensive because most of his statements were questioned these days, by the world at large. You make one dumb mistake in your life, he thought silently, and it follows you to the grave!

Jack was watching him. He grimaced. "Okay, Russell, I'll do whatever you want me to do, if you're that sure."

"I'll carry my cell phone out with me. If I call, come running," he added. "That's all I'll ask. Oh, one more thing," he said with a rueful glance. "Tell your boys not to drag me away in handcuffs in case any of the neighbors see me outside and get twitchy. Will you?"

Jack hid a grin. "Okay."

"What about me?" Mary asked.

"You go to bed and dream of brilliant summations," Curt told her. "While the FBI protects you."

"Gosh, lucky me," she drawled.

"Don't start that again, or I'll dribble honey into your bedroom and pour it over your feet. Remember the ants…?"

"You can't threaten women," she pointed out. "It's against the law."

"Who's threatening women? I'm only planning to feed ants."

She glowered at him, but he was already out the door with Jack while she was fumbling with her laptop's power switch.

It wasn't rainy, but the woods were damp at night. Curt was uncomfortable in his bed of leaves, with his cell phone in his pocket and his listening device in one ear. All he heard were crickets. There wasn't even an occasional loud howl from Big Red in his mother's living room. Since last night, the dog had been oddly silent.

When he'd returned home, after being arrested, he'd begged her to phone the pound and have the hairy menace taken away, but she was already attached to the big dog. In fact, she went out later in the day and bought the animal the premium dog chow in defiance.

Curt, taking matters into his own hands, had phoned veterinarians' offices asking about the big dog, but nobody had reported one missing. Probably, he summed up, the previous owner was enjoying his sleep and didn't want the nuisance back again.

After spending the evening fighting for enough space to sit on the sofa, and with a long-suffering sigh, Curt got up to prepare for his evening's work. When he left, Big Red was headed into his mother's room with her. He moved quietly to the dark back door, and went out to play spy.

He was watching the barn covertly, but it was empty and it remained empty. He knew he'd seen sign, positive sign, that the culprit had been skulking around the outbuilding. But he had no proof. And because he'd tipped off the man by alluding to a visit by the police, all the clues had been skillfully lifted.

That caused him to wonder if he had the right man. The potential federal witness, Abe Hunt, was a city boy, born and raised in Miami. He had no background that included outdoor activities, including scouting or other boyhood faculties. So how could a guy like that obliterate signs of his occupation?

There was another curious thing. The man's cousin, who lived down the street, had packed up his wife and kids and left town. Curt had gone by the house tonight, sneaking around its perimeters to make sure the family hadn't vacated it so the cousin could hide out there. But there was no sign whatsoever that anything had been disturbed since the family's abrupt departure.

The barn was empty and it remained empty. Oddly enough, the big dog wasn't howling at the window tonight. Everything was sublimely peaceful. Curt leaned back against a tree with a quiet sigh and watched the night go by.

Four

Curt dragged himself through his mother's back door at daylight, to be met by a wagging tail and a bark from the huge red dog.

"Isn't he sweet?" Matilda asked from the stove, where she was flipping pancakes on a griddle. "Come in and have breakfast, dear. You must be tired."

"Tired and all for nothing," he said, removing the black cap and jerking a paper towel from the roll to wipe off his camouflage paint. "There wasn't a peep out of anybody."

"I noticed. Big Red didn't bark."

He scowled. "Think that's why?"

"Well, he was howling and barking like crazy the night you and Mary got arrested, and you said somebody took food out of her kitchen. He even woke me up, just as they were driving away with you."

"He was outside," he pointed out.

"He was under my bedroom window, dear, where the basement door is," she corrected. "He's very loud."

"Yes, he is. Odd, isn't it, that he was barking there," he said almost to himself.

"Wash your hands, Curt."

He did, absently, at the kitchen sink. "You don't

suppose that our fugitive tried to hide out in our basement while we were tracking him down, do you?'' he asked, to himself.

''We don't lock the door,'' she replied.

''Today, I'm going to get a padlock and put it on,'' he said as he sat down to the table. ''If he did, he won't do it again.''

''Isn't it curious that a fugitive would try to hide out near an FBI agent,'' she mused as she served breakfast.

''I was thinking the same thing. And all the while his cousin lives down the street—when he isn't fleeing the scene—but there are plenty of safer places.''

''Just what I thought.''

After breakfast, and an errand that took him to the hardware store, Curt drove down to the district FBI office in Lanier County to see Hardy Vicks. He arrived just before lunch.

''I've had a wild thought,'' he told his superior.

''Yes?''

Curt leaned back in his chair. ''I'm not going to put it into words until I'm sure. But can you spare me two men for an around-the-clock stakeout?''

The reply was so loud that the secretary stuck her head in the door to see why her boss was laughing his head off.

''Never mind,'' Curt muttered. ''I'll ask the local police or the GBI or the sheriff's department. And if we catch who I think we might catch, the newspapers can give them the credit!''

''Russell, you're always sure you know what's going on," his superior reminded him, "and most of the time you haven't got a clue. You were still chasing down the blonde in San Antonio in that high-profile Texas murder case, when the lieutenant governor's wife was being booked for murder."

"She was a material witness and I caught her," he reminded the other man. "I even managed to have her extradited from South America to stand trial."

His superior's eyebrows rose. "Yes, I suppose you did." He thought for a minute. "Okay, I'll see what I can do about a surveillance unit, since this is a federal case. Where can we put them?"

"In my basement," Curt replied.

"Up to their necks in dirt with the snakes and spiders," the other man exclaimed.

Curt glared at him. "It's a walk-in basement. There's even a billiard table, if they're so inclined."

The other man grinned. "In that case, I might take the assignment myself. I'm partial to billiards."

Curt almost forgot himself and suggested that might be because the older man's head bore a striking resemblance to a cue ball.

"I'll get back in touch. It might take a couple of days, though."

"Okay," Curt said. "Let's hope the fugitive doesn't get spooked and run for it meanwhile."

"That's why we pay you, isn't it, Russell?" he was reminded blithely.

On his way out of the courthouse, Mary Ryan caught up with him. She was wearing a gray pantsuit and looked very professional.

"Any news?" she asked.

"Yes. My boss likes to play billiards," he said irritably.

She chuckled. "So does mine."

"It may take a couple of days to line up a surveillance team," he said impatiently. "But I think our fugitive's likely to take a powder long before then. When the police carried us off, the dog was howling under mother's bedroom window—right where the basement door is."

She whistled. "You think he might have been under your house?"

He nodded. "I went in this morning after breakfast to check it out," he said. "There were no obvious signs, but a couple of books were misplaced and the balls were set up on the billiard table. I always leave them in the pockets."

Her eyes narrowed. "He's blatant, for a fugitive, isn't he?"

He nodded slowly, with his hands in his pockets. "I was thinking that very thing. He acts less like prey than a predator."

"They won't want Abe Hunt to talk," she continued. "He could send his mob bosses to prison with what he knows."

"He could send one of them to his death. And Hunt might not be hiding from us at all," he added for her. "There might be a hit man after him, and that's why he's running scared. He's afraid of someone named Daniels."

She whistled. "Oh, that's just great. I'll sleep so

nicely, knowing there might be a hit man parked in my barn or your basement!''

"It doesn't make me any more comfortable," he told her. "And my mother's in the line of fire, too."

"At least you have the dog," she remarked.

He pursed his lips. "Another odd piece of the puzzle," he agreed. "Where did he come from? Where's his owner? Why is he living with my mother?"

"Because she likes dogs?" she ventured.

"He turned up at a strange time."

She glanced up and down the street. "I'm going to have a nice salad. Care to join me?"

He looked at his watch. "I might as well. By the time I get home, that soup mother promised to save for me will be in the dog."

She laughed delightedly. "Your mother's a character."

"You have no idea. When I was a kid, I never knew where she'd call from to say she was going to be late. Once she was behind a bank of police cars waiting for a sniper to be taken down. Another, she was racing to the scene of a drug-related bombing."

"It sounds like an exciting life."

His dark eyes sparkled as they walked into a nearby café. "It was. She had law-enforcement types around her half the time, men and women. It didn't take much guesswork to understand why she got so many scoops right from under the noses of the other reporters."

"But she retired."

"When I got in my middle teens, I started giving her fits," he confessed. "She gave up a higher-paying job to do feature work so that she'd be around when I needed her. I guess it was a good thing. I was headed straight to hell for a while. No matter how good a mother is, there's no real substitute for a father when boys are involved. That's not a politically correct statement," he added with a long glance. "But it's my opinion."

She smiled sadly. "I can't imagine life without my father."

"I'd like to meet him."

"Would you?" Her eyes brightened.

She was pretty when she was animated. He smiled down at her, and watched her cheeks color just slightly before she moved along in the line with her tray. When she lifted a glass to fill it with ice, there was the nicest little tremor in her long fingers. He felt pleasantly flattered.

Seated at their table, sharing a side order of vegetable chips, they talked about the mob case in Atlanta.

"If there really is a hit man camped out in our neighborhood," she said, "our fugitive must know it. So why is *he* there?"

"That's a question I wish I could answer. I didn't dare tell my boss what I suspected." He grimaced. "I got into some trouble in my last case. They've been giving me grief ever since I joined."

"From what they say at the courthouse, you had some help joining," she fished.

"Yes, from Marc Brannon. He was with them for two years. He's a Texas Ranger. I, uh, sort of worked with him on the Texas murder case. Actually, he's related to the vice president and the state attorney general, too.''

''You pulled strings,'' she guessed.

''It was the only way to get into the Bureau and stay out of prison,'' he chuckled. ''They had to agree that I did a decent job of investigation, just the same. But they think they're punishing me by sticking me up here in north Georgia, away from the action.''

''Seems to me you're right in the middle of the action, if what we're guessing is true,'' she commented.

''Just what I thought. So we have to handle this just right.''

''We?'' she queried, with her tea glass held suspended at her lips.

''I've had assigned partners who were less supportive,'' he pointed out, pursing his lips. ''Besides, you have connections. The police actually like you.''

She grinned. ''I never told you what my dad did for a living, did I?''

He shook his head, entranced.

''He's a cop.''

He chuckled. ''Now, why didn't I guess?''

''He's in administration since he got his degree, but he was a beat cop for years,'' she added. ''I learned a lot just by watching and listening.''

''That's how we all learn.''

''What are you going to do next?''

''I'm going to bug my basement.''

She grinned. ''How exciting! Care to bug my barn, too?''

''I suppose I'll have to, if we expect to catch anybody. None of the higher-ups have much confidence in my suspicions.''

She reached across the table and slid a long-fingered hand over his and smiled. ''You'll show them.''

His heart lifted. She made him feel capable of doing anything. His eyes brightened. ''Thanks.''

She shrugged. ''Sometimes, all it takes is having somebody believe in you,'' she said simply, and let go of his hand. ''I'll help any way I can,'' she added.

''I'll give that some thought,'' he promised.

Curt went back home, irritated with his lack of progress on the job.

His mother was sprawled on the sofa with her laptop while the big dog was lolling on its back on the carpet, sound asleep. It barely opened one drooping eyelid long enough to glance at him before it closed it again.

''Some watchdog,'' he muttered, sitting down across from her in a chair.

''Where have you been?''

''Trying to convince people to believe I'm not an idiot,'' he sighed.

''You're not an idiot, dear.''

''Thanks.''

''Can I help?''

He gave her a long scrutiny. ''Yes. You've had plenty of experience covering murder cases and racketeering. Who do you think is hiding out in Mary Ryan's barn?''

''Abe Hunt, your federal witness who won't testify,'' she replied with a smile. "Is that what your boss won't believe?"

He nodded miserably.

She shrugged and went back to her keyboard. "His misfortune. You catch your witness, dear, and let the others try to excuse their mistakes."

"You sound very confident."

"I raised you to be the best at what you do. And you are." She glanced at him with a whimsical smile. "So why are you sitting here doing nothing?"

He chuckled as he got to his feet. "I'm off to the basement to convert wire and batteries and lights into covert ops material," he remarked, stretching. "Good thing I know electronics."

"And you didn't even want to go to a technical school," she scoffed.

"I only did two semesters," he reminded her. "Just long enough to know that I wasn't cut out for television repair. But I learned how to make listening devices," he added wickedly.

She glared at him. "So I recall."

"I never told anyone except you what I found out," he protested.

"It was still illegal. Imagine, bugging the police chief's office!"

He grinned.

She waved him off without another word.

He didn't tell her that he'd learned most of the craft from an older student who was heavily into covert work, even back then. But he'd paid attention and absorbed all he could, because he figured to do federal law enforcement for a career.

It took most of the afternoon to string the wire—he didn't have the sophisticated bugs that were powered by tiny batteries. But what he had was workable, including a grid-pattern of weight-sensitive devices concocted of cardboard, wire and tape, which would reveal the presence of anybody weighing more than forty pounds. That left out most of the neighborhood dogs. He hooked his device to a central board with small lights and had his mother walk across to Mary's garden, ostensibly to pick a radish, but actually to let him test out his equipment.

Of course, if a hit man was really out there, and watching, he'd know what Curt was up to. But Curt was willing to bet that he was asleep somewhere, so that he'd be sharp and awake that night to continue his surveillance—assuming that Hunt was also going to move around at night.

None of which explained what Hunt was doing in this neighborhood in the first place.

If that was why the hit man was here.

If there was really a hit man.

For the first time, Curt was beginning to doubt his own assumptions. He'd made a lot of stupid mistakes, like not being quick enough to stop the Russian premier from being gored by a Brahma bull at the president's summer home in Texas. A week in the Okefenokee Swamp had cured him of carelessness, but he'd made other mistakes. What if he'd only made assumptions here that weren't true? If he didn't turn up the federal witness he was going to have egg on his face. He was going to be the laughingstock of the whole law enforcement community. He blanched at the thought.

Then he remembered Mary Ryan's words, and the look in her soft eyes when she'd told him she had confidence in him. And then he had his mother walk across Mary's garden, ostensibly to pick a pepper, and his homemade board lit up like a Christmas tree with every step she took. By gosh, he was good, and he was right, and he was going to prove it to those stuffed shirts at headquarters!

Late that afternoon, when Mary got home, he went across in his jeans and T-shirt to talk to her.

They went into her kitchen, but before she said a word, he held up his hand and took an electronic device from his pocket. This was an older one, but it worked just as well as it had when he bought it five years ago. He swept the room for bugs and found none.

"Just to be safe," he assured her, as he put it back in his pocket with a smile. "Be careful when you go out back. I've wired the yard."

She stared at him. "You've what?"

"Wired the yard. I've planted pressure-sensitive devices all the way to the barn and the street..."

"In my tomato plants?" she exclaimed, horrified.

He glowered at her. "Not in your plants. In the weeds. Those yellow things..."

"My marigolds," she wailed. "They're organic pest control!"

"Will you listen?" he asked with pure disgust.

"This is no time to get wild about a few flowers. This device might save your life!"

She took a deep breath. He couldn't be blamed for all her plants. The police department had walked over several while they were searching for footprints out there. "Okay," she said, gritting her teeth.

"When this is all over, we'll go to the garden supply store and I'll buy you ten flats of flowers," he promised.

"I grew these from seed..."

"Don't start that again!"

She put her hands on her hips and glared at him. "You have no idea what a garden represents, do you?" she burst out, furious.

He moved forward, caught her by the waist, swung her against his tall, powerful body, and kissed her fiercely.

She struggled for a few seconds, went still, and then slowly began to lean into him. Her hands rested at his belted waist then slid, caressing, into the small of his back. Her mouth opened under his, and his arms contracted, hard.

It had been a long time since he'd enjoyed kissing a woman so much. He hadn't realized how long it had been until she began protesting his bruising hold.

He lifted his head, dazed, to stare down into her misty eyes.

"You do that very nicely," she commented breathlessly.

"Thanks. So do you."

She searched his dark eyes. He looked back at her with barely contained passion.

"A garden represents the children you don't have," he murmured, watching her swollen lips instead of her shocked eyes. "You have to have something to nurture, so it's vegetables and flowers instead of kids." He kissed her again, hungrily. "You could try nurturing me," he suggested against her mouth. "My mother's tired of dirty socks on the bedroom floor and wet towels under the sink."

She laughed huskily. "You think I'd like wet towels under mine?"

"Why not?" he murmured, kissing her again. "We have similar professions and we're both nice people. We could raise lettuce and hell."

She nibbled on his full lower lip. "I'll think about it."

"You do that. In the meanwhile," he added wryly, moving her gently away from him, "we might get to the matter at hand. Which is, I've bugged your barn and my mother's basement and wired both yards. A dog can't walk around here without setting off alarms."

"How about a cat...or a mouse?" she asked with a pert grin.

He tapped her nose with his forefinger. "Don't make fun of my elaborate preparations. I'm going to catch somebody tonight, even if it's only a Peeping Tom. My reputation's at stake."

"I wouldn't say that," she said with a demure smile.

He grinned from ear to ear.

But although Curt sat in his basement until the wee hours, his board didn't light up. Nothing happened in the neighborhood. The dog slept like the dead beside Matilda Russell's bed.

Curt fell into bed at dawn, so tired and worn-out that he couldn't manage to keep his eyes open. It was early afternoon before he woke up.

He opened his eyes to a wet spot on his bare arm. He rolled over and there he was, the dog, sitting calmly beside the bed, hassling right over Curt's prone body.

"Oh, yuck," Curt muttered, wiping his arm on the sheet. "What's with you?" he demanded.

The dog kept panting. It really looked like he was trying to grin. He was beating time with his large tail at the same time. The *thump-thump-thump* was oddly calming.

With a sigh, Curt reached out a lean hand and rubbed Big Red's head gently. "You're not so bad, I guess...hey, what's this?"

He felt a lump on the clasp of the collar that had gone unnoticed. He sat up, wide-awake now, and unfastened the collar. There was something taped there. He removed the black tape to reveal a thin tube. It twisted open.

"This is a hell of a thing," he muttered to himself. He pulled out a thin roll of paper with writing on it.

"Curt, I've got lunch, dear!" his mother called from the kitchen. "Are you awake?"

"I'm awake!"

He opened the paper and looked at it with mounting curiosity. There were letters and numbers on it, but in no sort of order. It was like a code.

He got out of bed, securing the tube back on the dog's tossing neck as he protested the motions of Curt's hands.

"Found something," Curt told his mother as he strolled into the kitchen. He'd already swept it for bugs the night before, and he was certain they weren't being overheard. "Look at this."

He handed her the paper. She studied it with narrowed, intelligent eyes and handed it back. "Code?" she asked aloud.

He studied the numbers again. "Yes," he said. "It makes some sort of sense, but I can't untangle it."

"Where did you find it?" she asked.

"In a little tube taped under your new pet's collar," he told her. "And it looks as if it's been there for a while." He was worried. "What if the federal witness was trying to get in touch with me, and the dog was his messenger? I've blown days, because I didn't understand why the dog was here!" he exploded.

"None of us would have thought of looking for a message on a dog, dear," Matilda told him with an amused smile. "Sit down and have lunch. We'll look this over some more. Hear anything last night?" she added.

He shook his head. "It was as quiet as a church on Monday," he murmured, accepting a cup of hot coffee from his mother. "No lights, no sound, no nothing. It's the damnedest thing. I know somebody was hiding out in Mary's barn. I'm almost positive we had somebody in our basement. But everybody vanished.

Including Hunt's cousin, who left fire trails getting out of the neighborhood.''

"The cousins are back."

"What?"

"They drove by while I was having breakfast this morning," she said easily. "I watched them get out of the car. It was just him and her and their two kids, the boy and the girl."

"Nobody else?" he asked suspiciously.

She shook her head. "I kept a fairly decent watch on the station wagon, just to make sure nobody crawled out of it," she added. "But I didn't see a soul."

"Maybe they helped Hunt to go somewhere and then left him," he was thinking out loud. "That would explain the lack of activity."

"It would," she had to confess. "But what is that message all about?" she added, indicating the slip of paper in his hand.

He grimaced. "I don't know. The letters and numbers are jumbled, but even so, they make sense. It isn't a combination," he added absently, studying them. "Or a locker number, of any sort I recognize."

"Coordinates?" she suggested.

He shook his head. "Not possible."

"Read them to me."

"LPST23LBSDB129," he murmured. He shook his head. "See? No sense."

"Was there anything else in the tube?" she pondered.

"A piece of brown paper, apparently put there to hide this little slip of white paper...wait a minute!"

He got up and ran down the dog, who was wolfing down water. "Sorry, guy," he murmured as he untwisted the tube again. He opened it and had to use a car key to extricate the stiff little tube of brown paper that was concealed. He replaced the tube, stood up, and unfolded the stiff tube.

"Eureka!" he exploded.

Five

Curt barely took time to explain his find to his mother and put on his clothes before he rushed out to the car and drove himself, at unlucky speeds, to the courthouse in Lanier County.

Fortunately, Mary's court case had concluded early with a quick verdict. She was shuffling papers in the courtroom when Curt burst in.

"I need you," he said, barely giving her time to gather her briefcase before he took her hand and tugged her out of the courtroom and right out of the building.

"But I have to see the court clerk," she protested.

"You can phone and get your assistant to do it. We've got a break!" He put her into his car, got in, started it, and handed her the folded slip of brown paper.

"It's a pawn ticket!" she exclaimed.

"Yes! I've got something else, too." He fumbled in his pocket and handed her the jumble of letters. "Can you make out the code from what you've got in your hand?" he challenged, having already made the connections himself.

"Yes. Let's see… It's the Lanier Pawn Shop, this is the ticket, then there's another set of letters and numbers…'' Her head came up. ''If I'm right, this is a pawn ticket for a safe-deposit box key, which is located at the Lanier City Bank!''

He grinned. ''Sharp girl.''

''What do you think it is?'' she exclaimed.

''I have no idea. But with any luck, it's something concrete that will prove Hunt's mob boss committed murder to stop an investigation.''

She was as excited as he was now. They rushed into the pawn shop with the ticket. As they expected, they received a safe-deposit box key from the clerk at the shop. They then sped to the bank. They produced credentials and still had to get the bank president to preside over the opening of the safe-deposit box.

But when they inserted their key, there was a surprise waiting. The key didn't work.

''How can that be?'' Curt exploded. ''This is the right number. It's the right key!''

The bank president was scratching his head when the young woman who had been standing uncomfortably behind them spoke up tremulously.

''It wasn't my fault, sir,'' she moaned. ''They had credentials, too. They said they were from the Justice Department. They had the box drilled and the contents removed, and then we had to have the lock changed…''

The bank president was livid. ''You didn't say anything about this, Miss Davis!''

''Sir, I told my supervisor. You've been out of town,'' she added defensively. ''It was three days ago!''

Curt cursed under his breath. There went his evidence.

"We can have the box drilled again," the bank president said, disturbed.

"Don't bother," Curt replied quietly. "By now, every piece of evidence in it is gone. We've been beaten to the punch, royally. But thanks for your help."

"Damn the luck!" he exploded when they were driving back to the courthouse. "If I'd just examined the dog three days ago!"

"Who would have expected a stray dog to carry evidence of a crime?" she comforted him. "You're not superhuman, you know."

He grimaced. "I could kick myself. The evidence is gone, the witness is gone, and I'm in the doghouse again."

"I didn't see any other federal agents doing much better," she pointed out. "At least you've been trying!"

"For all the good it did me. I've been up all night staking out the neighborhood, and I have nothing to show for it. Except a few dead marigolds," he added with a rueful smile.

"I've got plenty left," she assured him. "Don't beat yourself to death over it. I could make supper for you tonight," she added. "Then we could go and play billiards in your basement. I love billiards."

"You do?"

She grinned. "My girlfriend and I used to be the terrors of the tables when we were in college."

He sighed. "That would make a nice end to the day. Something to actually look forward to," he added with a slow smile. "Thanks."

She shrugged. "What are friends for?" she asked, and she smiled back.

In the end, Mrs. Russell cooked for all of them. Over ham and potato salad with Matilda Russell's homemade bread, they had a lively discussion about the criminal justice system and the excesses of the twenty-four-hour news stations.

Afterward, leaving the dog with his mother, Curt led the way down to the basement and racked the balls on the billiard table.

"I never asked," he murmured. "Did you win your case?"

"Not my most recent one," she replied with a tiny smile. "I fought hard, but the jury didn't believe the poor man would do something so dishonest as to get his neighbor drunk and steal his land. However, I did win the one over the drug traffickers." She shrugged. "You win some, you lose some. That's life."

He let her go first. He was sorry when she cleared the table with expertise. He chuckled as he racked the balls again and cleared it himself.

Neck and neck, they shot for points until it grew late.

"I'm having a very good time," she said finally, "but I have a meeting at nine tomorrow morning. I'm going to have to...Curt?"

"Hmm?" he murmured, nudging balls into pockets to clear the table.

"What are those lights?"

He turned, only half concentrating on what she was saying. Then he noticed where her eyes were, and his heart stopped and started again. It was his board, the one he'd made and forgotten in the disappointment over the safe-deposit box. The grid pattern in Mary's garden was lighting up like a holiday ship making port.

"Somebody's in your barn again!" he exclaimed.

"How do you know?"

He explained, briefly, the grid pattern and how it worked. "See? He's just gone into the barn. We've got him!"

She gaped at him. "You're going in there all by yourself, huh?"

He went to the coat stand where he'd hung his shoulder holster without a word. He whipped it around his chest and checked his .45 automatic. His dark, serious eyes met hers. "This is where you go upstairs and phone Jack. Have him get in touch with Hardy Vicks. I don't care if he has to be dragged out of bed. I need backup."

She swallowed. "My dad taught me how to shoot."

He smiled gently, taking her by the arms and bending to kiss her with fierce delight. "I wouldn't risk you for all the tea in China, sweetheart," he whispered, and kissed her again when she smiled up at him.

"Don't get shot," she admonished firmly.

His eyebrows lifted. "I wouldn't dare. Go on."

She went up the inside staircase and he turned off

the lights. A minute later, he eased out the door, and the genial man of minutes before was eclipsed by a trained federal officer with nerves of steel and years of experience in risky situations.

There was, fortunately, enough cover to keep him hidden. He moved from his mother's backyard, past the carport, past the house next door, behind its carport, and into the small thicket of hedge bushes that led to the street. The view from Mary's barn was hidden by a growth of dogwood trees and boxwood shrubs, so he was able to duck and slide across the paved street. But then it was a matter of waiting for noise to camouflage his footsteps.

He waited until the sudden loud roar of a truck going along the highway a few hundred yards away disguised his movements. He rushed to the side of the barn, drew his weapon, took off the safety, and waited for another noise.

It wasn't long in coming. He heard a soft, whispery movement from inside the barn, as if someone was leaning against a wall.

His heart was rushing in his chest. It sounded loud enough that it could be heard a block away, although he knew it couldn't. He closed his eyes to concentrate on what he could hear.

The whispery sound came again. There was a flicker of movement, barely audible at all.

Curt had been shot once, early in his career. It had been a shoulder wound in a shootout with racketeers in New York City. It was the worst possible time to remember how much it had hurt. He couldn't think about pain. He had to think about his mother and even Mary.

He took two quick breaths when he heard the approaching echo of another big truck. *It's now or never, Russell,* he told himself firmly. He set his lips, took another breath, and rushed into the barn.

A big, heavyset man with wavy black hair gasped and threw up his hands in the bare gleam of light from the streetlight—the one that worked—nearby.

"Don't shoot!" the man squeaked.

Curt's blood was pumping madly. He had the pistol leveled at the man's gut. "Federal agent," he clipped. "Identify yourself!"

"Abe...Abe Hunt!"

Curt frowned. "Hunt?"

"Ye...yeah! Could you, uh, put that thing down?" he stammered, indicating the pistol with a nod.

Curt lowered it with a curse. "You idiot! I could have shot you! *What the hell are you doing in here?*"

"Trying to outrun Daniels," Hunt groaned, looking around wildly as he went toward Curt. "Man, you are slow as Methuselah! Didn't you get the message? I sent the dog...!"

Curt wasn't touching that. "Where have you been for the past few days?" he demanded. "You weren't here! The damned dog hasn't made a peep. Well, until now," he added, as the dog suddenly began to bay and howl so loudly that he could be heard even through the walls of Matilda Russell's living room.

"Oh, my God!" Hunt exclaimed. "It's him! It's Daniels! Redbone smells him...!"

Curt wasn't going to ask how the dog could smell

a man through a house. He'd seen bloodhounds track people in cars. Sloughed off skin was detectable even from the open window of a moving car, although most people wouldn't have believed it.

''Get down!'' Curt yelled, pushing Hunt ahead of him to the floor of the barn. It was dusty and dirty and, above all, safe. For the moment at least.

Hunt started to speak, but Curt snapped a faint blow against his arm, silencing him.

His eyes were growing used to the dark. His heartbeat was deafening him, but he knew his capabilities. If he could get a glimpse of their stalker, he could drop him. He was an expert marksman. Of course, there were other dangers—for instance, the man, Daniels, could just set fire to the barn and end the standoff. Old, dry, full of combustible material, it would go up in seconds with both men trapped inside.

Curt lay listening. If the man struck a match, in the silence unbroken except by the howling dog, he could hear it. He'd try shooting right through the walls if he had to. But he didn't hear a match.

He did hear a faint footfall, barely an echo of a leaf crunching. He closed his eyes, aware of Hunt's strained, loud breathing next to him. He jabbed the man again and made a motion with his finger to his lips. Hunt's breathing quieted.

Curt listened, cursing now the sound of another heavy truck passing within earshot, because it masked closer sounds.

Hunt was still alive. The hit man might have regained any evidence that Hunt could have used to convict the mob boss, but Hunt himself was the nail in the man's coffin. The hit man would go to any lengths to silence that voice, and Curt knew it.

He had to protect Hunt, no matter what the cost.

He waited in the semidarkness, his body tensed for action, his ears peeled, his every reflex honed to its finest edge.

But when the attack came, it was from a totally unexpected source. Only a faint creak heralded it.

It was enough. Curt rolled onto his back and fired over his head, at the hayloft where nothing was visible.

"You idiot, what are you shooting...look out!" Hunt yelled, and rolled quickly out of the way.

As he spoke, a dark form came hurtling down with the sound of automatic weapon fire bursting on the silence only for precious seconds.

Curt felt a stab in his arm as he fired again and again. There was a loud grunt and then the dark form crumpled. The weapon fire ceased.

Almost simultaneously, sirens burst on the silence.

"You okay?" Curt asked Hunt, who was dragging himself to his feet with his hands at his throat.

"Yeah," the man managed to say. "You?"

Curt wasn't sure about that. He didn't take time to check. He moved to the downed man, pushed him over quickly with the pistol leveled at his chest. An automatic weapon was held in a still hand. There was a dark stain on the man's suit front. He wasn't moving.

Curt bent, amazed at how painful the movement was, and dragged the automatic weapon from the man's clenched fingers, before he tossed it out of reach, just in case.

"Thanks, man, you saved my skin!" Hunt exclaimed. "Hey, you're bleeding…!"

Curt fell to his knees. It should be hurting, he thought dimly. His arm felt heavy. It felt wet, too. He had another pain, lower down, in his side.

"Russell! Russell, you in there?" came a familiar loud voice.

"Jack," he whispered. He couldn't talk louder. Funny.

"He's hurt! Come on in!" Hunt yelled, bending over Curt to keep him from toppling headfirst.

There were running footsteps, the sound of bolts being thrown on weapons, the clank of equipment.

"Curt!" Mary Ryan exclaimed.

"Miss Ryan, you shouldn't…!" the police chief protested.

It did no good. She was right beside Curt, checking him with trembling hands, touching him.

"He's been shot. Twice I think," she said quickly. "Where are the paramedics?"

"Right behind us," one of the SWAT team members volunteered. "Hurry it up, guys!" he called to two men with a stretcher.

"That's Erskine Daniels," Hunt was telling the policemen, pointing to the downed man, who was in bad shape, but still alive. "I'm a federal witness, Abe Hunt. I know plenty about the trial that's going on in Atlanta. I saw the head boss pop another potential witness and dump him in the Chattahoochee. You get me to a safe place, and I'll sing like a bird! But fix that guy first, will you?'' he added, nodding toward Curt. "He saved my life!''

"We'll fix him,'' one of the paramedics promised, working in the spreading light held by a police officer. "He's been hit twice, once in the shoulder and once in the side, but I think he's going to be fine.''

"Oh, thank God,'' Mary Ryan moaned.

There was a howl and another howl, and Matilda Russell walked into the barn.

The police chief threw up his hands. "This is my crime scene!'' he yelled.

Matilda just smiled at him and walked right to her son, kneeling. "My poor boy,'' she said, touching his cold face. "You'll be fine, son. Just fine! Can we get you anything?'' she added, ignoring the paramedics and the cursing police chief.

But Curt was drifting away into merciful unconsciousness in a wave of nausea.

Beside him, the big red dog was licking his face.

"Redbone, you big dope,'' Abe Hunt exclaimed on a chuckle. "I send you out with a message that might save me, and what do you do? You move in with strangers and forget me!''

"Is he yours?'' Matilda Russell asked quickly.

Hunt nodded. "He was,'' he added ruefully. "I guess I can't take him with me where I'll be going. Right, guys?'' he asked a newcomer to the scene, Hardy Vicks from the FBI.

"That's right,'' the older man agreed. "Damn, that's Russell!'' he exclaimed when he saw Curt on the floor. "Is he dead?'' he asked quickly.

"Of course he's not dead!'' his mother huffed.

"He's my son. He's a Russell. You'd have to put a stake through his heart first. These are just itty-bitty flesh wounds."

"You'd know, I guess," Vicks muttered sarcastically.

"I was a reporter. I was actually shot covering a riot in Atlanta," Mrs. Russell told him haughtily. "Took two bullets, right through the upper leg. Missed the bone by half a centimeter."

He was impressed. He moved closer. "You his mother, you said?" he asked.

"I am."

He studied her closely. "He's not bad," he murmured, sparing Curt a glance as Mary Ryan walked beside the stretcher the paramedics were rolling him out on. "I have to admit I'm impressed. He took down a hit man and saved a government witness all by himself, from what the policemen told me."

"He did," Matilda agreed. She studied the taller man. He was about her age. Bald, but that wasn't a bad thing. She found bald men rather sexy. She smiled. "I don't suppose you'd give an old lady a ride to the hospital? Mary will go with him in the ambulance. There won't be room."

"It would be my pleasure!" he replied. "But I don't see any old ladies," he added gallantly. "I'm divorced. You got a husband somewhere?"

She shook her head. "I was widowed years ago."

He smiled. "I was shot once, too."

She smiled, glancing worriedly at her son as they moved him. "I need to get to the hospital. But I have to do something about the dog," she murmured vaguely, glancing at Abe Hunt.

"You can keep him," Abe Hunt said with a grin. "I'd like knowing he had a good home."

"Thank you, Mr....?"

"Hunt," he volunteered. "Abe Hunt. And if you ever need anything, anything at all, you just let that guy know," he indicated Special Agent in Charge, Vicks. "He can get word to me. I know people all over."

Matilda had visions of a strange man appearing at her door with a baseball bat offering to break legs of potential abusers. She cleared her throat. "Thanks, Mr. Hunt. I'll take good care of your dog."

"He's sorta stupid, but he's got a good heart." He bent to pet the dog before he was led away by two men who had accompanied the SAC.

"Come on, Big Red," Matilda told the big dog, tugging at his lead.

"Here, let me do that. He's a handful for a dainty little woman like you," Vicks offered, taking the leash. "I hear you have a billiard table!"

Curt woke up hours later in pain. He opened his eyes. His mother and Mary Ryan were sitting beside the bed talking animatedly.

"He has cousins in Cordele," Matilda remarked, "where my uncle lives. Imagine that! And he loves billiards. I invited him over for supper Friday night. Curt will be out of the hospital by then. You can come, too, dear, and I'll make some more rolls."

"I'd enjoy that," Mary replied.

"Who has...cousins in Cordele?" Curt managed in a hoarse whisper.

"Why, your boss, dear, Special Agent in Charge, Hardy Vicks. I was very impressed with him," she added. "He said you did a great job."

"He has an ulterior motive. He likes billiards," Curt murmured with all the humor he could muster, then he groaned. "Hurts."

"That thing injects painkillers automatically," his mother said, indicating the IV that was pumping fluids into him through complicated electronic machinery. "It should start working pretty soon."

He sighed heavily. His arm felt strange. His belly hurt.

"Don't pull at that IV," Mary said, laying a gentle hand on his arm. "Just be still and ride it out. You'll be home before you know it."

He opened his eyes and looked up at her with a faint smile. "I got shot."

She shrugged. "Nobody's perfect. You saved Mr. Hunt. The hit man was wanted for at least two murders." Her dark eyes narrowed. "He would have killed you and Mr. Hunt if you hadn't had good hearing. He was waiting in the loft. Just waiting. He knew Hunt would be back. The only loved ones Hunt has in the world are his cousin and that big red dog. Hunt told us he couldn't leave them. Turns out Hunt was hiding out in the barn not only trying to protect himself from the hit man but trying to protect his cousin as well. And that's what Daniels was betting on." She closed her eyes for a moment. "He would have killed you," she repeated.

Curt caught her soft hand in his and held it tight. "It wasn't my time," he said huskily.

"I'm glad," she replied, her heart in her eyes.

"Mary's coming to supper Friday," Matilda remarked, delighted at their apparent closeness. "So is Agent Vicks," she reminded them.

"We can play billiards," Mary offered.

He glared up at her. "You can play billiards while I watch," he corrected. "I'll give you some pointers. I want you to beat the pants off Vicks. He thinks I'm an idiot."

"He does not," Matilda said smugly. "In fact, he's given you a glowing report and recommended you for promotion."

Mary looked worried. "Yes, he said something about them giving you a much better position in a big city."

He was barely lucid, but he heard the disappointment in her tone. "Honey, there are plenty of jobs for assistant prosecutors in cities all over the country," he said comfortingly.

"Yes, but I work in Lanier County," she moaned.

He linked his fingers with hers and closed his eyes. "We'll talk about it when I get out of here. I'm so sleepy…"

He drifted off again, still holding Mary's hand tight.

Matilda gave her a curious, but approving, glance. "I think he's making plans."

Mary smiled slowly. "I wouldn't mind."

"He's a good son. He'll make a wonderful husband."

"He might not have that in mind," Mary reminded her.

Matilda only smiled.

Several days later, Curt was bandaged and stitched and lounging around his mother's living room with the big dog at his feet.

"Imagine sending evidence through a dog," he remarked to the people sharing the room with him.

"It was a good idea," Vicks said lazily, drinking coffee on the sofa after a big meal. "But nobody would expect a dog to be carrying secrets. It's like those message tubes they tied to homing pigeons during World War I."

"They actually awarded a medal to a pigeon in France," Matilda volunteered. "He carried a message that kept American troops from firing on a position until the French could pull back their men."

"She's full of little facts like that," Curt teased her.

"You should write a book," Agent Vicks told her. "All that trivia and no place for it in nonfiction articles."

"A book," she mused.

"Sure!" Vicks put down his coffee cup. "I know this guy who used to work for Interpol," he added. "He told me about a slave racket on the coast of West Africa where a blond white woman would sell for half a million dollars back in the twenties."

"Oh, that would sell fiction," Curt said sarcastically.

"Remember *The Sheik* back in the twenties, and Rudolph Valentino?" his mother replied.

"Before my time," he drawled.

"Before mine, too, thank you very much, but it made exciting reading," Matilda mused. "I'd like to hear some more about that."

"I'm at your service. Uh, about that billiard table," he added, rising.

Matilda chuckled. "Come along. I wield a mean cue stick, though," she warned.

"Oh, I like a woman who can use a stick," Vicks replied with a chuckle.

They excused themselves and went down to the basement.

Curt was watching Mary quietly, and without smiling. She sat stiffly in a big armchair, trying not to look as uncomfortable as she felt.

"Well, it's all over now except the trial," she said. "I guess I won't have a part in that, because it will be a federal case. But I'd really like to be in the audience..."

"Mary," he said softly.

She stopped in midspate and lifted both eyebrows.

"Come here."

Six

Mary just sat and stared at him. She was a modern woman. She didn't answer to commands. She didn't do what she was told.

He smiled slowly, his dark eyes twinkling. "Come on."

She got up without understanding why, and went to him.

He drew her down gently against him, wincing as he moved to position her cheek against the shoulder that didn't have a bullet wound.

"It will take a little work," he murmured as he bent, "but we'll get the hang of it…"

His mouth covered hers. She touched his cheek while he kissed her. She smiled under the warm, hard crush of his lips. It was like coming home. She'd been worried about him during his hospital stay, although she'd tried not to let it show. Now that she knew he would recover, the relief made her reckless.

He eased her down on the sofa, overcome by her response and his hunger. It had been a long, long time since he'd wanted a woman so much.

But the pain of the wounds was inhibiting. He groaned and his mouth found its way to her soft breast through the fabric covering them. He rested there with a husky laugh.

"I can't," he whispered. "I want to, you don't know how much! But it hurts too much."

She sighed and stretched and relaxed under the warm, hard press of his body. "I'm not in a hurry. Are you?" she teased.

He looked down at her with real emotion. He touched her soft mouth and studied her intently. "I don't do affairs. My mother raised me very strictly."

"My father raised me very strictly, too," she replied with a smile. "I guess that means we can't have sex on your mother's sofa."

He nodded.

"I have a sofa."

He grinned. "As you said, we're not in a hurry." He bent again and kissed her gently. "And I'm now officially on sick leave."

"Are you saying something?"

"Yes. We can get to know each other."

"That might be fun."

"Indeed it might." He bent again. He kissed her hungrily, only barely noticing the pressure against his side until it got wet.

"Am I bleeding?" he murmured against her mouth.

He lifted up and she looked over. There he sat. The dog. Drooling on Curt's hip.

"We have got to do something about that dog," Curt muttered as the dog grinned at him.

"I have an idea," Mary replied, but she wouldn't say what it was. Not then, at least.

*   *   *

Three months later, during a hiatus from Curt's new duties working out of the Atlanta FBI office at the Richard Russell Federal Building, he and Mary Ryan were married at a small but simple ceremony in Lulaville. The police and the SWAT team turned out, along with the Lanier County courthouse staff and the local FBI office. In fact, Hardy Vicks sat with the family, very close to Matilda Russell, who looked younger and happier than her son had seen her in years.

The dog, decked out in flowers, sat in front of the church with one of the ushers and was hustled into Agent Vicks's sports utility vehicle, along with Matilda Russell, after the service.

"They wanted us to go to a reception," Curt told Mary with a husky chuckle. "But I told them we had to rush to catch a plane."

"Do we?" she asked, close beside him in the front seat of his dark sedan.

"In a manner of speaking," he replied, driving faster.

Barely forty-five minutes later, Curt checked them into one of the fanciest hotels in the northeastern metro of Atlanta. Uniformed porters met them at the door to take their luggage while a valet parked the car.

"We have reservations," he told the clerk with a sly grin at Mary, who gave him a wide-eyed stare. "Mr. and Mrs. Curtis Russell," he added.

"Yes, sir," the clerk replied with a pleasant smile

and a meaningful glance. "Uh, congratulations, by the way."

"Thanks," Curt replied, glancing at his beaming bride.

Once they were registered, the bellhop followed right along with their luggage on a tall cart. As they went down the hall to the bank of elevators, the sound of loud singing came from the balcony above.

"The marines landed last night," the bellhop told them. "They, uh, like to sing the song. Anybody who gets in the elevator with them gets to sing it, too."

Mary burst out laughing. "You're kidding!"

The elevator door opened and two marines, one male and one female, both sergeants, turned to look over the new arrivals.

Curt held Mary's hand reassuringly as the doors closed.

"We like to sing," the male marine said.

"Very much," the female sergeant agreed, moving closer. She was easily six feet tall.

"Now, isn't that a coincidence?" Mary asked, nodding. "I like to sing, too!" And she immediately launched into "Over hill, over dale, over trusty mountain trail...!"

"No," the male marine said at once, shaking his head. "No, no, no, that's the *army* song. You have to sing *our* song."

She stared up at him. "I just got married. Can we sing the 'Wedding March' instead?"

Before the words were out, the elevator paused on the next floor, the door opened, and four more marines crowded onto it, making barely enough space to breathe for all the occupants and the luggage carrier and the bellboy.

"She just got married," the female sergeant said loudly. "She says she wants to sing the 'Wedding Song'!"

The new arrivals blinked. They were both holding thick short glasses with barely an inch of liquid left. They grinned.

"Okay!" one of them agreed. "Let's go, marines! Da da da DUM, DA da da DUM..." He stopped and blinked at the others. "What are the words?"

"Never mind," Curt said, shaking his head. "It's better your way. Come on, sweetheart, let's sing the marine song." He raised his voice. "From the halls of MontezuuuuuUHma...!"

Hands went over ears. Buttons were pressed. The elevator stopped and disgorged almost an entire company of marines.

"Please," the female sergeant pleaded. "Don't *ever* sing our song again...!"

The elevator doors closed on the plea.

Curt burst out laughing. After a minute, so did Mary and the bellhop.

The bellhop opened the curtains, pointed out the wet bar, whirlpool bath and the closets and left with a nice tip.

Curt locked the door behind him, turned around, and pursed his lips as he studied his pretty new wife in her nice oyster-white suit.

"Reservations in the nicest hotel in the metro area," she murmured with a beaming smile. "You sweetheart, you!"

"Nothing's too good for my best girl," he said gently, walking toward her. "You were the prettiest bride in Georgia, and I love you to distraction."

"I love you, too," she admitted, linking her arms around his neck. She sighed. "Thank God you didn't go out in a hail of bullets. I'm so glad you've recovered with no residual damage. It was a wonderful wedding ceremony. And now, here we are, all alone together with no pending court cases and no fugitives to pursue." She sighed again, although her expression was mischievous. "What *shall* we do with the rest of the day…?"

His hard lips cut her off. He kissed her hungrily. Their courtship had been, largely, an old-fashioned one. It had been, as the saying went, a long, dry spell.

Her lips parted eagerly. She reached up to hold him, feeling his body tauten with desire as she answered his long, slow kisses.

The teasing stopped suddenly as he lifted her and carried her to the big, king-size bed. In between warm, lingering kisses, he got rid of the obstacles, including the ankle gun he was never without.

"You wore a gun on our honeymoon?" she exclaimed, sitting up.

He pushed her back down again. "It's a precaution."

"Against what, for God's sake?"

"Intruders singing the marine hymn…come back here!"

He turned her, and his mouth found all the warm, soft, secret places, making her body sing with delight. He liked the husky little sounds she made when his mouth covered her breasts and suckled them. He liked the way her long, elegant legs wrapped around the back of his, the way her body lifted to tempt him into intimacy.

He wanted to take forever, but he was too hungry. His hands moved into more delicate persuasion, and she moved quickly to accommodate him. His mouth ground into hers as he possessed her, feeling her body ripple, feeling the faint hesitation as she accepted him.

"It's been...a long time," she groaned.

"You were married," he whispered gruffly.

"I was married when I was eighteen."

"Right."

"I was also divorced when I was eighteen."

"So?"

"Are you really that thick?" she exclaimed, lifting in a sudden high arch when his mouth touched her in an unexpected place.

The thought suddenly got through to him. He lifted his head fractionally to meet her shy eyes. "You mean, you haven't, since you were eighteen?!"

"I'm old-fashioned," she replied.

He let out a ragged breath. "I love old-fashioned women," he murmured, his eyes alive with feeling as they searched hers. His hips moved abruptly, and he smiled at her expression. "How old was he?"

She swallowed. "Eighteen."

His body poised. "Eighteen."

"And I was his first girl."

He looked as if he'd swallowed the pillow. "Oh."

She moved experimentally. "Neither of us knew much, and I didn't like it much, so I didn't really miss it when we separated." She moved again, gasping. "But I like it...with you. I love it with you!" Her nails scored gently down his back. "Could you do that again, what you did when I gasped?"

"You haven't stopped gasping," he pointed out. "Not that I'm complaining!" No kidding. It would take a mortician half a day to get the smile off his face if he died right now. He moved away a little. "Okay. Is *this* what you want me to do...?"

She really gasped then, and her hands became frenzied, holding on to him wherever she could reach while he taught her new ways to experience sensation. Somewhere in the middle of the lesson, it became fierce and urgent. She reached up toward him and felt her body explode into little tiny bits of flame. She sobbed endlessly, clinging, until she slowly became aware of the man straining against her in rough shudders, his breath jerking out breathlessly at her ear.

Minutes later, the ceiling came slowly into focus above her. She felt drained, sensuously exhausted, and very proud of herself. Apparently, she was damned good at this, a natural, because he'd certainly enjoyed it. She could tell, even if she didn't have a lot of experience.

"I may give up law and do this from now on," she murmured with her eyes closed. "I have definite potential!"

He chuckled. "You can pin a rose on that!"

She rubbed one leg slowly against his. "You have definite potential, too," she said sensually. "Maybe we can stretch our honeymoon out by another four or five months?"

He laughed out loud. "Now, that's what I call incentive!"

She rolled onto his chest and kissed him softly. "I want to keep the dog."

It was the last thing he expected to hear. His eyes almost popped. "You what?"

"I want to keep Big Red. Your mom doesn't really have room for him, but we could live in my house and fence in the yard and the garden, and he could have lots of space to run."

"Oh, no. Not the dog. Not that dog…!"

"Please?" she murmured, kissing his chest. "Pretty please?" She kissed a hard nipple and started sucking on it gently. He was lifting up, and breathing hard, and even gasping by now. "Pretty please with sugar on it…?"

"Okay, you can have the dog. That, and anything else you want," he choked as he moved over her with intent. "Anything!"

"The dog," she agreed, reaching up to kiss him as he moved into possession. "And one…more…thing."

"What?" he panted.

"Don't ever…sing…the marine song again."

"Don't…?"

But she kissed him passionately and he stopped thinking or talking, in that order.

* * *

Three hours later, they lay sprawled together, totally exhausted and almost asleep. "You said we were rushing to catch a plane," she reminded him with a grin. "What a fast plane it was!"

"Very high-flying, too," he murmured with a weary chuckle. He pulled her close and kissed her with his last ounce of strength. "Next time, we try for the sound barrier."

"Next time," she agreed, closing her eyes.

He was almost asleep when the phone rang.

He picked it up, murmuring into the receiver. "Ummmhmmm," he said. "Ummhmmm. Ummh… what?" He sat straight up in bed. "You're kidding!"

Mary opened her eyes and watched him react to what was obviously shocking news. He spoke in monosyllables, finally laughing and wishing the other person luck and promising to speak to them later.

He hung up the phone and lay back down, looking astonished.

"What's wrong?" Mary asked gently, leaning over him to trace patterns in the hair on his chest.

"They didn't want to waste the minister and the decorations in the church," he said, dazed. "There was an audience, too. So they went ahead."

"They who?"

"My mother and Agent Vicks," he said on a sigh. "They got married!"

"They did!" she exclaimed, wide-eyed.

"I guess there are worse things than having two FBI agents in the same family," he said, glancing up at her.

She looked uneasy.

"Yes?" he prompted.

"You know Dad couldn't come for the wedding, even though he sent us that nice tape of congratulations," she offered.

"Yes."

She cleared her throat. "He's in Virginia."

"In Virginia."

She nodded.

He frowned. "Where in Virginia?"

"I think they call it Quantico?"

"No. Oh, no. No!"

She grimaced. "He's been in law enforcement his whole life. Now he has a son-in-law in the FBI. He just wants to keep it in the family."

"He's joined the FBI!" he exclaimed.

She bent closer. "Well, yes. So now it's really an agency family, isn't it?" She wiggled her toes and smiled as she put her mouth gently over hers. "And just yesterday, I got an application form...!"

He rolled her over and moved closer with intent. "I don't want to hear it," he told her. "Not another word."

"But, Curt," she teased, big brown eyes twinkling with humor.

"We'll catch 'em, you prosecute 'em. Deal?" he teased back.

She chuckled. "I was only kidding," she confessed. "But you have to admit, it would be the story of the century."

"We'll have a bigger one, you wait and see."

* * *

And they did. Twenty-five years later, their two sons and their daughter were all three inducted into the FBI as special agents on the same day, with their proud parents, and grandparents, for witnesses.

* * * * *

Coming soon from MIRA Books, watch for

DESPERADO

by international bestselling author
Diana Palmer

Cord Romero's sizzling adventure unfolds in a searing, explosive story where one man and one woman confront their splintered pasts and walk a precarious tightrope between life and death.

This long-awaited tale will be available in a special hardcover edition in July 2002 wherever MIRA Books are sold!

This deeply moving novel proves once again that nobody tells women's stories better than Debbie Macomber!

DEBBIE MACOMBER

BETWEEN FRIENDS

Debbie Macomber tells the story of a remarkable friendship—a story in which every woman will recognize herself...and her best friend.

The friendship between Jillian and Lesley begins in the postwar era of the 1950s and lasts to the present day. In this novel, Debbie Macomber uses letters and diaries to reveal the lives of two women, to show us the laughter and the tears *between friends*.

Available the first week of June 2002
wherever fine hardcover books are sold!

MIRA®

MDM905

JOAN JOHNSTON

The Hazard-Allistair feud had endured for generations—and after meeting proud, stubborn Harriet Allistair, Nathan Hazard could see why. Harriet had come west to Montana, convinced that inheriting her uncle's farm offered the chance to prove herself to her family—and most importantly, to herself.

From his neighboring ranch, Nathan is counting the minutes till frustration and desperation drive her off "his" family's land. But what he hasn't counted on is an "Allistair"—least of all, newcomer Harriet—getting under his skin, making him wonder if ending the feud once and for all could mean a new beginning for them both.

"Like Lavyrle Spencer, Ms. Johnston writes of intense emotions and tender passions that seem so real that readers will feel each one of them."
—*Rave Reviews*

Available the first week of June 2002 wherever paperbacks are sold!

A Wolf in Sheep's Clothing

MIRA®

New York Times Bestselling Author

FERN MICHAELS

GOLDEN LASSO

After inheriting a ranch in the beautiful Arizona desert, Jan Warren put all her money and dreams into making a success of *Rancho Arroyo*. But the resort needed work and Jan faced many difficulties—difficulties that were not at *all* helped by the commanding presence of Derek Bannon.

Owner of the Golden Lasso, the neighboring ranch and vacation hot spot, Derek was determined to buy her out. But was it his business agenda that threatened her so? Or was it the man himself? Somehow a business venture had become intensely personal and the stakes were dangerously high—her trust and her heart.

"Her characters are real and endearing, her prose so natural that it seems you are witnessing the story rather than reading about it."
—*Los Angeles Sunday Times*

Available the first week of June 2002 wherever paperbacks are sold!

MIRA®

USA Today Bestselling Author

KAREN

THE STONE FOREST

HARPER

One warm night sixteen years ago, sisters Jenna and Amanda Kirk disappeared. Days later, Jenna was found wandering alone, with no knowledge of her sister's fate. Now, desperate to uncover the truth about what happened that night, Jenna returns to Stone County, Indiana...and faces her darkest fears to expose a legacy of murder.

"Mystery, intrigue, love—it's all here."
—Rendezvous
on *Shaker Run*

On sale June 2002
wherever paperbacks are sold!

MIRA®

If you enjoyed what you just read,
then we've got an offer you can't resist!

Take 2
bestselling novels FREE!
Plus get a FREE surprise gift!

Clip this page and mail it to The Best of the Best™

IN U.S.A.	IN CANADA
3010 Walden Ave.	P.O. Box 609
P.O. Box 1867	Fort Erie, Ontario
Buffalo, N.Y. 14240-1867	L2A 5X3

YES! Please send me 2 free Best of the Best™ novels and my free surprise gift. After receiving them, if I don't wish to receive anymore, I can return the shipping statement marked cancel. If I don't cancel, I will receive 4 brand-new novels every month, before they're available in stores! In the U.S.A., bill me at the bargain price of $4.74 plus 25¢ shipping and handling per book and applicable sales tax, if any*. In Canada, bill me at the bargain price of $5.24 plus 25¢ shipping and handling per book and applicable taxes**. That's the complete price and a savings of over 20% off the cover prices—what a great deal! I understand that accepting the 2 free books and gift places me under no obligation ever to buy any books. I can always return a shipment and cancel at any time. Even if I never buy another The Best of the Best™ book, the 2 free books and gift are mine to keep forever.

185 MDN DNWF
385 MDN DNWG

Name	(PLEASE PRINT)	
Address	Apt.#	
City	State/Prov.	Zip/Postal Code

* Terms and prices subject to change without notice. Sales tax applicable in N.Y.
** Canadian residents will be charged applicable provincial taxes and GST.
All orders subject to approval. Offer limited to one per household and not valid to current The Best of the Best™ subscribers.
® are registered trademarks of Harlequin Enterprises Limited.

BOB02-R   ©1998 Harlequin Enterprises Limited

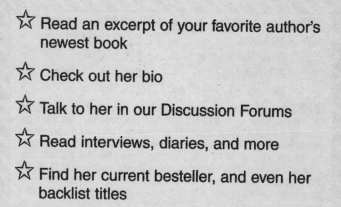